SOMETHING FOREVER

RACHAEL HARRIET

PRAISE FOR SOMETHING FOREVER

"Something Forever" is utterly brilliant. A page turner that will leave you obsessed and wanting more of Whitney and Liam.

— MEG JONES, AUTHOR OF "INVISIBLE STRING"

A delightful and engaging romance that kept me eagerly turning pages.

— KATIE VAN BRUNT, AUTHOR OF "FOR THE PLOT"

An absolutely hilarious enemies to lovers romcom. The witty banter will suck you right into the story and the lovable characters will charm you immediately.

— ALEXIS JONES, AUTHOR OF "ANYWHERE FOR YOU"

To my parents, who show me everyday what a real marriage looks like.

1

WHITNEY

Nothing good has ever come from a rash decision.

This is my mantra.

Structure, stability, and reliability. The simple tenants by which I live my life. So far, they have not let me down. I have never come to a conclusion without crafting a highly detailed and aesthetically pleasing pros and cons list. A pros and cons list is infallible, and it is the only way to be sure that every choice I make is the right one — that I'm not leading my life down the wrong path simply by making a spur-of-the-moment decision. I always consider every possible outcome before acting, which is why the words that just came out of my mouth are a shock to me more than anyone.

"I'm sorry, what did you just say?" Dan, my boss, asks, his graying hair slicked back in a greasy man-bun.

"I quit," I repeat, an out-of-body sensation seeming to take hold of me. "I quit," I say a third time, just because it feels so damn good.

Dan stutters, furrowing his brow. "You can't quit!"

"I just did," I grin, another laugh escaping me.

"But... why?"

There are many reasons I could give Dan for my departure. The not-so-subtle misogyny that I've dealt with as the office manager at the world's dumbest tech start-up being high up on the list. Last week, Jeff — a serial sexual harasser and absolute menace — left a sticky note left on my computer with a crude drawing of a stick figure woman being bent over a desk. Also, no matter how many times I've reminded him that my name is Whitney, he still calls me Brittney. I'm 99% certain he does it on purpose to make me feel small.

Secondary to the inhospitable environment might be that BeanLife is everything that is wrong with the world, and I've been pushing pencils for their ridiculous agenda for the past three years. It's an app to find the nearest coffee shop, like people don't have the internet. Why would they need an app to tell them there's a Starbucks around the corner? More importantly, why have I wasted so much of my life here?

I know why: the salary, benefits, and reliable routine that it has allowed me. Still, all the bright-siding in the world isn't enough to make up for the fact that I am not meant to answer emails all day long.

"It's just time," I reply diplomatically to Dan. "I'm ready to move on to something else."

"Oh, come on," Dan scoffs. "Don't feed me some line. Why are you really leaving?"

I should just leave it, but I'm already deep in my throwing-caution-to-the-wind moment, so I shrug and give Dan the truth: "Honestly? This workplace is toxic, the kitchen always smells like fish, I'm one of two women on the entire floor, and I couldn't give less of a fuck about our mission. If someone wants a cup of coffee, it's easy to find one. They don't need a stupid app made by a bunch of frat bros to tell them where they can get a cold brew. It's a bad idea, and the world doesn't need it."

With that, I walk out of Dan's office. I pass by the desks of people staring at me, slack-jawed. Clearly my outburst wasn't very quiet, but I don't care.

I'm free.

It doesn't take me long to pack up everything at my cubicle, but I do steal a box of tissues as a final petty gesture.

Sharon, the aforementioned other woman in the office, stares at me from across the office, as shocked as the rest of the staff must be, but her surprise morphs into an expression that almost looks like... satisfaction?

"Good for you, Whitney," she says in a motherly tone.

"Thanks, Shar," I say with a smile. "Good luck."

Tucking my box under my arm, I strut down the hallway, hoping I can steal a bit of that luck for myself.

By the time my adrenaline subsides, I'm stumbling up the stairs to my apartment, clutching my box of belongings to my chest. Now that the rush has faded, I'm left with the painful reality that I am unemployed with no real plan. It took me *three weeks* to decide on a dress to wear to my college reunion, two of which were spent scouring the product review sections of multiple websites. I don't normally surprise myself, so I have no idea what makes this day different than every day before it. It just felt... right. It was like my feet carried me into Dan's office, like some alien had inhabited my body for those brief minutes in which I changed my life forever.

Now, the worry is settling in, my chest is tight, and my stomach feels twisted up in knots.

Trying to shake off my growing anxiety, I push the door to my apartment open to find my roommate, Olivia, standing in the living room with two suitcases and a guitar case, looking like she's been caught with her hand in the cookie jar.

"Uh, hey?" I greet her, dropping my box onto the floor near the entrance.

Her face scrunches into a guilty frown. "I'm so, so sorry,

Whitney. I was gonna text you, and I really hate to leave so quickly, but listen — I found a subletter, and he'll be here in a couple of days."

Her words are swirling around in my head, but nothing is really computing. Maybe I'm still running on the adrenaline from my first ever impulsive decision.

"What?"

"I'm sorry. It all happened so suddenly, and I just couldn't turn down the opportunity."

"What are you talking about?" I ask, confused.

"I got an offer to open for Young the Giant on their US tour, and we leave tomorrow."

"Oh, wow. Wait, so you're... moving out?"

Olivia has been my roommate for a little over a year, but we aren't friends. We coexist, but we don't really know each other. I know she's been trying to make it as musician and works as a waitress somewhere in the Lower East Side, but other than that, I don't know much about her. She spends a lot of time out of the apartment, so I rarely see her.

"Yeah, I am. Sorry again. I meant to talk to you about it, but it's been a crazy twenty-four hours. My friend is coming for my boxes tomorrow, and the subletter will be in sometime next week."

My mouth is opening and closing like a fish.

Boxes. Her stuff is in boxes. Because she's moving out.

"Oh-kay?" I manage.

"I'll text you everything you need to know about the sublet. He's got the key already. Thank you so much for everything."

Olivia brings me in for a hug that I think I reciprocate, but my limbs are sort of moving of their own accord. She brushes past me, yanking her suitcases behind her, and clamors through the front door without looking back. Just like that, she's gone.

Wow.

I know she said it was just the tour, but part of me feels hurt that my roommate is leaving me behind. That she didn't care enough about our sort-of-friendship to give me an advance notice. That she chose today, of all days, to announce her swift departure. Okay, so maybe she had no way of knowing that today was going to blow up in my face, but now I've not only quit my job, but I'm completely alone.

My mind reels, snagging on a detail that Olivia mentioned.

"I'll text you everything you need to know about the sublet. He's got a key already."

He's got a key?

My new roommate is a guy?

A guy living here? In *my* apartment? Oh, no. Oh, no, no, no. I haven't lived with a man since my ex, Christopher, and I certainly never planned to again until I got married, which is many years off. Decades, even. Boys are irresponsible! Boys are messy! Boys are gross! It was bad enough having to deal with those assholes at my job, but what if my roommate is some creep? How can I even trust living in the same apartment as some strange guy I've literally never met? He could be a murderer. He could be a mansplainer. He could be the type of person that claps when planes land and knows how NFTs work.

Okay, so maybe I'm being childish, but the point is my apartment is my happy place. My sacred place. My lavender scented, perfectly decorated haven. Fall is just around the corner, and I plan on turning this place into a veritable Pinterest board of autumnal cheer. If a man moves in here, it's going to screw everything up. He'll leave his sweaty man-things everywhere and just... ugh!

I groan into the empty room and take a gulp of my coffee, praying it'll wake me up from this nightmare scenario I've entered.

It doesn't.

This cannot be happening.

Freaking out, I grab my phone and send a text to Olivia.

> Whitney: Sorry, did you say the subletter you found was a guy?

Her response comes in quickly.

> Olivia: Yes, his name is Liam. He's the best!

Suppressing a growl, I reply immediately.

> Whitney: I really don't want some random ass guy living in my apartment.

> Olivia: I promise, you've got nothing to worry about. Besides, he works nights like I did, so you'll never see him.

I scowl down at my phone. Am I really going to get into this fight with her over text? Whatever. I'll just have to wait for this Liam guy to show up and inform him that the room is no longer available. Rolling my eyes, I send a text to my best friend, Abbi, to relay my two shocking tidbits of news.

> Whitney: I quit my job and Olivia is moving out.

Her response comes through immediately, two texts in quick succession.

> Abbi: OMG WHAT!!

> Abbi: Drinks at Rocka Rolla at 7? Tell me everything.

I reply, letting her know I'll meet her at our favorite local bar. It's a divey spot that serves frozen margaritas in giant goblets. We like to sit in their backyard and make bets on who can finish their drink the fastest.

I imagine that tonight I'll come out victorious.

Abbi's been my best friend since I moved to the city. She's more like my mom than me — a total free spirit. Where my mom prefers crystals and Coronas, though, Abbi is more of a CrossFit and cosmos kind of girl. Still, I guess I am drawn to my opposite, or maybe I was subconsciously looking to fill that mom-sized hole in my life when I met Abbi a few months after finishing school and moving to Brooklyn.

I'm about to start wallowing in self-pity — or maybe I should just start drinking? — when I see my phone buzzing with an unknown number. Usually, I'd ignore it, but something tugs at my chest. Maybe it's because of the shit show today has been, but I have the urge to answer.

"Hello?"

"Hello, is this Whitney Rhodes?"

I pause, wary. This day has already been a complete mess, so it's not like it can get any worse. "Yes, this is she."

On the other line, I can hear papers shuffling. "Ms. Rhodes, I'm so glad I reached you. It's been a nightmare trying to contact all the next of kin."

"Sorry, who is this?"

"I'm your grandmother's attorney, Trent Wilson. I've been tasked with her last will and testament."

"My grandmother?"

"Agnes Rhodes."

My mind is spinning. My mom is the only family I have. The only family I've ever known. Whenever my mom would talk about her parents, which was rare, it was always in the past tense. I guess I assumed they were dead. I never really thought about it. I accepted a long time ago that it was just me and my mom.

"Your inclusion in the will is somewhat extensive. There's a letter to you, as well as your portion of the inheritance, though there's a complication with that as well. She was a very... eccentric woman."

I open and close my mouth, trying to form a response, but nothing comes out.

"Are you able to come to New Haven?"

"What?" I manage.

"If not, I can send everything over, but these things are easier in-person."

"I'm in the city. Will the rest of my... family be there?"

"You're the first person I've managed to get in touch with. Her daughter Caroline — your mother, rather — seems to be completely off the grid. It's really just the two of you and a few of your grandmother's friends in the area. Your grandfather, Joseph, passed a few years back."

My mind is reeling, trying to process the information I am receiving. I had two grandparents. *Living* grandparents that I never got to know, and now it's too late. Meanwhile, my mom is nowhere to be found as usual. In the wind.

"I'll call my mom. I don't know if her number is the same, but she usually checks in with me every few months, and it's been a while, so I'm sure I'll hear from her soon."

"If you do speak with her, please tell her to call me."

"Can you just... email me everything? To be honest with you, I didn't even know I *had* a grandmother until the start of this conversation. I just quit my job, my roommate is moving out, and I am, like, completely freaking out right now."

"I understand," Trent says, his tone sympathetic. "I apologize for springing all this on you. I can certainly email you the relevant documents and information, but... well, as I mentioned, your grandmother was quite eccentric and had her own way of viewing things. I had no idea you were estranged, and to be honest, I'm quite surprised."

"Why?"

"Well, your inheritance is... significant."

"Significant?" I say, squinting. "How much?"

"One million dollars."

My jaw hits the floor. "Did you... " I swallow the lump in my throat. "Did you just say a million dollars?"

"That's correct."

My breathing increases, black spots starting to appear in the corner of my vision. "Is this some kind of prank? Is Abbi behind this?"

"I assure you, Ms. Rhodes, this is no prank."

"What... how... I don't understand."

"There's also the slight issue of the amendment clause to the inheritance."

I squeeze my eyes shut, pressing the bridge of my nose with my thumb and forefinger. "What do you mean, amendment clause?"

"Well, it's stipulated that the inheritance be paid out in three parts," the attorney says plainly, "the first upon your marriage."

A burst of laughter escapes from me. "I'm sorry. I thought you said 'marriage'?"

Trent pauses on the other line. "I did. In order to receive the first part of the inheritance, you must be married. The second and third are paid upon the subsequent years of marriage."

My brain just... breaks. There are no thoughts inside of it. No words on my tongue. Zero.

"Ms. Rhodes? Are you still there?"

"Sorry. Um, yes, I'm here," I say, dragged back to earth. "So, not only do I have a grandmother I knew nothing about, but she's also left me a million dollars, but only if I'm married, and only if I stay married for... "

"Three years at least."

Brain. Cannot. Compute.

Trent sucks in a breath. "I'll just... email you the details. You give me a call back if you have any questions. I'll be available."

Words. Where are words?

"Nice speaking to you, and I am very sorry for your loss. Goodbye, Ms. Rhodes."

Trent hangs up, and I set the phone down on the counter.

I can't believe this. Agnes Rhodes. I've never once heard that name before. Eighteen years of raising me, and my mom never mentioned her own mother. How is that even possible?

My blood boiling, I try to take in a few deep breaths to calm my panic. My first thought is that my grandparents must have done something terrible for my mom to remove them from our lives completely. After all, she wouldn't have cast them aside for no reason. But another thought crystallizes and hardens inside me, remembering the nights we scraped together the last of her tips from the diner to buy frozen pizzas. How I'd hustle the drunks at the local bar into thinking I couldn't play pool and smirk at their shocked glares as they reluctantly handed over twenty-dollar bills. I'd run home with my winnings in my pockets, and we'd use the money to fill the gas tank so we could make it to a new town and do it all over again. Days and nights on the wide open road. Untethered, clinging to each other, parent and child merged into one.

We had nothing.

There were times I didn't understand it, our nomadic existence. Whenever we'd settle somewhere, I'd be the new girl at school, struggling to make friends. It was as if my peers could tell I didn't belong in their world of pleated skirts and study dates. Just as I'd start to finally feel like maybe I could fit in, we'd be on the road again, headed somewhere new. I'd beg my mother to tell me why we had to go — why we couldn't stay in any of the places we'd been to.

"We're not meant for there, peanut. How much better is this? Just the two of us, completely free."

I didn't feel free. I felt lost. By the time I turned sixteen, I was as different from my mother as I could possibly be. I wrinkled my nose at her cigarettes and beers that I used to think were cool. She'd remind me of my scheming days at those dive bars, and I'd curl my lip in anger, frustrated that she'd roped me into her lifestyle from day one. I wanted nothing more than to settle down somewhere, to have a normal teenage life. Instead, I floated, belonging nowhere, finding nobody. I was desperate to go to college, despite my mother telling me over and over that I didn't need that to have a good life.

Resentment churns in my gut at how things might have been different. That whole time, I had two grandparents living in New Haven, probably in a classic New England style mansion; while we'd been scraping pennies together at a rest stop in the middle of Iowa, they'd been scraping their silverware against their finest china.

I know I should call my mom, but I can't. I'm too angry and shaken right now. I'll end up saying something I regret. I'll probably announce that I'm unemployed, and she'll try to convince me to go on some wild adventure with her. She's the only family I've ever had, but sometimes I just don't understand her. I think we're just too different. Maybe if I were more carefree, more like her, it would have worked, but I'm just not. I'm particular and anxious and I like my comforts. The life that I'm building for myself is the type of life that I always wanted — stable, ordered, and 100% *mine*.

Well, the life that I *was* building before I blew it up over the course of a single day.

How am I standing in the same place I was before this call?

The apartment looks different, feels different, somehow. Heavier. Emptier.

Gasping for another deep breath, I feel the familiar prickling on the backs of my eyelids, a pressure building in my nose and chest.

Great, now I'm going to cry.

I should have trusted my mantra.

Nothing good has ever come from a rash decision.

2
———

WHITNEY

After eating an entire pint of ice cream, I spend the rest of the day binging my comfort TV show, trying to distract myself from my imploding life. I can usually tell how depressed I am by what teen drama I'm watching. *One Tree Hill* is when I know I'm on the decline, *Gossip Girl* is getting into pretty dire territory, and *Glee* is when I know I've hit absolute rock bottom. Still, my favorite has always been *Gilmore Girls* because Lorelai and Rory always reminded me of my mom and me. It used to be us against the world.

Now, it's just me.

And potentially a million dollars.

I get to Rocka Rolla a few minutes late. Abbi is already in the backyard with our drinks, her fiery hair tied into a messy bun that somehow manages to look both stylish and chaotic. When she sees me, she shrieks and throws her arms around my neck.

"Oh my God! My girl is a free woman!" she shouts as we both sit down. We're getting side glances from other people sitting on the patio, something that happens often when I'm with Abbi given that her voice is louder than any sane person's probably should be.

She picks up her margarita and lifts it against mine. "To spontaneous life decisions." She grins. We both sip our drinks and Abbi leans forward. "So, tell me everything."

I sigh, trying to figure out where to start. I haven't even told her about my inheritance. How do I explain the shit show that is the past twelve hours of my life?

"I just... snapped. Walked right up to Dan and told him I was done."

"Are you sure you and I haven't been *Freaky Friday*'d? Because spontaneous quitting is much more my groove."

I chuckle, shaking my head. "I wish. Then I'd be going home to a hot basketball player instead of finding out my roommate is moving out. Olivia got some tour gig that required her to leave immediately, and now some random guy is supposed to be taking her place."

Abbi frowns. "No way. You gotta vet him first. He could be a Craigslist murderer for all you know. My ex once had a roommate who used his toothbrush. Nasty shit."

"Thanks, Ab," I say, grimacing through a wave of nausea. "I'm feeling really assured now."

She smirks. "Maybe he's one of the good ones. You never know."

"Knowing my luck, he's probably Ted Bundy's grandson."

"I don't think Bundy had kids."

I give her my best glare, but she just cackles in response and downs the rest of her cocktail.

"Come on," she urges impatiently, "drink number one should be a distant memory by now."

I snort and down the drink. When I'm finished, I bang my fist on the table for good measure, startling the people around us. "Same again?"

"You know it."

I get the second round and return with two more margaritas, setting them down on the table.

"The loser next to us just tried to hit on me. As if I'd ever go out with a guy who wears Kanye merch," she says, her voice carrying through the garden.

"Pretty sure he can hear you, Ab." I glance to the right where a kid, who can't be older than twenty-three, is frowning at us.

She shrugs. "Who cares? Anyway, since you're a free agent, what's next for you?"

I grimace, trying to figure out how the hell to phrase this. What's the best way to explain that phone call?

"Well, actually, I have more news, and this one is a real doozy."

"There's something more newsworthy than Whitney Rhodes making her first ever spontaneous decision?" she teases.

"My estranged grandmother who I didn't even know existed passed away and left me a million-dollar inheritance."

Abbi's jaw drops. "Oh my God. What?"

I nod in disbelief. "Yeah. It's crazy."

"Whoa," she breathes out. "I'm so sorry about your grandmother."

"Thanks," I reply numbly. "It's weird. I know I didn't know her or anything, but I can't help but feel a sense of grief, like I've missed out on an important relationship. I had this whole family that I never knew."

"It's pretty fucked up your mom never told you about them," she says.

Abbi knows all about my strained relationship with my mother, and I'm sure she can tell that this news is only adding fuel to the fire.

It's quiet for a moment before Abbi speaks again, awe in her voice. "So, a million bucks?"

I hold my hand up. "There's a catch."

"Ugh!" she says, throwing her head back dramatically. "There's always a catch."

"I have to be married — and stay married for three years — to get it."

It's so quiet you could hear a pin drop. I've never seen Abbi so speechless. She's always the quickest to come up with a retort or something clever to say.

I take a large gulp of my margarita. "Whenever you're ready."

"So... could you just... repeat that for me?"

"I have to get married and stay married for three—"

"No right, so I heard you correctly, then." She nods and then turns to face me. "So, I suppose my next question is: what in the ever-loving fuck?"

"I know."

"Wow. This is so crazy."

I shake my head, chuckling, the sound turning into a groan halfway through. "Abbi. What am I going to do?"

She puts her palm on my back, rubbing soft circles. The motion reminds me of when my mom used to rub my back when I was sick. A small, familiar comfort.

"You should probably call your mom."

"She won't even answer. I bet she's holed up in some motel somewhere," I grumble. "I haven't been able to get in touch with her for weeks. I think she ditched her phone."

Abbi is quiet for a moment. "It's a lot of money, Whit."

"I know."

"You could do a lot with that money. Pay off all your loans. Finally open your salon."

The truth I've been trying to ignore hits me all at once then, fueled by the alcohol and openness with Abbi. My dream. I've wanted to open my own hair salon for years. Ever since I was a kid, salons were a safe place for me. When I was on the road with my mom, she'd drop me at the strip mall, and I'd find my way to a place where I met all kinds of women. Beautiful women with problems and ideas and *dreams.*

All I ever wanted was to create that same sort of space for other people, but life got in the way. I ended up taking an office job for the benefits a cosmetology career couldn't offer me, but I always missed it. Always dreamed of having my own little haven. The picture that Abbi paints is almost too good. It's the things I never thought would be possible, especially not all at once.

It's the possibility of my dreams finally coming true.

"It's crazy that I'm even considering it."

"Even crazier not to. It's a million dollars."

I shake my head. "I can't get married. I'm not even dating."

"It's not like you'd actually be getting married. It'd be more like a business arrangement, right?"

"I guess so, yeah."

She shrugs. "So, it's not even a big deal. Sign some papers and bam, you get a million bucks. Honestly, this sounds like every girl's dream. Or maybe the plot to a Hallmark movie."

"It gets paid out in installments over the three years, so I'd have to stay married for at least that long. I wouldn't get all the money at once."

"Still, it's worth it. I mean, come on, Whit. You've always made excuses for why it's not the right time for your salon, but now you've got the money, so just get over your scaredy cat shit and do it!"

Abbi always has a way of making the most difficult tasks sound like a walk in the park. It's very annoying.

"It's not that simple," I mutter.

"Yeah, well, it ain't rocket science either, babe."

I chug the rest of my drink and sigh, resting my head in my arms with a moan. Abbi pats my back. "Cheer up, champ. You're basically a millionaire. You can get any guy you want to marry you."

If only that were true.

WHEN I GET HOME from the bar, my plan is to go straight to bed. Even though I spent all day on the couch, I feel completely drained. I'm sure the multiple margaritas didn't help, but at least I'll be able to fall asleep without my thoughts distracting me.

After speeding through my skincare routine, I lay down, exhausted, but I'm distracted by the buzz of my phone. I check it and find an email from Trent, reading through it quickly to see that he's attached the terms of my inheritance and a letter from my grandmother. Curious, I click on the attached document and zoom in so that I can read it:

> To my granddaughter,
> If you are reading this, it means that I never had the pleasure to meet you. I do not know what your mother has told you about us, but it is my hope that despite our distance and separation she has shared with you some of the fond memories we shared during her childhood. The day I gave birth to Caroline was the happiest day of my life. Every mother knows that their greatest gift in the world is their child, and that losing them is the most terrifying horror imaginable.
> Your mother was always a bit of a wild child. I never understood why she so resented the life we led. At the time, I chalked it up to teenage angst and tried not to let it get to me, but your grandfather was more sensitive to her attitude. He believed it was my job to

keep her under control and was angry when I failed to do so. When she came to us at sixteen and told us that she was pregnant, I couldn't believe it. Joseph demanded that she marry the father of the child immediately, but she refused. He told her that he would not have a bastard raised out of wedlock in his home.

I think of that night quite often, mostly with regret and shame. Regret that I did not speak up. Shame that I allowed my husband to throw our only child out into the streets. A few days after your mother left, I begged Joseph to reconsider. I heard she had been spending the night at a friend's house, but I knew that couldn't last long, and I feared that if she left town, we would not be able to reach her again. He told me that she was no longer our daughter and forbade me from contacting her. I obeyed, though the pain was unbearable. After a few months, I couldn't take it anymore. Without Joseph knowing, I managed to find out where she was staying and went to see her. I begged her to come back home, but she refused. She told me that she was leaving town, and that she never wanted to see me again.

Over the years, I endeavored to stay in touch with her, sending letters often. I told her how dearly I wanted to meet you, and always sent her money, which was often returned to me with a note to leave you both alone. For years, I tried to convince your mother to bring you home to us, but every attempt was unsuccessful. Eventually, I started to lose hope. Then Joseph passed, and I was alone. I hate to admit it, but the truth is that in the end, I simply gave up.

I am sorry that I never had the chance to meet my only granddaughter. My wish is that this gift bestowed onto you may help you in your life, wherever you may be. As for the matter of my condition, I desire a different path for you than your mother. I am hopeful that these funds will assist you in raising your own child with the support of your marital partner.

Very sincerely yours,

Agnes Rhodes

I set my phone down, reeling. Licking my lips, I taste a familiar salty flavor and realize that I'm crying. I wipe at my face, taking a few deep, steadying breaths. I'm surprised by my intense reaction, but I think the events of the past two days are starting to catch up with me. I feel tired all the way down to my bones.

Closing my eyes, I fall back against the pillow and hope that life doesn't have any more curveballs to throw me.

3

LIAM

"Can I get two rum and cokes and whatever IPA you have on tap?" The lanky skater boy in front of me slams his hand on the counter, a fifty peeking out from under it.

I raise my eyebrows, scanning him. He's barely passing for twenty, and even though my boss told me to stop carding the people that come in here, something about these NYU trust-fund kids gets me aggravated. Probably their practiced look of poverty that they seem to wear as some sort of badge of honor, as if I can't tell that their baggy, half-ripped t-shirt is actually designer and costs as much as I make in a week.

"ID?" I ask as his friends join behind him, a trio of what can only be called boys.

"Sure," he says casually, opening up his wallet and handing me his ID, which is definitely a fake. Maybe one of those batch-order ones that all the college kids tend to bring in here. Why they feel the need to come all the way out here to Abe's Pub and not some trendy spot in the village, I'll never understand. But I acquiesce. I give the kid back his ID and line up the drinks and slide them to him.

At least he leaves me a solid tip.

The night is only getting started. It's not even eleven, but by the time midnight hits, I know I'll be deep in the swing of things. The place tends to get packed with a combination of locals and hipsters. I tend to ignore the latter, but then again, these days I tend to ignore everyone.

"Liam, we've got a delivery comin' in tomorrow. Can you come in early?" Abe, my boss and the namesake of this place, chimes in from behind me.

It's rare for him to be here, but my coworker Darius called to say he's running late and won't be in until midnight. So, I'm stuck manning the bar alone until then, which is a recipe for disaster since Abe isn't much help when it comes to pouring drinks. He might take one or two of the regulars who tend to come by, but I'm basically on my own.

Not that I mind being alone. I'm used to it by now.

"I can't. I'm moving into a new apartment tomorrow. Got kicked out of student housing, so I had to find a new place," I tell Abe.

"You're still in student housing? Didn't you drop out months ago?"

"It's been less than two months, and it was under... unique circumstances, so they made an exception," I explain. "The new place is a lot closer, so it'll cut my commute in half. I'll be positively cheerful."

"Believe that when I see it," Abe offers, and doesn't say anything else. He knows not to pry about any of our personal lives, which is something great about this job. While I may have to pour drinks as random folks share their whole life story, nobody asks about mine.

Which is good, because my story isn't one with a happy ending.

"I can come in at five earliest," I tell him.

"Thanks, son. You're a real help."

I grin sloppily at him, tossing my rag over my shoulder. "Stop flirting with me, old man."

He chuckles and shakes his head, walking into the back office and leaving me to tend to a few women who have just walked in wearing matching cowgirl costumes. Likely a bachelorette or birthday party.

I have a feeling this is going to be a long night.

THE NEXT DAY, the movers arrive at my place first thing in the morning.

I would have asked friends to help me move, if I had any of those left. All my Columbia buddies have stopped making an effort with me. To their credit, they reached out countless times after Luke's funeral to check in on me, but I ignored nearly every text and call.

Eventually, they stopped trying.

Last night was exhausting. A group of drunk girls at the bar kept asking me to pronounce random words. Apparently, they'd seen it in a scene in *Love Actually* and wanted to test the legitimacy of it. Which is how I got trapped repeating *vodka* and *beer* back to them until closing. I'm pretty sure they were flirting with me, but even when I blatantly ignored them, they didn't seem to get the hint.

To tell the truth, I haven't been interested in touching anyone since Luke died.

Glancing around at the empty apartment that Luke and I used to share, a pit gathers in my stomach, tight and unyielding. Shaking my head, I swallow the lump in my throat and slam the door behind me. No use dwelling in the past any longer. I have to start focusing on what semblance of a future I can scrape together.

I'm on my way to the new place when I call Olivia. She and Darius used to hook up, and she'd come around the bar a lot to meet him near the end of his shift. I'd mentioned that I was desperate for a new place last week, since my student housing extension was up at the end of the month. A few days later, she called me to tell me she was leaving her place and wanted to sublet.

So, maybe my luck is starting to turn.

"Hey! How's it going?" Olivia answers, muffled sounds of laughter and music behind her.

"Alright. I'm on my way now. You left the keys for me, yeah?"

"In the lockbox attached to the gate."

"Anything else I should know?" I ask. She hasn't told me much about the place, but my desperation overrode any hesitations I may have had about such a fast decision.

"Well... my roommate was less than enthused when I told her I was moving out and a guy was taking my place."

"Didn't you ask her about me before?"

"Not really. I had no time! Anyway, she'll deal with it."

I roll my eyes and bite my tongue, not wanting to stir anything up. "Great. Love moving into a place where I'm not at all wanted. Thanks so much," I say sarcastically.

"You're welcome," she says brightly.

I hang up the phone as I pull up to the apartment, my irritation growing. It's hot as hell, the August humidity sticking to my skin. After finding the key and letting myself into the apartment, I glance around, feeling like an intruder.

"Hello?" I call out, wondering if my new roommate is here, but there's no response.

I glance around, taking in the apartment. It's nice. There's a unique style to the decor, somewhere between modern and maximalist. I usually prefer a simpler look, mainly because I can't be arsed with decorating, but something about the splashes of color and how alive the place feels — plants everywhere, artwork on the walls — makes the place feel homey.

It takes the movers almost two hours to get all my shit inside, and I spend the rest of the day unpacking. It's late when I find a box of bits that I've been ignoring. I already know what I'm going to find there. With a sigh, I pick up the box and lift the top to see its contents. The first thing I find is a photo of me and Luke in our freshman dorm.

We look so young. Happy.

Naive.

"Can you hand me the microscope?" Luke asks from beside me, his head bent over his desk while I look at our latest results on the computer screen. We're the last ones left in the lab, as usual. We've been running this experiment for weeks with no results, and I'm pretty sure we're close to killing each other. Between the time spent side-by-side in the lab and the three feet of distance between our beds in the dorm, we're practically inseparable.

I've never had a friend like this. A best friend.

I slide the microscope over to him, and he looks through it, then pushes it away with a sigh. "I'm exhausted," he announces. "Should we call it a night and grab some pizza?"

"Believe it or not, I actually have plans."

He glances over at me with mild surprise, his eyebrows raised. "Liam Clark. Do you have a date?"

I shrug, the corners of my mouth lifting. "Maybe."

"Who is she?"

"Claire? From our physics seminar. She asked me out last week."

"My boy's getting out there!" he whoops, pushing back from the table. "Damn. I guess I'll stick around here."

"Not gonna hit up Sophie?"

"Nah." He shakes his head. "We ended things."

"Oh," I reply dumbly. "What happened?"

He shrugs, then smiles, but it doesn't quite reach his eyes. "She wanted more than I could give her, I guess."

"I'm sorry, man," I offer. Luke and I don't talk about our feelings that much with each other. Sometimes, he'll confide in me, and I always appreciate it when he does, but most of the time — when we're not working — we just have fun together. "I can reschedule with her if you want to hang for a bit longer?"

"No way," he replies quickly. "This is a rare opportunity. You might never get another date, Clark."

I shove his shoulder lightly, and we both laugh. Packing up my stuff, I sneak a glance in his direction. Ever since last semester, he's been working a lot harder. It feels like every time I see him in our room, he's sitting in his bed with papers strewn around him, a frustrated grimace on his face.

"See you later," I tell him as I head out, and he waves in my direction with a half-smile, turning back towards the microscope.

I'm halfway down the hallway when I realize I left my coat on the back of my chair. There's no way I'll survive the walk to the bar in the frigid December air without it, so I double back to the lab. When I step back inside the sterile room, I see Luke, bent over the desk, his head in his hands. I'm about to call his name when I hear a low, choked sound and notice the shaking of his shoulders.

He's crying.

What do I do? Should I go over there and try to comfort him? If I asked, would he tell me what's wrong? Does he even want my help?

If it were me, and he caught me crying, I'd be embarrassed. I'd probably try to play it off somehow, make it seem like it wasn't that big of a deal. Make up some excuse about something being stuck in my eye or some shit.

Indecision keeps me rooted in place, unsure what's the best move *right now. Wanting to protect my friend's pride while worry and sympathy flood my system. Another sob racks through Luke, and I tense.*

What the hell am I doing? Just standing here like an idiot, watching my friend cry?

My gaze flickers over to my jacket, and I tense my fingers. Wrapping my hand around the doorknob, I take a silent step back, and tug the door closed, not making a sound. I'll have to brave the cold, but at least nothing has to change between Luke and me.

I'm not running away, I tell myself.

This is for the best, I tell myself.

But as I wrap my arms around myself, stepping out into the crisp air, I can't stop seeing Luke's slumped, defeated figure in what is supposed to be our happy place. I can't stop replaying the image of my best friend, crying and alone, and wondering: did I just make a huge mistake?

MY CHEST ACHING WITH AGONY, I press the backs of my shaking hands into my eyes with a sigh. Every time I think of that night, I hate myself. Hate that I couldn't see whatever it was he was hiding behind his eyes. Hate that I walked out of that room instead of sitting next to him, wrapping him in a hug, and asking what was wrong. Hate that I feel like it's my fault. All of it. My fucking fault.

My phone buzzes with an alarm telling me it's time to head to work. It's the last place I want to go, but I'm relieved to have the distraction. At least it's something to do, so I don't have to sit here and wallow in memories.

It's time to move on.

The only question is... how?

4

WHITNEY

My first day as a soon-to-be-married woman begins with a meeting with a lawyer. As solid as Trent seems, I figure I should get a second opinion. I find some guy online and fork up an obscene amount of money to meet with him and go over the inheritance documents. My hope is that the whole marriage clause isn't legally binding and, somehow, I can access my inheritance another way.

No such luck.

After two hours of research, there's not a single loophole to be found. It looks like if I want my money, I'll have to put a ring on it and soon. If I don't complete the terms of the marriage clause, my entire inheritance sum gets passed to the next beneficiary, whoever that is.

When I get home that afternoon, something is different in the apartment. At first, I'm not sure what it is. I think maybe it's me — that my new mission has somehow changed my perspective on life — but then I realize that's ridiculous, and what's changed is that in the entryway where my shoe rack is, there's a pair of size twelves sitting on the ground.

Men's shoes.

He's here? Already?

I tiptoe towards the kitchen, listening intently for any indication that he's here.

What am I doing? Sneaking around my own apartment like some thief in the night? This is my home! Part of me wants nothing more than to march right up to his door, introduce myself, and explain that he really cannot be living here. But a bigger part of me needs to shower. Like, now. So instead of confronting my mystery roommate, I go to my room to get my towel. It's not until I've stripped down and wrapped my towel around me that it occurs to me.

I have to share a bathroom with this man!

What if he's in there?

What if he's shitting?

Okay, Whitney. You really need to get it together.

Ignoring the crazy voice in my head that happens to be my own, I slip out of my room and down the hall to the bathroom, which is mercifully empty. I take my time in the shower, shampooing and conditioning my hair and even doing a face mask, if only to prove that this bathroom is mine, and I will not be changing my habits for anyone.

When I get out, the apartment is still quiet, so I slink back to my room and order some ramen for delivery. I open and close every app on my phone and doomscroll on Twitter for at least twenty minutes before I finally give up and take out my notebook.

Step one: get married

I start over.

~~Step one: get married~~

Step one: meet a man who is not insane (difficult)

Step two: get married

Pushing down the urge to stop there, I finish my list with a grimace.

Step three: business plan for the salon

Step four: find location

Step five: think of trendy name

I put the list away when my food arrives and eat in the kitchen, looking over my shoulder every five minutes, wondering if *he* will make an appearance. But there's nothing. Not even a peep from his side of the apartment. Once I finish eating, I try to keep working on the list, but it suddenly looks pathetic. It feels like my brain is devoid of any good ideas, and the list of potential names for the salon is downright criminal. *Hair Haus?* I hate myself for even writing that down.

Instead, I decide to download Hinge and make a profile, spending way too long trying to come up with responses to the prompts.

What I'm looking for? A fake husband.

*You should *not* go out with me if...* you don't want to get married.

All I ask is that you... marry me.

That's how I fall asleep: with my phone in my hand, open to a photo of a man holding a fish.

I WAKE TO COMPLETE DARKNESS, my throat dry and itchy. Checking the time, I realize it's almost three in the morning. I reach over for my water and find it empty. With a sigh, I roll out of bed and trudge into the kitchen. The light from the fridge is blinding as I pour from the Britta. I chug it down in three gulps, then pour another glass and close the fridge.

I hear something, and I turn around.

"*Ahh!*" The scream bursts out of me when I see the silhouette of a man in my kitchen. I stumble backwards and flip on the light switch, the fluorescent bulb glaring as I blink furiously, trying to take in the scene in front of me.

"Christ, that's bright," the man says.

Holy hell.

He's *hot.*

Like, really hot.

He's shirtless, standing in nothing but his boxer briefs, his rich brown hair tussled in a mess on his head. Dark tattooed lines cover his broad chest and toned arms, and boy is there a lot to cover. His jawline is sharp, and he's scrubbing his scruffy beard with his very... large... hand. Usually I'm more into a cleaned up, preppy sort of guy; my ex was that type; but something about this man's rugged, messy look has my nerve endings tingling.

I need to get laid, like, yesterday.

"Um. Hi?" I squeak.

He eyes me, his dark eyes pinning me in place as he scans me from head to toe. His gaze is intense and causes all sorts of unexpected somersaults in my stomach.

"Hi," he replies, brushing past me towards the fridge. He pulls out a carton of orange juice — my carton of orange juice, actually — and takes a long pull. Straight from the bottle.

"Is that my orange juice?" I ask.

He turns and finally pulls the jug away from his mouth, wiping his lips with the back of his hand. He doesn't say anything as he puts it back in the fridge and closes the door.

"Well?" I prompt him, getting frustrated by his brick wall demeanor.

He just shrugs.

"Night," he says, pushing off the counter and heading back towards his bedroom. I hate myself for the way my gaze watches him go, tracing the muscular lines of his back.

What the hell was that?

First of all, it definitely *was* my orange juice, so we are going to need to have a conversation about that. Secondly, he is so rude! Why was he being so standoffish? He barely even said a word to me and we're going to be living together for God knows how long! Well, not for very long, I hope. Third... wow. I mean, wow. What is the guy, a male model? A firefighter? Some kind of walking cologne ad? This is worse than any other scenario — not only do I have some random guy living with me, but now I'm attracted to him.

Flipping off the lights, I drag myself back to my bedroom. The grumpy roommate will have to wait until the morning.

The next day, I wake up with my body sprawled across my bed like a starfish. It's late in the afternoon, and there is definitely some drool on my pillow. My unemployment has officially reached depressing territory.

Get up and get your life together, woman!

With a sigh, I turn out of the bed and grab my robe, wrapping it around my body and dragging myself to the bathroom. I scrub my face, the cold water jolting me awake, then saunter into the kitchen. The first thing I do is take my orange juice out of the fridge, eyeing the jug like it's got some bacterial disease. I put it back immediately, opting for coffee instead.

Memories of my late-night encounter with my new roommate flash through my mind, and I'm only alone in the kitchen for a few minutes before the Grump himself comes sauntering into the room. His eyes flicker briefly in my direction as he approaches the coffee machine. He pops in a pod and turns, leaning against the counter, his expression blank. As he reaches his hand to scratch the back of his head, his shirt rides up, revealing those toned muscles and dark lines that I ogled over last night.

My stomach drops at the sight.

"So, what was your problem last night?" I ask, my walls raising.

"My problem?" He raises his eyebrows and turns his back to me, picking up his coffee cup and walking over to the couch.

"You barely said a word to me," I say with a definite edge to my voice. Much to my own frustration, I follow him, sitting in the chair across from him.

"It was three in the morning," he grunts and spreads out on the couch, his huge body taking up what feels like half the room. "I was half-asleep."

I huff out a breath. "Well, nice to meet you. Really, I just need to tell you that I'm sorry for whatever deal Olivia led you to believe there was, but there's been a mistake. The room is not available."

"You mean my room?" He narrows his eyes at me.

"It's not your room," I retort.

"Well, I'm living in it."

"For like a day!" I screech, shocking myself by how upset I'm getting. I'm usually much calmer than this. "Look, I don't even know you. You can't live here. It's too weird."

"Oh, come on, love. You'll hardly notice I'm here," he replies, his British accent coming out stronger than I noticed it before, along with the condescension dripping in his words.

"The bottom line is you cannot stay here."

"Why not?"

"Because! I don't even know you. I don't even know your name."

"My name is Liam. Born outside London, moved to the States to live with my dad when I was in high school, stuck around here to get a couple degrees, then fucked that off. Now I'm a bartender, and I mind my own. There, now you know me." He pushes off the couch, making a move to leave, but I stand, stopping him.

"That is not good enough. That's barely anything," I tell him.

He frowns down at me, his gaze pinning me into place. "That's more than most people get."

"Don't you want to know my name? Know anything about me?" I cock my head to the side, trying to match the intensity of his gaze.

He sighs heavily and rubs his stubble with his hand, a gesture that seems to be common for him, and one that I find myself staring at with way too much interest.

"Alright. What's your name, then?"

"Whitney."

He motions for me to keep going, then folds his arms as though growing impatient.

Realizing I don't know what to say, I let honest words tumble out of me. "I'm not really from anywhere. I grew up on the road with my mom. I just quit my job which is really unlike me because I'm a Virgo which means I rely on structure and organization and lately I feel like a total mess, which is not good because now I have a complete stranger moving into my apartment."

He stares at me, unblinking.

"So... okay. I feel worse," I say.

He still doesn't respond.

"Well, maybe you'd like to discuss which shelf in the fridge you'd like to be yours? I prefer the top, but if you want the top, I can be middle and we can split the bottom."

"Sure," he replies, looking bored.

God, would it kill the guy to smile?

"Listen, buddy. I don't know what your last roommate dealt with, but I won't take your bad attitude all the time. The least you can do is try to be nice, or just tell me if you're in a bad mood."

Without warning, his bored expression turns harsh — livid.

His jaw locks, and he stares down at me, his chest rising and falling. Inexplicably, my gaze is drawn to the deep green shade of his eyes, speckled with hazel in the morning light.

"I don't care, princess. I'll pay you rent on time, and you'll hardly know I'm here. Now fuck off and let me be." He barks the words out, and before I can respond, he sweeps past me and stomps down the hall, slamming his door behind him.

I'm left gaping, standing in the living room like an idiot.

He is... the worst!

I can't believe he just told me to fuck off to my face.

I don't know if anyone has ever said that to me before. Actually, I know nobody has ever said that to me before, because most of the people I associate with are civilized, kind individuals who use their words to communicate. I have half a mind to call housing authority and get him forcibly removed from the premises. Do the police do that? Who do you call to get your stranger-turned-roommate to get out?

Whatever. Forget him.

It's time to focus on the important stuff. The salon. The husband hunt.

Is it too soon to start shopping for giant scissors?

5

——————

LIAM

Even when things are looking up for me, I still act like an arsehole.

I mean, for Christ's sake, this beautiful bombshell of a woman is helping me out by letting me stay with her, and what do I do?

I tell her to fuck off.

When I first saw her in the middle of the night, I thought I must be dreaming. I dragged myself to the kitchen half-asleep, only to find a gorgeous woman standing there in nothing but an oversized t-shirt and panties. The soft whites of her thighs sticking out from the hem of her shirt, her sleepy brown eyes drooping in the low light, her messy blonde hair cutting off to reveal the nape of her neck...

It wasn't just a dream: it was a wet dream.

Then she opened her mouth and all that flew right out the window. At first, I thought she seemed like a ray of sunshine, but her words struck me like lightning.

"I don't know what your last roommate dealt with."

My fist clenches involuntarily at the anger her words stir up within me. I know she didn't mean anything by them. It's not like she'd have any way of knowing how that exact phrase would hit me in my most vulnerable spot.

My weakest point.

The thing is... she's right. Luke did have to deal with my crap when we lived together. He was always the one cleaning up after me, picking up after my shit both literally and metaphorically.

At least I have the rest of the night to think about what a dick I was. It's early evening on a Sunday, so the bar is pretty quiet, with Darius and me behind the bar. We've only been working together for a short time, but he's easy to talk to, and he always knows how to get me laughing, even when I'm in a mood. Which is quite often.

"What's wrong with you?" he asks from beside me. "You're grumbling like someone pissed in your cereal."

"I'm not," I protest weakly, but he just clicks his tongue and turns away from me, shaking his head. "It's my flatmate. We got into a row," I admit.

"Can you talk normal? Like, what the fuck are you saying?"

Darius has a running joke that he can't understand me because of my accent. Though, come to think of it, I'm not sure how much he's actually joking.

I chuckle at that. "My roommate and I got into an argument."

"What did you do?"

"Why do you assume I did something?" I shoot back, and he just raises his eyebrows at me as if to say *seriously?*

"I was kind of a dick to her. She didn't really deserve it, to be fair. She just hit a nerve."

Darius shrugs. "Just apologize. Bring her flowers or some shit."

"Amazing advice, Darius. You should be a therapist." I wipe down a glass and replace it on the rack. He grumbles in response. "Nah, you're right. I'll apologize. Flowers I didn't think of. Could be a nice touch," I say. "Maybe she'll get over it by the time I get home."

"Yeah, cause chicks just love to get over things."

I roll my eyes at Darius. "I swear, you're more of a prick than I am sometimes."

"Proud of it, too."

"How's your brother?" I ask him. Darius' younger brother, Jackson, is a super smart kid, but lately he's been skipping school. Apparently, Jackson wanted to go to college, but his dad told him he should just get his GED and work at the sanitation department with him. Darius has tried to convince him to finish his classes and apply for a few programs, but he's been hard to get through to.

"He's alright," Darius replies. "But he still doesn't listen to me. Just thinks I'm his dumb big brother. Maybe..."

"What?" I pry.

"Maybe you could try to talk to him? You went to college, right?"

"Yeah, I did," I reply, trying not to think about Luke. Hating that every memory of my schooling is tainted by his absence.

"He won't listen to me, but maybe he'd listen to you. If I bring him round next shift, can you try and talk to him?"

"Sure thing," I tell Darius, but my mind is still elsewhere.

Why can't I seem to shake off my stupid row with Whitney? It's not even that big of a deal. I'll do what Darius suggested — buy the girl some flowers and call it a day. Like I told her, we aren't friends, we're roommates, and that'll be that. Maybe it's because I've got nothing else to think about. My life is so empty these days, my little spat with my roommate is the first interesting thing that's happened to me in weeks. Well, I guess getting the room in the first place was a nice change of pace from slumming it in student housing, being taunted by the thoughts of what could have been. I swear if I had to spend another minute seeing folks cramming for exams like their lives depended on it, I was gonna lose my head.

Worse than that were hearing the bloody parties. Remembering all the late nights Luke and I had together, crashing frat ragers and drinking their beer until we stumbled to some bar in the Village, trying to find girls to talk to. More often than not, Luke would be the charmer and I'd strike out, leaving me to stumble back to our place while he stayed the night with his new friend. It's not that I can't get women, but whenever I stood next to Luke, it was obvious which of us was the better man.

He'd always been better than me, and this argument with Whitney just proves that.

On my way home from the bar, I pick up a bouquet of flowers from the bodega and bring them back to the apartment. As I ascend the stairs to my new place, I brainstorm what my apology note should say.

Thanks for letting me stay with you. Apologies.

I got you these flowers. Sorry I was a dick.

Sorry I told you to fuck off. Here's some roses.

Shaking my head, I turn the key in the lock, thankful that she didn't change them in my absence. I half-expected to come home and find myself homeless, but nothing in the apartment has changed.

My phone buzzes in my pocket and I slip it out, my dad's name flashing across the screen. I've been dodging his calls for a bit, so I figure I should answer.

I pick up. "Hey."

"Liam! How you doin'?"

"I'm good, Dad, thanks. How are you?"

"Fine, fine. Listen, Stacy's got a work trip coming up in a couple of months, so I thought I'd head up to the city to come see you. See what you're cooking up in that lab of yours!"

Shit.

Oh, sorry Dad, did I forget to mention that I've dropped out of grad school and I'm now a bartender at a shitty dive? It's not the type of announcement one generally wants to make over the phone — or at all, for that matter.

"Oh, cool," I say, hoping my voice sounds neutral. "When are you thinking?"

"First weekend of November."

"Won't I see you at Christmas?" I try, hoping I can put our reunion off a little longer.

"You don't want to go to Brighton to see your mum for the holidays? You know she's been dying to have you over there, and she loves Christmas."

Ever since my parents split when I was fifteen, I've been the pawn between them. The annoying thing is they are both so bloody nice about it, insisting the other one should have more time with me. I'm half-convinced neither of them wants to be stuck with me. They're on good terms now, but there was a bit of a bad patch when I didn't speak to my mum for a few years. There was a lot I didn't understand; I thought she'd cheated on my dad, but really they'd already been separated for a while and hadn't told me about it. Then, I didn't get why she wouldn't move to America with us to make it work, why she would let her whole family disappear across the ocean just to date some bloke she hardly knew. Now she's been married to that bloke for ten years. Dad met Stacy when we moved to Philadelphia, and they've been together ever since.

"I dunno if I wanna go all the way home, Dad. It's a lot."

"I know you've got your feelings about Simon, but you really ought to get to know him more. He's a great guy, and he really loves your mum."

"I know that," I grumble. I hate that any mention of *Simon* causes me to regress into an angsty teenager with step-daddy issues. It's pathetic. "It's not about him."

"Then what's the problem?"

I sigh. "There's no problem."

"Great! Then I'll see you in November, and I'll let your mum know you'll come for the holidays."

"Lovely," I mutter sarcastically. This is why I've been avoiding his calls. He's got a way of roping me into whatever he's got planned.

"Any hotel recommendations close to your dorms? I don't want to have to take a cab everywhere."

"Nobody takes cabs anymore, and I moved."

"You moved out of the dorms?"

Shit. How do I explain this without telling him that I've dropped out?

"Yeah, um. Just felt like it was time to be a bit more independent, you know? Plus, there were bad memories and all..."

"Right. Right."

It's quiet for a moment.

"Well, what's the new place like?"

I glance around and take in my spacious room. "It's great. It's a two-bed in Bushwick. It's really nice, actually."

"That's awesome. I can't wait to see it. You got a pull-out couch?"

"I think it's a futon? It's my flatmate's."

"Even better. You know how much a hotel room costs these days? It's insane. Inflation is out of control."

I don't bother to answer. He's mostly talking to himself, and I don't feel like complaining about the price of eggs. (Although, seven dollars? What a fucking joke.)

"Well, as long as your flatmate doesn't mind, I'd love to crash! We'll be boys on the town. Boys in the house!"

I suppress the eye roll that threatens to burst through me. He really is the lamest guy I know.

"I'll ask her," I tell him.

"Oh, a lady flatmate? How progressive."

"Yes, Dad, men and women can live together, you know."

"I know. I watch reality TV. Stacy likes the live-in ones. Like *Love Island.* You should try that, by the way."

"Alright, Dad, I gotta go."

I don't, but once he gets going about *Love Island,* he never shuts up.

"Listen, son, before you hang up. I just want to say... or ask, really... how you holding up? You know, if you ever want to talk about Luke and what happened, I'm here for you."

My spine turns to steel at the softness of his words. The pity in his voice seems to shatter through me. I blink into the empty room, my stomach churning uncomfortably.

"I've really gotta go, Dad."

"Liam—"

"Bye," I manage before hanging up.

Great. Now I have to figure out how to tell my dad I'm a disappointment with no future and how to ask my new roomie if my 50-year-old father can move in with us for a weekend. I'll save that for another time. November is months away.

I find a vase in the top cabinet and put the flowers out on the dining room table, scribbling a small note:

Whitney,

Really sorry about the other morning. You caught me on a bad day, and you didn't deserve my attitude. Hope you like roses.

It's not great, but at least it's earnest.

Let's hope she doesn't burn them.

6

LIAM

When I wake up, it's pouring. I hate the rain. Part of why I was eager to leave London and live with my dad when I was younger was to get away from the terrible weather. Not that New York is so much better, but I prefer the seasons to the constant rain and fog. The only problem is that even now, in the dead of August, I feel cold inside. Have for the past six months.

Ever since I watched them lower Luke's body into the ground.

After dragging myself to the shower, I go to the kitchen and see a note sitting on the counter next to the bouquet I got for Whitney.

Thanks for the flowers.

That's it?

This is from the girl whose grocery list on the fridge has exclamation points after every single item. That's the loudest period I've ever seen.

So, she's definitely not over it. Why do I even care? I fucked up, I apologized, and now it's done. If she can't forgive me, that's on her. Staring at the note, I crumble it in my hands and throw it away. Why does the thought of her being upset piss me off so much? She said thank you. It's done.

Later, I'm in my room finishing the last of my unpacking when I hear a knock at my door. Turning down the music blasting from my speaker, I answer. "Yeah?"

"Can I come in?" Whitney's voice asks from behind the door.

"That's generally what 'yeah' means."

The door opens, her bored expression meeting mine. "'Yeah' doesn't always mean enter. You should be more precise," she says in a matter-of-fact voice.

I suppress an eye roll, knowing that if I react to her attitude I'm only going to make things worse. "You're right. Sorry about that. I'll be more transparent in future," I reply.

She narrows her eyes as if she doesn't believe me, then huffs, crossing her arms. "How do you want to handle rent and utilities? Venmo, or...?"

A moment stretches between us. I can't stop looking at her eyelashes. Why are they so long?

"Is there another option coming, love?"

"Don't call me that." She shifts her weight. "Olivia always Venmo'd me."

I smirk. "Venmo works."

"Cool," she replies.

"Was there something else?" I prompt, trying to keep my voice as light as possible.

"Yes." She stands rod-straight, her chin lifted. "I was wondering if you'd like to do a chore wheel."

I blink at her. "What's a chore wheel?"

"It's a wheel you spin to decide what chore you do."

Is she serious? I try my hardest not to smirk. "There's only two of us. Why would we need a wheel? I'll clean up after myself."

"In case we wanted to mix it up and have different chores," she clarifies.

"Then we can just switch. Bloody hell, you're a handful." The words slip out before I can stop them.

"Excuse me?"

"Fuck. I'm sorry. I didn't mean that," I admit. "Just tell me what you want me to do, and I'll do it, yeah? I don't need a wheel."

"Fine. Forget it," she grits out, turns on her heels, and struts out of my room, slamming the door behind her.

Well, I fucked that one.

Seriously? What the hell is it about this girl that has my heckles raising? It's like no matter what comes out of that perfect mouth of hers, I turn into the worst version of myself. Maybe if I stopped counting her eyelashes or staring at her lips, she wouldn't bother me so much.

I realize with a grimace I forgot to ask her about my dad staying with us in November. Whatever. I still have a few months, so I'll get around to it. Hopefully by then we'll be on better terms, or at the very least, our conversations won't end with a door slam.

A guy can hope.

My phone rings with an incoming call from my mum. I stare at it for a few seconds, thinking. I really don't want to get into the whole me-dropping-out-of-school thing right now — or ever for that matter — but I can't avoid her forever. All I can hope is that Simon isn't on the call. He loves to slide in on our conversations and ask me questions about my life and call me *buddy*.

"Hello?"

"Liam, darling! You're alive! I'd never know it given how little I hear from you."

There's that passive aggressive charm I know and love.

"Hi, Mum. Sorry it's been a while. Things have just been..." I trail off, unsure of what I was going to say. Horrible? Depressing? Filled with dread? "Before you say anything, I'll come over there for Christmas, if you'd like."

I haven't been home in a while, so I'm not surprised when she squeals in glee on the other line. The sound of it sent a wave of guilt through me, my stomach knotting.

"Simon! Simon, come here!"

I suppress an eye roll as I hear Simon's voice on the other line.

"You're on speakerphone, honey," my mum says.

"Hi, Simon," I say, trying to keep any irritation from seeping into my tone.

"Alright, Liam?"

"Yeah, you?"

"Grand, yeah."

This is the extent of my relationship with my stepfather.

"Liam's going to come for the holidays. For Christmas!"

My mum is thrilled, and I can't help a small smile that I've pleased her with this. I suppose I'll tell her about dropping out when I visit them.

"Will you stay for the new year?"

I shake my head. "Probably not. Rather be back in the city."

"Can't wait to see you, mate. We've been thinking about you over here. Really just hoping you're alright." Simon's tone is friendly but laced with pity.

I hate that fucking pity.

"Simon," my mum whispers in warning.

"All good over here. Listen, I've gotta run, but I'll send you flight details whenever I figure them out. Text you about dates and all."

"I'll get your room set up. Did I tell you it's our gym now?"

Always comforting to hear that your mum and stepdad have

turned your childhood bedroom into their own personal fitness haven. "Thanks, Mum."

"Alright, love. Be safe over there. Don't be a stranger," she says. "Oh! I'm gonna send you a care package."

"You really don't have to," I protest.

"Oh, stop. You know you love my candles and soaps."

I sigh dramatically. "I've moved, so I'll send you my new address."

"I thought you were in Columbia housing?"

This is it. The moment I should tell her. Just say it.

Mum, I dropped out.

"Just felt weird without Luke there. I'm in Brooklyn now," I say, chickening out yet again.

"I'm so sorry, Liam," my mum replies. "Isn't that a bit of a journey for you?"

It would be if I were still going to class.

"Don't mind it. Just get some studying in," I lie. It feels foreign on my tongue, and another pang of guilt hits me in the gut.

"Alright. Send me your new address. Talk soon, darling."

"Bye, Liam," Simon adds.

I say goodbye and hang up the phone, shaking my head. What a disaster. I had my chance to tell the truth and I didn't take it. Suppressing a sigh, I vow to tell them the truth when I visit in December. I just have to figure out how the hell to tell my mum that her dreams of her son being a scientist are crushed.

Falling back against my pillow, I feel a sense of restlessness down to the tips of my fingers. Taking a deep breath, I roll over and open my messages, typing out a text to Grayson, Luke's dad.

Liam: Hey. Can I come over?

WHEN I GET to Long Island, he's waiting for me at the station, standing next to his truck.

"Liam!" he calls, waving me over. He brings me in for a back-slapping hug, wrapping his arms around me. When he pulls back, he's grinning from ear-to-ear. "Wow, you look like crap, son."

I laugh despite myself. "Yeah, yeah. I know."

"Seriously, when's the last time you slept? Burning the midnight oil in study hall?"

Ever since Luke died, we've kept in touch, mostly through phone calls and the occasional visit. I try not to bother him, but when things get a bit much, or I feel like being around my parents without being around my parents, I take the LIRR out to Jamaica.

He climbs into the truck, and I follow him. This is the part I was dreading. It's bad enough that I haven't told my own dad that I quit school. I can handle his disappointment. In fact, I'm probably used to it by now. But Grayson? I don't know if I can handle letting him down.

"Yeah... I kind of dropped out, actually."

Almost as soon as we've started driving, he slams on the brakes. "What? Liam—"

"Jesus! I know, I know." I cling onto the door as a car honks behind us. "Just... can we not talk about it? That's not why I'm here."

He sighs and shakes his head, setting off again. "Alright. No problem."

When we get to the house, he insists on making coffee and puts some cookies on a plate for me. Whenever I'd come stay with Luke, they'd send us both home with enough food to feed an army. I'm sure today will be no different.

"Listen, Mr. Monroe, the reason I asked to come over today is because I wanted to talk to you about something."

"C'mon, man. How many times I gotta tell you? Call me Grayson."

I run my hand through my hair. "Alright, Grayson. The truth is... I've been thinking about this for a while, and I want to do something to honor Luke. To carry on his legacy. I'm thinking if I can somehow raise money to set up a scholarship in Luke's name, then—"

"Son..." Grayson interrupts me, tears gathering in his eyes. "That's incredible, but you don't have to do that. You should be focusing on your own future."

"I want to. I feel like I owe it to him. To all of you."

The truth is that this idea has been eating me up for months. I don't just feel like I owe it to him, I *know* I do.

He shakes his head. "You don't owe us anything."

"Please," I insist. "Let me do this."

"Alright." He rubs the back of his neck. "But there's something you should see." He gestures for me to follow him, and he leads me to Luke's room.

I linger in the doorway, stuck by an invisible barrier of sentimentality and grief. I've only been here a couple of times before when Luke brought me home for Thanksgiving, but both times were enough to leave an impression on me. As all childhood bedrooms are, it's his all over, exactly the same as the last time I was here.

Grayson reaches under the bed and pulls out a cardboard box. He puts it on the bed and turns to me. "I'll give you a minute alone."

He leaves, and I sit against Luke's bed, already feeling a pressure building in my chest. I don't know what's in this box, but

I'm sure whatever it is won't be easy for me to see. Talking about Luke is hard enough. If it's photos...

Taking a deep breath, I lift the lid off the box and peer inside. Inside is a handwritten plan for a foundation focused on tutoring students and helping them find scholarships to universities of their choice. It supports low income and first-generation high-schoolers interested in pursuing higher education, but who may not have the means.

Reading further, I find detailed notes, pages and pages of Luke's inspiration laid out in full.

Mission Statement: making large, structural changes to effect individual change and ensure the success of every participant.

Wow.

I knew that Luke had big ideas, but I had no clue that he'd already started an entire business plan for a his very own foundation. Forget my scholarship idea — I have to do this. I have to finish the work that Luke started. It's what he would want.

The only question is... how the hell am I going to pay for it?

7
———

WHITNEY

I have decided that I simply no longer care about my new roommate. So what if he's a jerk of the biggest proportion? I don't care. He's just my roommate. We don't have to be friends. In fact, we don't even have to speak.

We can simply coexist.

It's not like Olivia and I were ever close, so I don't know why this bothers me so much. Maybe the difference is because she never outright hated me, which is the general feeling I get from Liam at all times. I thought British people were supposed to be nice, but clearly not. I guess he's more of the Gordon Ramsay variety.

Whatever. I don't have time to waste thinking about Liam. I should be focusing all my energy on figuring out a business plan for the salon. If I get everything together, I'm convinced somehow the universe will reward me with a husband.

Right?

I spend a few hours working on the business plan and budget spreadsheet. I figure the inheritance should be more than enough to front the cost of renting a place and other upfront costs. Feeling positive about my productivity, I pivot to the fun stuff — interior design. Pinterest becomes my best friend, and I spend the next few hours saving photos and thinking of color palettes.

After a few hours of work, I'm feeling exhausted and slightly dejected. Even though planning for the salon is exciting, without the money secured, it's nothing but a pipe dream. I close my eyes, feeling raw and emotional, a voice whispering in my head that *I'm alone.* It might not feel so true if I'd dated anyone since Christopher, but I've been nursing that wound since college, and in the three years since then, I've barely made it three months with any of the guys I've dated. Some of them were fine, but the truth was, I have walls up the size of Everest.

I text Abbi, knowing she's probably at work. I don't think she's ever been further than five feet away from her cell phone at any given moment, so I'm not surprised when she responds right away.

> Abbi: How's hubby hunting?

> Whitney: Awful.

> Abbi: Why don't I come over tonight and we can brainstorm? I have some ideas.

> Whitney: Should I be scared?

> Abbi: Terrified.

> Whitney: Don't put anything in writing. The FBI agent reading this will come for us.

> Abbi: See you after work. I'll bring wine.

I decide to distract myself by cooking dinner, but end up burning it. After I finish, I go to grab some silverware, yanking on the drawer, jiggling it left and right. It's always a pain in the ass; it's broken, and I can't figure out how to get it back on the tracks.

"What did that drawer ever to do you?" a voice drawls from behind me, and I turn sharply to see Liam leaning against the doorframe with a smirk.

I blink, trying not to stare at the spot where his t-shirt rides up, revealing a strip of tanned skin. I turn away from him, shaking my head.

"Ugh. It's been broken forever," I reply. "You have to jiggle it open, FYI."

He slips past me to fill up a glass of water while I slam the drawer shut and cross to the dining room to eat.

"Thanks for the heads up," he replies.

Why does he have to say everything with that teasing, sultry tone of voice? It's like he's purposefully trying to rile me up.

"My friend Abbi is coming over tonight," I tell him. "She's very loud, so I apologize in advance."

The corners of his mouth turn upwards, a small dimple forming on one of his cheeks. The sight of it sends a fierce blush to my cheeks, another wave of mortification rushing through me. This guy has done nothing but antagonize me since he's shown up, and here I am fawning over his every micro-expression.

"I'm off tonight, but I'll keep to myself. Wouldn't want to spoil your girls' night."

I can't tell if he's trying to bait me, so I don't respond. Thankfully, he goes back to his room, leaving me to eat in peace. As soon as he's gone, I exhale in relief, shaking my head. What the hell has come over me? I should be focusing on my business plan, not getting distracted by some jerk.

Abbi texts me to let me know she's on her way, so I clean up and light a candle.

Of course, I burn myself again, thinking about said jerk.

Once she arrives, we settle on the couch with a bottle of wine between us.

"Okay, Operation Matrimony is in action. What have you tried so far?" she asks, her tone serious.

"Mostly an embarrassing number of texts and calls to randos in my phone. Lots of getting hung up on. A few people calling me clinically insane."

"Well, they aren't wrong." She smirks.

"Ha-ha," I deadpan.

She chuckles. "This is harder than I thought it would be. You know what? We should just get you on Hinge. Put serious relationship and start swiping. Find someone who seems cool, intro the idea on date two or three... totally chill."

"I already tried Hinge, and I chickened out. I barely swiped on anyone. Also, I don't think there's a chill way to ask someone to marry you on a third date."

"Can you stop ruining all the fun?" Abbi groans. "Give me your phone. Let's do it together."

She takes my phone and makes me pick out my best photos while she answers all my prompts and starts swiping. I notice her thumb swiping right very often.

"Abbi, you can't swipe right on everyone."

"Why not? It doesn't matter who he is. It's not like he has to be hot or anything."

"Why don't *you* just marry me?" I groan. "It's only three years."

She throws daggers at me. "Shane definitely better have proposed by then. Sorry babe, but I'm spoken for."

I groan, and she exits Hinge.

"Okay, time for Plan B. Let's start calling your exes."

"I only have one ex, Abbi, and you know there's no way I'm calling Christopher."

"Fine, then let's try *my* exes. One of them owes me a favor, I bet."

"This is a pretty big favor," I tell her. She scrolls through her contacts until she lands on one and holds it out to me.

"I can't do this."

"Yes, you can," she encourages me. "If anything, you should offer like, 100k or something. It's hardly any of it, and I bet someone would do it for that little."

"Not if they find out I'm getting a million," I grumble.

She throws her hands up. "It's not like you're going to call him up and say 'hey, I just inherited a million bucks from my granny, but I can only get it if I'm married. What do you say?'"

"Shh! My roommate is home," I say in a low voice.

"Oh my God." She glances down the hallway. "Why didn't you tell me? He's here? I want to meet him."

"Trust me, you don't."

She rolls her eyes and points to the phone. Reluctantly, I press call and hold the phone against my ear.

"Put it on speaker!" she whisper-yells, grabbing for the phone, but I yank it out of her grasp. She throws her body over mine, reaching over my head to try and grab it, but I don't let go.

"Stop it!"

"I want to hear!"

Trying and failing to shove her off me, I turn away, trying to tuck the phone to my ear.

"Hello?"

We both freeze at the sound of the male voice coming through the phone.

"Abbi?"

My eyes wide, I shove the phone towards her, shaking my head. She shakes her head back at me, gesturing for me to take it back. After a few moments of silent communication, she relents, pressing the speaker button.

"Hi, James," she says, her tone sweeter than honey. "How are you?"

"Uh, I'm alright. What's up?"

"Just hanging with my friend Whitney. You remember Whit, right? Gorgeous blonde? Legs for days? Impossibly cute?"

I glare at her, and James chuckles slightly.

"What do you want, Ab? I haven't heard from you in two years, and you call me out of the blue to set me up with your friend?"

"Excuse me! Can't an ex-girlfriend want to reconnect just for the hell of it?"

"I'm engaged. You'd know if you hadn't blocked me on Instagram," he replies.

Abbi's eyes widen and she stares down at the phone. "Uh, you're breaking up—can't—going through tunnel—"

She hangs up the phone, tossing it onto the couch between us.

"Seriously?" I quirk an eyebrow at her.

We descend into a fit of giggles. After our laughter subsides, we chat for a few more minutes. She gushes about Shane; she's expecting him to propose any day now, especially since she's been dropping major hints that she's ready. Last time I hung out with them, she spent the whole time showing him wedding photographer Instagram accounts and asking what he thought of them.

Abbi has never been one for subtlety.

It's late when she finally leaves, kissing me on the cheek. "You're gonna find someone. I know it," she says.

I shrug. "We'll see."

She grabs both my shoulders. "You are not losing out on that money, Whitney. I swear to God, we will find you a husband."

I nod, feeling suddenly emotional. I really, really want to

make the salon a reality, but the more time that passes, the more I'm starting to doubt this entire plan. Too much can go wrong. Too much is at stake.

And I'm no closer to figuring any of it out.

8

———

LIAM

Is it technically eavesdropping if it's mostly unintentional?

It's not like I had my ear to the door, praying to catch a bit of my roommate's conversation. Whoever her friend is, she's the loudest person I've ever had the (not) pleasure of listening in on, so it's not my fault that I overheard every word they were saying. I suppose I could've put my headphones in, like a decent lad would.

Too bad there's none of those around here.

Instead, since my door was wide open, and Whitney's friend was screaming like a banshee and at one point singing *Here Comes the Bride,* I'm now aware that my new roommate is in the market for a husband.

When I first hear their debate, I could hardly contain my laughter. What a ridiculous pair these two are — like a modern-day *Thelma and Louise*, cackling like hyenas and from the sound of it blowing through wine like it's water.

But then I heard the number.

A million dollars.

That's a lot of money.

No, correction: that's a *fuck ton* of money. Enough money to get started on Luke's foundation. To make his dreams a reality, even if he's not here to see it. Selfishly, there's part of me that hopes that if I can see this through, I'll finally be able to move on.

Slinging my bag over my shoulder, I check my piece of paper again, making sure I'm at the right room.

304.

I shouldn't be so bloody nervous. It's just a roommate. It'll be awkward at first, yeah, but then we'll just be normal. Pushing the door forward, I walk in and see a tall, Black guy with braids laying in the bed on the right, reading a book.

"Hey," I greet him.

His head shoots up and he tosses the book to the side, sitting up. "Hey! You my new roomie?"

"Yeah, I'm Liam."

"Whoa. You British?"

I chuckle. "Apparently."

He smiles widely. "Awesome. First day of college and I've already got a cool British roommate. I'm Luke." He slips his hand into mine in a bro-shake. Shit. He's a fucking cool guy, isn't he?

"Where are you from?" I ask him.

"Long Island." He sits back down on his bed. "I hope it's cool I took the right side. You wouldn't have liked me on the left, trust me."

I'm not sure what that means, so I just drop my bag on the other bed and roll my suitcase over to the corner. I take in the room, which isn't huge, but it's not terrible, either. Luke has a TV set up on his side and what looks like a video game console.

"What's your major?" Luke asks from beside me.

"Biological sciences. You?"

"Chemistry. I bet we'll have classes together," he replies. "I don't know if you like gaming, but I set up my PS5 and I've got tons of stuff.

Skyrim, 2K, Elden Ring, GTA. We could play together, or you're free to use it whenever."

"Thanks, mate. That's golden."

"Yeah." He rubs the back of his head and smiles ruefully.

"I'm just gonna unpack." I gesture towards my stuff, and he nods, looking slightly disappointed.

It's quiet for a while as I start putting my clothes into the dresser. After a few minutes, Luke pipes up again. "Sorry if I'm being annoying as shit. To be honest, I'm really excited about college. I'm the first in my family to go, and I'm just... yeah. It's a lot of pressure and excitement, but you know, if you ever want me to shut up, just say it. You can definitely be straight with me."

"You're not annoying. If you're bothering me, I'll just tell you to fuck off, won't I?"

He smiles, wide and clear. "Dude. You rock."

BLINKING BACK TEARS, I refocus. I need to get started on Luke's plan. Already it feels like everyone else from school has forgotten him. Somehow, they can go on with their studies and their jobs and not feel this crippling sense of... wrongness.

One million dollars. Is that much money worth getting married for? To Chore Wheel Girl?

I have to think about this rationally. Pros and cons.

I already live with her, and we'd only be married on paper. From her lips, after three years we could cut each other loose. It's not like I'm getting into a relationship anytime soon. So, really, my life wouldn't change at all, I'd just be half-a-million richer. I could honor Luke and find some way to fill this emptiness that exists inside me, do something that Luke would be proud of.

Just do... *something.*

All I have to do is get Whitney to marry me, and I can finally figure out some way to stop this endless sense that I failed Luke, that I'm the one responsible.

I know what I have to do.

I need to convince my new roommate that I'm husband material. Unfortunately, my schedule never lines up with Whitney's long enough for me to talk to her. Every time I get home, she's gone. I'd almost think she were avoiding me if I thought she cared about me even slightly.

If I go out there now, she'll know that I know that Abbi is gone. And if she knows I know that, then she knows I can hear from my bedroom. And if she knows that, she'll know I'm a nosy bastard.

I'll deal with this tomorrow.

I wait until things go quiet and then make my way to the bathroom, ready for a shower instead, towel in hand.

"Hey."

I turn, startled despite my embarrassing eavesdropping. "Sorry. Didn't mean to disrupt, just heading for a shower."

Her brow furrows and she smirks — a tipsy smirk. "You don't have to apologize for showering."

"Right."

"Just letting you know Abbi left." She offers a small smile, then turns around to resume tidying up. Chore Wheel Girl in action.

Chore Wheel Girl.

"You know what," I say before I have time to talk myself out of it. "I thought about your chore rotation thing, and it's a great idea. We should do it."

Her head snaps towards mine, her face clouded in skepticism. "Really?"

Really, Liam?

"Absolutely, yeah."

Absolutely, yeah?

She narrows her eyes further. "I thought you hated it."

I shrug. "Well, I changed my mind, didn't I?"

She glances away from me, still seeming unsure. "Okay," she says finally. "If you really want to."

"I really do," I say, trying to inject as little sarcasm into my voice as possible.

"Well..." She perks up, smiling now. "If you want, we could make the wheel together? Like a craft project?"

I force a smile to match hers. "I love crafts."

Who am I?

"Great, let's do it tomorrow night!" She claps, an even wider smile spreading across her face. It's like her face comes alive when she smiles. She should do that all the time. "We can drink wine! And I'll make a charcuterie board!"

"Yay!" I flash a thumbs up.

Now I just have to figure out how to propose.

9

———

LIAM

The following evening, I walk into the kitchen to find Whitney sitting at the counter with an unopened bottle of rosé.

"You want some?" she asks.

"Sure," I reply. She tugs at the silverware drawer, the motion smooth and easy ever since I fixed the thing. After she told me it wasn't working, I took it upon myself to mend it, and it turned out to be a simple task.

Whitney's brow furrows, and she looks at me. "It's fixed," she says in awe.

I shrug, glancing away from her bright brown eyes. "It was easy to do. I can show you how if you want."

A smile spreads across her face, and I can't help but stare at the sight. I'll fix a hundred drawers if it means I can see that damned smile on her face one more time. "Thank you for doing that," she says.

"No big deal."

She pours me a glass of wine and hands it to me, clinking her glass against mine.

"To new beginnings?" I offer.

"If you're waiting for me to forget that you told me to fuck off, you're out of luck."

Despite myself, I laugh. "So, chore wheel?" I prompt. Whitney grabs a shopping bag and empties out the contents on the counter.

"I am so excited. I may or may not have spent $100 at Michael's." She plugs in a glue gun and hands me a packet of construction paper.

"Wow," I chuckle under my breath. "You were serious about that craft stuff."

"Absolutely," she replies, tossing me a packet of glitter. "I have a scrapbooking addiction."

She spends the next ten minutes showing me exactly how she wants to build the wheel and assigns me to cutting duty, noting that it's one of the only things I can't screw up. I'm elbow deep in glitter and glue when I finally set my tools down and take a deep breath.

"I have something I need to ask you," I start, not totally sure how to breach this topic with someone I hardly know.

"Is it about the shade of pink? Because I was also thinking it's *too* pink."

"It's not about the pink," I cut her off. Reaching across the counter, I place my palm over hers, and meet her eyes. Her hands are soft and warm. I blink at her, and the corners of my mouth tilt upwards automatically, bracing myself for her reaction. I'm sure this will go over like a pile of bricks, and yet I find myself excited for her reaction. I take a deep breath, and pose the question I've been waiting all day to ask:

"Will you marry me?"

WHITNEY LOOKS like she might be in shock. She's gaping back at me, her mouth opening and closing like a fish, staring at me like I've grown a second head.

"Listen, I'll be straight with you. I overheard you gossiping with your friend about your... dilemma," I tell her.

That gets her attention. She snaps her gaze to me, her eyes hard. "You were eavesdropping on me? In my apartment?"

"Our apartment," I correct her.

She rolls her eyes. "Oh, please. It's mine, and I don't gossip. Two women talking is not gossiping."

I hold my hands up in a gesture of surrender. "Do you have to take everything I say as an insult?"

She narrows her eyes. "Maybe because your tone is insulting!"

I pinch the bridge of my nose, inhaling and closing my eyes. *Ten, nine, eight, seven, six...*

When I feel calm enough to not say something stupid, I open my eyes "Bottom line is I'll do it. I'll marry you."

She whistles out a laugh. "Wow. I actually don't need your offer, but good to know my private conversations aren't as private as I thought."

"Come on. I heard you. You need the money to start your business."

"That was *private!*" she seethes. "As in, not for you to hear."

"I wasn't intentionally listening to your conversation. It just happened," I explain.

"Well, next time, put some fucking headphones in."

It's quiet for a moment, so I press on. "What's holding you back? Talk me through it."

"I don't even know you!" she exclaims, throwing her craft supplies in the air. "And what I do know of you is really not winning me over. You've already told me to fuck off and ruined my craft night."

"Pretend you do know me. Talk to me."

She sighs, a heavy, lengthy sound, and reaches for her wine, taking a deep gulp. "Well, besides the fact that *I don't know you*, and that this is probably illegal, I am actually looking for... *it*." She shifts, her cheeks coloring slightly.

"Looking for what?"

"Love. A relationship. And maybe... marriage at some point," she admits.

"Okay, well, maybe that's still possible. What's our timeline? Three years only, right?"

"Stop acting like this is happening!" she replies, her voice rising. "But yes. At least three years for everything to be processed. It's not a single payout, she has it spaced out in three parts."

Now, that stops me.

"Wait, the money won't be immediate?" I clarify.

"No, only the first part."

I push off the counter and head for the living room. "Alright, well, forget it then."

She follows me and tugs on my shirt sleeve, stopping me in my tracks. She narrows her eyes at me. "What does that have to do with anything?"

I smirk down at her. "Well, sweetheart, I'm only doing this for the money."

"What the hell do you mean? It's *my* money."

I shake my head. "Nah. You're gonna split it with me, *wife*."

She almost spits out her wine. "There is no way." Her voice is ice cold and her gaze even colder.

I shrug like I couldn't care less. "Alright, good luck finding someone else to marry you. You're such a peach, I'm sure you'll have no problem at all."

She ignores my insult. "Why do you need the money?"

"Like you said. It's *private.* I don't care what this business venture is that you're using your half for, so don't ask about my half. That's my one condition. We split the money, 50/50."

"We are not doing this!" she exclaims, throwing her hands in the air.

"Listen, I'm not thrilled about the idea either. The last thing I want to do is marry you."

"Gee, thanks. You really know how to propose to a girl."

"The point is, I need the money and so do you. This is a win-win opportunity for both of us and nothing more than a business deal. There's no need to think any more into it."

"How about this... " she trails off, her voice dripping with honey. "You marry me, and I won't kick you out of my apartment."

I rear back, shocked. I definitely underestimated this woman.

"You can't do that," I stutter. "I live here now."

She laughs. "Oh, yes I can. You are not on the lease. You haven't paid me a dime —"

"I Venmo'd you for utilities and sent Olivia the rent!"

She shrugs. "Doesn't sound very legally binding to me, and I'm pretty sure if I called the landlord or the cops, you'll be out on your ass before you can say *'til death do us part.*"

A growl escapes me, my body tightening with anger. This is not going the way I expected.

"What about you? If you kick me out, who's gonna be your rent-a-husband?"

"So it's a mutually beneficial agreement. You marry me, you can stay here."

"I still want a cut," I shoot back. "That's a shitty deal for me, and you know it."

She eyes me, her expression wary and suspicious. I'm absolutely certain she's going to tell me to bugger off and pack my shit when she crosses her arms and meets my gaze head-on.

"70/30."

"50/50," I retort.

"65/35, and that's my final offer. I could kick you out right now, you know."

I pause. Thirty-five percent of a million bucks is certainly enough for me to honor Luke. Plus, I really can't afford to move again right now.

"Deal."

I stick my hand out, waiting to shake. She stares down at it, a mixture of uncertainty and excitement on her face. Something about the openness of her expression churns in my gut, but I don't have time to examine it.

She's about to meet my hand when she suddenly pulls back. "Wait. What's our dating policy?"

"What do you mean?"

She shifts on her feet. "Like, this marriage is obviously fake, and if it's going to last three years... it's not like you're going to be celibate that whole time, right?"

I blink back at her. How had I not considered this? I'd honestly assumed this conversation would not come up, and sex has been the last thing on my mind lately.

"That won't be an issue," I say.

An awkward silence settles between us.

"Well," she starts. "We're only married on paper. I guess it's okay with me if you see other people as long as you're... discrete about it. I feel like it wouldn't be fair to expect either of us to just stop having sex..."

I don't bother replying.

She nods, mostly talking to herself at this point. "Okay. That works. We can both see other people, but we have to pretend it's real for everyone else. We can't tell anyone. Well, besides Abbi. I already told her."

"I'm not going to tell anyone."

It's not like I even have anyone to tell.

"Alright, then. I think we've got a deal." She reaches out and shakes my hand before collapsing onto the couch. "Am I really doing this?" she says out loud, more to herself than to me.

"Hey, we shook on it. No backing out on me now, Rhodes. Or shall I say, the future Mrs. Clark."

She shoots daggers at me, her eyes wide. "Oh my God, shut up. There is no way I am taking your last name."

I guess we'll see about that.

10

WHITNEY

I am officially an engaged woman.

I have a *fiancé*.

Technically, neither of us have rings, so I guess it's not a completely done deal. Well, it won't really be done until someone says, 'I do'. Still, rings or no rings, I'm freaking out. After Liam and I shook last night, I spent the remainder of the evening chugging red wine and watching *Love Island* in a fruitless attempt to distract myself from my impending marriage.

I'm almost regretting quitting because I don't even have work to distract me. I have lots to do with the salon, but I can only dedicate a few hours a day to that before I start to feel agitated, worried that it's not going to work out, or worse, that I'll pour all this money into my idea only to discover that I can't do it. Still, now that I know the marriage deal is secured, I can at least start making plans. As soon as the certificate is signed and the first check is on its way to my account, I'm going to start looking around Brooklyn for a location.

Cycling between dread over the salon's potential failure and disbelief over my new relationship status, I decide to text Abbi and tell her that I have updates on the hubby hunt and need to meet.

I'm sipping an Aperol Spritz at the Italian restaurant across from her office when I spot her red hair at the entrance and wave a frantic hand in her direction.

She crosses the room and flings her arms around me. "You crazy bitch," she laughs into my hair. "Tell me everything. Wait, where's the waiter? I need a drink for this."

Once she has a glass of wine in hand, she leans closer to me. "Okay. Spill."

I shake my head. "I can't believe this is happening. I can't believe I agreed to this."

"Wait. Back up. Who's the guy?"

I pause, unsure how she's going to react.

"It's my roommate."

It's silent for a moment before Abbi throws her head back, cackling. She laughs for a full minute and doesn't stop despite my shushing and eye-rolling. The elderly couple sitting next to us eyes her like she might be a real-life witch.

"Oh my God." She wipes at her eyes. "This is amazing."

"No, it's not. It's probably the worst idea I've ever had, and you were there that time I took six jello shots."

"That was epic. But this... wow. The grumpy roommate. I was not expecting that."

"I'm freaking out. I barely know this guy, and what I do know of him, he seems like the world's biggest jerk. Now I'm going to chain myself to him for the next three years? What the hell am I thinking?"

"Oh, calm down. It's perfect. The universe knew you needed a husband, and it sent you a tattooed hunk."

"He's like, the rudest guy I've ever met."

"Come on, he can't be that bad. I'm sure you're exaggerating it."

"Nope. He sucks."

She rolls her eyes. "Whatever. I'll bet you fifty bucks you guys sleep together eventually."

I gape at her. "That will never happen. He doesn't even think of me like that."

She raises her eyebrows. "Oh, but you think of him like that?"

I shift under her knowing gaze. When you've been friends as long as Abbi and I have, it's impossible to hide things. She always knows when I'm lying, and worse, she seems to have some sort of Whitney-radar that tells her when I'm horny.

"Oh my God," she cackles again, throwing her head back. "You totally want to fuck him."

People around us turn again, some giggling, the elderly couple next to us gaping in horror. If I weren't so used to it, I'd be mortified.

"I do not!" I protest. "I just... haven't been with a guy in a while, and he's really muscular."

"I bet you're flicking the bean to him."

"Oh my God." I laugh despite myself. "No way. That position is reserved solely for Dr. Spencer Reid, and you know it."

"This is very unlike you, Miss Virgo," Abbi observes, her brow furrowed. "First the impulsive quitting, now an impulsive engagement. What's going on with you?"

"I don't know," I reply honestly. "As out of control as I feel, it's also sort of... liberating. It feels like I'm finally taking my life into my own hands."

The waiter comes over and we order some appetizers to share. I manage to divert the conversation to her new project at work for a while, but she's relentless. She's paying the bill when she leans back in her chair, her scrutinizing gaze making me fidget in my seat.

"I love this unemployed look on you. Do you have a new

skincare routine or something? I feel like you are literally glowing."

"Stop it." I glare at her, knowing it won't deter her in the slightest.

"I'm serious!" she exclaims. "I bet it's the pheromones, trying to attract your mate, *Liam*."

"You've got to stop."

She just laughs loud enough for the entire restaurant to hear. "You guys are absolutely going to fuck."

"No way. We already discussed it, and we're both allowed to see other people as long as we are respectful about it."

She raises her eyebrows. "I bet you'd like to respectfully jump his bones."

"Would you stop?" I groan.

"I'm telling you. Fifty bucks says you guys sleep together."

I lift my drink. "Make it 100, because I am 100% sure nothing will ever happen between me and Liam."

She clinks her glass against mine with a knowing grin. "You're on. Just don't come crying to me when the dick is so good you can barely walk straight."

11

LIAM

It's been a week since Whitney agreed to marry me, and I haven't heard anything from her. I assume our agreement is still on, but I'm starting to get nervous. What if she changed her mind? What am I supposed to do then?

I've drafted eight texts to Luke's dad to tell him I am working on a plan to honor Luke and deleted all of them. The only idea I've had is setting up a scholarship in his name, but I don't really know anything about that. Still, I can't help but feel excited about it. Finally, I have something to focus on.

Something important. Worthwhile.

Besides, I'm really starting to get sick of the smell of beer following me everywhere I go. I feel like it's seeped into my pores. Plus, the stench reminds me of the way the lab smelled so *clean* — like sanitizer and latex gloves. I loved that smell. That's how I used to smell. How I used to feel.

Clean.

I didn't get home until four in the morning last night, which has been typical for me lately. Working all night and sleeping all day. Closing my eyes, I try to imagine what Luke would say if he saw me now.

Man, you're a mess. Real women dig white coats, not White Claws.

He'd shove me and smile that foolish grin of his, the kind of smile that seemed so real and so deep. I used to look in his eyes when he laughed and swore he had this sort of spark, this light that felt wholly permanent somehow. I took it for granted. Didn't realize how rare and special it was to find someone like him, someone who really seemed to brighten the world no matter where he went. That's one thing I always admired about him — how genuinely *good* he was. I should have told him. Maybe if he'd known, if he'd understood how much everyone who met him looked up to him, maybe things would be different.

I push any thoughts of Luke from my mind and kick off my blankets, deciding it's time to get up. I'm brewing coffee in the kitchen when Whitney shuffles in, a fluffy pink robe wrapped around her.

"Hey," she says.

"Hey," I reply.

It's quiet. Is she going to say anything about the wedding plan? Do I need to get rings? Shit. Of course we need rings. Am I supposed to be in charge of that?

She crosses the kitchen and pulls out the blender. "Are you around this weekend?"

I lift my coffee to my lips. "I have a shift Friday night and Saturday night."

She just hums in response.

"Why?" I ask.

She shifts on her feet, reaching for a banana. "Well, I was thinking we should probably go to Vegas to get married since it's the shortest waiting period for a marriage license. Then we can fly back here and... be married."

"I can trade my Saturday shift," I tell her. "If you can get us flights for Saturday morning, we can get married Sunday and come back Monday?"

She tosses the banana and some strawberries into the blender. "That works. Do you want me to book them?"

I lean against the counter, watching her. "Sure."

She adds oat milk and protein powder. "Can you send me your... license or something? I don't know. That feels really intimate."

"We're about to be legally married, but booking a flight for me is intimate?"

She rolls her eyes. "Can we just do it now? I'll go get my laptop."

"Okay."

She leaves the room, her unblended smoothie sitting on the counter. I set down my coffee cup and cross over to the blender, plugging it in and running the pulse setting for a few seconds. When she comes back into the kitchen, I'm pouring the liquid into a mason jar and sticking one of those twirly straws she's always chewing on into the glass.

"You didn't have to do that," she says as I slide the smoothie across to her.

"It's fine." I shrug.

We browse online for a few minutes before Whitney books flights for the both of us. Once those are set, I call Darius, basically begging him to take my shift. After I hang up, I wonder if I should have told him I'm getting married. Maybe he would have been excited for me.

Across the counter, Whitney is typing rapidly on her laptop, her eyes darting across the screen. She looks so focused, those chocolate brown eyes zeroed in on whatever she's working on.

Chocolate brown? What the fuck?

My curiosity gets the best of me. I clear my throat and slant my gaze towards her. "What are you working on?"

She glances up at me, wariness written all over her face. I feel a sudden churning in my gut. I've really been a dick to her if she doesn't even want to answer a simple question like that.

She sighs. "It's my business plan. The business I need the money for."

"What kind of business is it?"

"It's a beauty salon," she replies with a soft smile.

I'm surprised by that. Sure, Whitney is gorgeous, and I realized that the second I laid eyes on her. Her short blonde hair that cuts off just at her slender neck, her freckled cheeks and slim, symmetrical face. She's fucking stunning, but she doesn't seem like the type to be concerned about having perfect hair or a face of makeup.

"What made you want to do that?"

"I spent a lot of time in salons when I was kid. Since my mom and I basically lived on the road, she would leave me for long periods to do my own thing. I'd often hang in one of the local hair salons and talk to the ladies who worked there. It felt like a safe space for me, a constant in a world where nothing else really was."

I find myself oddly fascinated watching her speak. She's got this gleam in her eye, a fiery passion behind her words that makes me want to keep listening.

She shrugs. "Yeah, that's it. I don't really know what I'm doing."

"I'm sure you'll figure it out. It sounds really cool."

She nods, and it's quiet. For the first time, I feel a comfortable silence settle over us, like I don't need to say anything. Like we can just sit here, together, and that's enough.

12

WHITNEY

The morning of our trip to Vegas, I shoot up in bed at the crack of dawn. After triple checking my suitcase, I go into the kitchen and quickly make a couple of sandwiches for the flight. Everything is ready.

Except I haven't heard a peep from Liam's room.

I knock on his door, softly at first. There's no response, so I knock again, harder this time, but still nothing.

Glancing at the oven clock, I shake my head and open the door. The room is a dark cave, the blackout curtains drawn so not a sliver of light can get in. Liam's muscular figure is sprawled across the bed, and he's shirtless.

Very shirtless.

For a moment, I just stare at him, taking in the broad lines of his shoulders and the dark ink splattered across his arms and chest. I've never really looked at his tattoos or studied his body, but he's incredible. Ignoring the sudden flush of heat rushing through me, I cross the room and nudge his sleeping form, trying to wake him in the least intrusive way possible. He doesn't seem to even register my presence.

I nudge him again. "Liam. Wake up," I whisper into the darkness.

Nothing.

"Liam!" A little louder now. "We have to go!"

He stirs, grumbling into his pillow.

"Get up!" I say, sounding too much like my mother for my liking. "I'm calling the car in ten minutes."

He lifts his head slightly. "What time is it?" he rasps, sending another strange flush through me.

"A little past five."

"Isn't our flight at ten?" he mumbles into the pillow.

"Yes. It's a forty-five-minute drive to JFK. If we leave before six, we'll be there a bit before seven, and that gives us three hours to get through security."

Finally, he opens his eyes. "Three hours? Are you insane? Go back to bed."

I roll my eyes. "Liam. Get up. I will be calling the car in ten minutes, with or without you."

"Yeah? Gonna say the vows without me, too?"

I throw my hands in the air. "Ugh. Just get up! Please."

He rolls over, facing away from me. "Fine. Get out so I can get dressed."

I glance around at the messy room, barely visible in the darkness. I don't see a suitcase anywhere. "You're packed, right?"

"Sure, sunshine. Now get out." Before I can duck, he sends a pillow flying in my direction, hitting me square in the chest. Taking the hint, I slip out of the room, slamming the door behind me.

Twenty minutes later, my thumb is hovering over the Uber app impatiently. I'm about to lose my shit when Liam finally stumbles out of his room with a duffel bag over his shoulder.

"Great! Let's go!"

He blinks slowly. "How do you have this much energy?"

"I'm a morning person. Haven't you realized that by now?"

He shrugs and sits across from me, setting his bag on the ground. "I guess."

I call the car and the app says it's five minutes away. I take a deep breath, unsure how much to reveal about my fear. "Also... I'm kind of a nervous flier."

He puts his head in his hands, closing his eyes. "Lovely. You're not going to vomit, are you?"

I shake my head. "Probably not."

"Thank God."

We're quiet on the ride to JFK. All through security, we barely engage in conversation. I comment on the length of the line, and he says nothing in response. When we finally sit down at the gate, we have over an hour until boarding starts.

He turns his full gaze onto me, his eyes hard. "What did I tell you? I could've slept another hour."

I shrug. "Better safe than sorry."

"I'm already sorry," he mutters under his breath. I try to hide my chuckle at his grumpiness, which I'm starting to find entertaining. He stands and gestures at the Starbucks. "Want a coffee?"

"Oh, sure. I'll take a—"

"I got it," he cuts me off and walks away without another glance.

I take out my iPad and connect to the Wi-Fi, downloading a few Netflix episodes for the flight. Ten minutes later, Liam returns with two drinks and a bag. He hands me one of the cups and the bag.

I eyeball the two items. "What is this?"

"Iced oat milk latte and a cake pop. What does it look like?"

My mouth hangs open in shock. "How do you know my Starbucks order?"

He just shrugs in response. "You've left like four of those cups in the trash and I saw you eating a cake pop twice in the last week. Don't know how you can stand them. They taste like balls of sugar."

"What a great new term of endearment for you, Sugar Balls." I open the bag and sure enough, there's a brownie cake pop sitting inside. "Thank you, Liam."

He just nods curtly, avoiding my eyes. He's acting like it's not a big deal, but I'm surprisingly touched that he noticed anything about me other than what an annoyance I am.

While I finish downloading a few episodes of *Stranger Things* onto my iPad, Liam takes out a book. I slant my gaze over to read the title — it's a Vonnegut book.

He catches my eye. "What?"

"Nothing. I was just wondering what you're reading." He opens the book to the first page. "I liked that one."

He glances up again. "You've read it?"

"Yes, women *can* read you know."

He shakes his head. "Why do you do that?"

"I was joking."

"It wasn't very funny," he says bluntly, his eyes falling back down to the page. "If this is going to work — you know, me being your *husband* and all — you might want to give me some benefit of the doubt. Stop assuming the worst."

I huff and cross my arms. "I was *trying* to be friendly! Make small talk about *Sirens of Titan*. Maybe we have that in common."

He shrugs. "I guess we'll find out once I finish."

I sigh and turn back to my iPad, feeling frustrated that my efforts at conversation turned into another argument. Maybe I am being too harsh on him. But he started it by acting like a jerk the last few weeks we've been living together.

"I liked *Slaughterhouse Five*, so I thought I'd try another," Liam pipes up from beside me. I glance over at him, and his gaze meets mine, open and... warm?

I realize he's trying, too. He's giving me an olive branch.

I smile softly. "Yeah, I liked that one too. I thought he'd be insufferable and pretentious, but he's actually got a really interesting style."

He hums in agreement and turns his gaze back to the book. I let my eyes wander over his face, his sharp jaw line, his speckled green-hazel eyes, his soft brown curls and rugged beard that I want to reach out and touch. It would be a lot easier to hate him if he weren't so absolutely gorgeous. I force my gaze back down and pretend he's not there.

When the flight starts boarding, I slip my iPad into my bag. Of course, I want to wait until the last second to board, but Liam stands when they call our group, glancing back at where I'm sitting.

He smirks. "Surprised you aren't the type to wait by the sides to board, blocking everyone in your path."

I shrug, my nerves already starting to come on. My stomach is churning with anxiety. Why did I think I could handle this? Why didn't I realize Liam would be sitting right next to me when I inevitably freak out? I should see if they can switch our seats. Maybe there's an empty one in the exit row.

"Whitney?"

Liam's voice jolts me out of my spiral, and I force what I hope looks like a real smile and grab my bag. "Yep! Let's go." I inject as much cheerfulness into my tone as I can, but it doesn't help — I sound frantic.

As we make our way onto the plane, my fingers and toes are tingling with a familiar dread, and it only intensifies when we take our seats. When they finish boarding and announce that the doors are closed, my chest starts to feel tight. Gripping the sides of my seat, I inhale, willing my heart to stop racing.

You're fine, you're fine, you're fine.

The pilot comes over the intercom, announcing that we'll be taking off soon. I think I hear a flight attendant say something nearby, but I'm starting to really feel like I'm going to be sick.

Nope, not fine.

"Y'alright?" Liam's deep voice interrupts my panicking.

I think I manage a nod, but all I can feel is the growing tightness in my chest. I'm starting to feel like I can't breathe, like I really might be losing air.

"Are you sure?"

I'm going to die.

"Whitney?"

I can't do this. Why did I think I could do this? I just can't.

"Are you okay?"

No. No. No.

"Whoa, Whit. Breathe. Just breathe."

I want to speak, to tell him that I'm trying to breathe, but I can't. I feel the warmth of his hand on my arm, gripping it lightly.

"Come on. In for four seconds. Breathe in — one, two, three, four. And hold it for one, two, three, four. Now exhale. That's right. Just like that."

I listen to his words. I let them be a tether, something to hold on to, to cling to in desperation. Something about the soft commanding tone in his voice makes me want to listen. I keep breathing like he says until I hear the pilot announcing that we're cruising at 10,000 feet.

Opening my eyes feels like a herculean effort, but I manage to blink a few times and focus on the feeling of my body in this seat. I take another shaky breath, and exhale with a whoosh.

I'm okay. The worst is over. We've taken off.

Except now that I can breathe normally, the embarrassment

is setting in. I don't dare look to where Liam is sitting beside me. His hand is no longer wrapped around my arm, but I can still feel him. I can feel his gaze heavy on my face, warming my cheeks to a bright shade of red. My nose tingles and there's pressure on the backs of my eyes, a telltale sign that I'm close to tears.

Do not cry.

I blink furiously, forcing the tears back, praying they don't break through the dam I'm building inside. Brick by brick, keeping my emotions locked away.

"Is that what you meant when you said you're a nervous flier?" Liam finally asks from beside me, his voice surprisingly soft.

"I guess," I squeak, a shudder running through me. I rub my hands over my arms, feeling suddenly cold.

Liam reaches above me and closes my AC duct, pushing it away from me. "Does that happen every time you fly?"

I shake my head. "I try not to fly that much. I drive whenever I can."

He nods but doesn't say anything else.

Flattening my lips into a straight line, I take another deep breath. "Sorry. And... thanks."

"Don't worry about it."

The rest of the flight is less eventful. Liam reads his book and says nothing else about my panic attack. I distract myself with Netflix and avoid thinking about the warm feeling of Liam's arm pressing against mine.

A few hours later, the pilot announces that we're landing, and my whole body tenses once again. I don't know if I can handle another panic attack right now. I will definitely cry, and any ounce of dignity I have left will be completely shredded.

Suddenly, I feel Liam's large, warm hand wrapping around mine. He brushes his thumb against the back of my hand.

"Does this help at all?"

All I can manage is a slight nod, unable to focus on anything but the sensation of his thumb rubbing soft circles on the back of my hand. Such a small movement should not be causing this kind of reaction in me — my heart is still racing, but for an entirely different reason.

"You can lean on me if you want. I dunno. Whatever would make you feel better, or if I can help somehow... " He looks more unsure than usual, his brow furrowed as he gazes down at me. Something about the doubtful hope in his expression cracks through my anxiety.

"Thanks," I whisper, closing my eyes and resting my head against his shoulder. I do the same deep breathing he coached me through earlier and it really helps. That and the feeling of his hand on mine, his fingers still brushing soft circles on the back of my hand.

For just a moment, I'm not so scared.

13

LIAM

We land in Vegas in the early afternoon and go straight to the hotel. Whitney passes out in the cab ride over, unsurprising as she didn't sleep at all on the flight. She was too busy freaking out.

I had no idea how to handle something like that. Luke was always the supportive guy, the guy you'd want around in a bad situation. I, on the other hand, am a fucking mess when it comes to emotions. So, when Whitney started having what I can only assume was a panic attack, I just made stuff up based on films I've seen. People always say to breathe, and the counting thing made sense in the moment. It seemed to help her, and God knows why, but I really, really wanted to help her in that moment. Maybe it was the look in her eyes, or maybe it was the threat of tears, but I couldn't just sit there and do nothing.

We pull up to Caesars Palace, and I nudge her awake. "Did you have to book us at the biggest place?"

She shrugs. "Go big or go home, baby. It's Vegas."

I blink heavily. This girl surprises me more and more every time she opens her mouth.

The hotel is huge, and the lobby is a whirlwind of activity.

Whitney makes us stop on the way to take a picture with a Roman warrior before we check in, and I have to urge her multiple times to stay on task, pulling her away from distraction after distraction.

When we get to the desk, the girl behind the desk pulls up our reservation, which I discover is for only one room.

I turn to Whitney. "Seriously? You only got one room?"

She smiles brightly at the girl checking us in before grabbing my arm and pulling me to the side. "How suspicious would it be for a married couple to have separate rooms? What if the cops come after us and start asking questions?" she whisper-yells at me.

"Don't you think you're being a bit intense about all this?"

She looks me dead in the eye. "I'm being thorough, Liam. Be glad I got us two beds, and let's hope the feds don't come sniffing."

Shaking my head, I follow her as she turns back to the desk. She finishes checking us in, and I grab our bags. On the lift, I lean down and breathe against the back of her neck. "Any other precautions I should know about? Think the *feds* will find us if we don't consummate the marriage?"

She shoves me, and I stumble to the side with laughter.

"Not funny," she mutters.

We walk down the hallway until we find our room. I tap my key and open the door, stepping back and gesturing for her to go ahead. I follow her into the room, and I don't know why I'm surprised when I see that there is in fact only one bed.

One king-sized bed in the center of the room.

"What the hell?" I say, but I doubt Whitney can hear it over her own laughter. I turn to her, and she's bent over, slapping her knee like a crazy person.

"Of course. Of course it's one bed."

"What's so funny?" I ask her.

"It's just so... cliche," she says through her laughs. "So *classic.*"

With a groan, I turn on my heels and slam the door shut. "Come on. Let's go downstairs. They obviously made a mistake. You did book double beds, right?"

"I told you. I would've booked two rooms, but this is our wedding weekend, *sweetheart.*"

"Cut it out," I growl. "We're getting a second room."

"Obviously."

We're silent on the ride down, and I can tell she hates every moment of it.

There's a line downstairs now, and it takes us a few minutes before we can talk to someone, who tells us that the hotel is completely sold out — because of course it is. I argue for a few minutes, and they offer to bring up a cot as soon as any come available, so we head upstairs, both more frustrated than ever.

When we get back to the room, Whitney drops her bag and crosses towards the bathroom.

"I'm gonna shower."

"Cool."

She closes the bathroom door, leaving me alone in the silent room. I fall back against the bed with a sigh. This trip is not going well so far. What's next? An Elvis impersonator as our officiant?

How the hell am I supposed to share a bed with Whitney? As much as the girl drives me crazy, I'd be an idiot not to notice how sexy she is. She better wear a full PJ set. I usually sleep shirtless, but the idea of my bare chest pressing against her...

Fuck.

Pillow wall. That's the only solution. We'll have to cling to our sides like our life depends on it. There can be absolutely no touching, not after how my body reacted to our handholding on the plane. My pants were tightening just from rubbing circles on her bloody hand. What the hell is that about? One minute she's Chore Wheel Girl with an orange juice obsession, the next she's making my body react for the first time in months.

It's not like there haven't been opportunities to have sex. Women at the bar have propositioned me once or twice, but I just haven't felt like it was worth it. Like I was worth it. So, I haven't thought about it. But now...

I hear the shower turn off and sit up in bed. Shaking my head, I open my bag, pretending to unpack. There's barely anything in there since we're only here for the weekend, but I have nothing else to do, so I might as well pick a drawer. I hear the bathroom door open behind me and make the terrible mistake of turning at the sound.

Whitney is standing in front of me in nothing but a towel.

Holy shit.

Our gazes meet, and her eyes flare with something dangerous before she looks down.

"Forgot my stuff," she mumbles and crosses over to her own bag before scurrying back into the bathroom.

There is no way I am going to survive this weekend.

14

WHITNEY

Staring at my reflection in the hotel bathroom mirror, I run my hands along my dress, spreading out the wrinkles. I've been hiding out in here for the past twenty minutes. I've already dried my hair, done all my makeup, and gotten dressed for the ceremony. Now I'm just stalling.

Liam knocks on the door. "You okay in there?"

I clear my throat. "Yep! Almost done!"

"Well, can you hurry? I've gotta piss."

My fiancé, ladies and gentlemen.

When I come out, Liam is sitting on the bed scrolling on his phone. He tosses it to the side and glances in my direction before doing a full double take, his eyes scanning me from head to toe. The look sends a flush right through me.

He clears his throat and leans forward. "What, *ah*, are you wearing?"

I can't hide the blush on my cheeks as I glance down at my white dress. "I have a weird thing about weddings. I don't know. I kind of like the traditions."

"Really?"

"Don't make fun of me."

"I won't," he promises. "What traditions?"

I shift on my feet. "Well, no dad to give me away, obviously... but I at least wanted to wear white. I got these shoes from a thrift store my first year of college, so... something old. Wore blue eyeshadow for the something blue. It's dumb, I know. I don't even have the other two."

He smiles softly, his eyes crinkling at the corner. I don't think I've ever seen that smile on him before, and now that I've seen it, I feel greedy. I need to see it again.

"Here." He stands, reaches into his pocket and pulls out a gold band, holding it out to me. "Here's your something new."

I step toward him and blink down at the ring, unexpected moisture forming in my eyes. "Oh."

He shifts, closing his hand into a fist. "You don't have to. It's just from the pawn shop. I saw it on my way home from work and I thought—"

"No!" I reach for his hand. "You just surprised me, but I love it. Thank you."

"I'll hold onto it until the ceremony." He slips the ring back into his pocket and brushes past me, heading into the bathroom and closing the door behind him. I sit on the edge of the bed, taking a few deep breaths.

It's just a stupid ring. It doesn't mean anything.

The door opens and Liam comes out, cuffing the sleeves of his button down. He opens the closet and takes out a suit jacket, pulling it on. I've never seen him in anything but a t-shirt. He looks incredible. He smirks and reaches for my hand, pulling me to stand next to him and turning us towards the mirror. Standing side-by-side like this, we actually look like a real couple.

"As for the something borrowed," he starts. "I think I qualify. You've only got me for three years, so I can be your something borrowed."

I smile. "Okay. I guess that counts." I turn towards him and flatten the lapels of his jacket, running my palms against his broad chest. "Come on, let's go get hitched."

WE DECIDE to get married at A Little White Wedding Chapel. Liam protests, but I figure if I have the chance to tie the knot in the same spot that Judy Garland did, I'm taking it. Thankfully, the officiant is dressed in a button down and slacks. Liam swore that if we were married by anyone dressed in a costume, he'd walk out the door. So far, everything is running smoothly. We don't even have to say vows or anything. It's all perfect, until...

"By the power vested in me by the state of Nevada, I now pronounce you husband and wife. You may now kiss the bride!"

Oh shit.

In all my anxious preparation for today, I forgot about this part. How did I forget about this part? It's like, the big thing. The main course. The final boss at the end of the video game.

Is Liam expecting us to kiss? The minister (if I can technically call him that) is definitely expecting it given the way he's currently glancing between us with a confused expression on his face. We're both frozen solid. He's probably used to drunken fools whose lips are basically attached. Meanwhile, we look like a couple of wax statues at Madam Tussaud's.

The clock is ticking, and I can't take any chances about the legitimacy of this thing, so I lean in and press my lips against his. He's frozen for a moment, but he softens at the contact, opening his mouth and meeting my kiss. He tastes like mint and cherries, sweeter than I was expecting, and I don't want the brief contact to end. My lips are still tingling when I pull away and glance at the officiant.

"Congratulations! Now, please move forward. The next appointment is starting in five minutes."

He starts pushing us off the faux-altar and gestures for the couple behind us to step forward. Now, *they* look like a real couple. She's clinging to his side like a sloth on a tree, and he's staring at her like the sun rises and falls in her eyes. It's surprisingly sweet, and I'm hit by an unexpected pang of jealousy. Liam's hand settles at the base of my spine, pressing me forward, and I stumble a bit, dazed from our kiss and the unwanted feelings of desire it stirred in me. Sure, I knew I was attracted to Liam, but he wasn't supposed to be a good kisser. A great kisser, in fact.

Liam gets all the forms we need while I wait outside, staring at my left hand and the shiny ring that is now part of me. Maybe it's the Nevada sun bearing down on me or the after-effects of Liam's lips on mine, but I'm starting to feel dizzy.

This is real. I am married.

"Hey," Liam's gruff voice interrupts my spiraling. "You ready to go?"

When we get back to the room, things are... awkward. We're both eyeing the bed like it might bite us if we sit on it. I hover near the doorway while Liam takes off his jacket and throws it onto the chair in the corner.

"Sweating my arse off in that thing. This city is a fuckin' sauna."

"I kind of like it. It's so dry."

He doesn't reply. He just stares out the window at the twinkling lights of the Vegas nightlife. It's still early, and something tells me we'll be delaying sleep as long as humanely possible.

"Do you want to go get dinner? I might hit the casinos later or see if I can get tickets to a show. I've heard the Blue Man Group is fun. *Ooh*, or Cirque Du Soleil? They are so impressive. We could go together!"

He raises his eyebrows at me in a gesture that reveals his obvious disapproval. How do I already know how to read his nonverbal communication?

"Forget it. I'll go by myself," I tell him, stung. I don't know why I even invited him. Every time I try to be nice, he throws it back in my face. I turn away from him, but he reaches out and grasps my arm lightly.

"I'll come, but no Blue Man Group. They freak me out."

I can't help but laugh. "Seriously?"

"They're creepy. Who willingly paints themselves head-to-toe like that?" He shudders, and I laugh again. "Let me shower and we'll go, alright?"

"Okay. I should probably change out of this dress… "

While Liam showers, I change into a denim skirt, tank top, and my platform Doc Martens. Once he's done in the bathroom, I touch up my makeup and meet him in the hallway. He's wearing a t-shirt and backwards baseball cap, and he strides to the elevator with barely a glance in my direction. He's shaved his beard down to a light stubble, and it looks soft and clean.

Hello to you, too!

Why, yes, you look lovely.

I look nice, too? Thanks so much!

Tired of conversing silently with myself, I turn to Liam. "What do you want for dinner?"

"Whatever you want."

I take a deep breath, reaching for my inner patience. I'm gonna need a lot of it tonight.

"Can we go to the Trevi? I want to see the fountains, and I'm in the mood to stuff my face with breadsticks and pasta."

He scrolls on his phone. "Sounds good to me."

"Can you at least pretend you like spending time with me? I get that this whole situation isn't ideal, but I'm trying to make the most of it."

He slides his phone in his pocket and turns to me, studying my face. "I like spending time with you."

"Oh, really? You sure have a way of showing it. You barely even look at me, for God's sake!"

He blinks, his face impassive. "I didn't realize it bothered you."

"Yeah, well... "

The elevator doors slide open, and I strut through the lobby towards the exit.

Forget this.

He follows after me as we head out to the Strip. He grips my wrist, tugging me back towards him. "Hey, slow down a sec."

I huff out a breath and glare up at him.

"I didn't think... look, that's just how I am, alright? I'm sorry if you took it as something against you."

"Forget I said anything. It doesn't matter." I tug against his hold, but he keeps me firmly in his grip.

"We're stuck together for the next three years, so let's be clear. You've gotta tell me when I piss you off 'cause I can't read your mind, and I'll probably do it a lot. I'm sorry I've been a dick, yeah? I'm excited. We'll go to dinner, and then we'll see the Cirque thing. Alright?"

I nod, shocked by his earnest response. "I only wanted to go out because—" I cut myself off abruptly.

You idiot.

"Because what?"

My cheeks flame. I press my lips together, not wanting to spill the truth I've been trying to ignore all day. When I suggested we go to Vegas this weekend, I knew what I was doing, but I really hoped Liam wouldn't find out and read too much into it. It's just another day, after all.

"*It- my bir-day,*" I mumble under my breath.

"What was that?"

"It's my birthday," I repeat.

He rears back, surprise coloring his features. "Why didn't you say anything?"

"It's not a big deal. I just didn't want to sit in a hotel room all night."

He blinks. "How old are you?"

"Didn't your mother teach you never to ask a woman that?" I tease, trying to avoid the sudden intensity in his gaze.

"I think I should know how old my wife is."

He's got me there. "I'm twenty-six. How old are you?"

"Twenty-seven."

"What's your sign?" I shoot back, wanting more information now that's he's finally sharing something with me.

"My what?"

"Your astrological sign. I'm a Virgo," I explain.

He shrugs. "Dunno. My birthday's April 21st."

I grin at him. "Of course. Taurus."

He narrows his eyes at me. "Are you going to tell me what that means?"

"Not a chance," I sing back at him, linking our arms together and tugging him along. "Now tell me what time you were born so we can figure out your moon and rising."

15

—————

WHITNEY

"Come on, just open your gullet and knock it down," Liam says, tilting his shot glass towards me. It's our third one of the night, and we haven't even gotten our entrees yet. I suppose the Vegas waiters are used to this level of drinking during dinner, since ours didn't bat an eyelash when Liam proclaimed we *needed* to take another shot.

I scoff. "Open my gullet?"

"Yeah, come on. Don't be a—"

"If you say *pussy,* I'm going to be highly offended," I interrupt him with a near-growl.

"I thought offended was your resting state," he shoots back.

Refusing to justify that with a response, I follow his instructions and take the shot down in one gulp, shuddering when the liquid makes its way down my throat.

"Hey! We were supposed to cheers for your birthday," he says before downing his own, handling it like a champ. The man doesn't even flinch.

When our food arrives, we stuff our faces in silence, both of us having drank too much on empty stomachs. Liam excuses himself from the table to use the bathroom and returns a few minutes later.

"You look weird," I tell him, studying his expression.

He scoffs, avoiding my eyes. "Finish your spaghetti." He points to the nearly clean plate in front of me.

"Did you just pull trig?"

"Did I *what?*"

"Pull trig. Vom. Throw up. Are you sick?"

He throws his head back, laughing like I told the world's greatest joke. "I did not throw up, but thank you for your concern. In fact, we should get another shot."

"Please, no." I shake my head and lift the bottle of wine sitting between us. "We still have this."

We both finish eating, polishing off the bottle of wine. They clear our plates, and I'm studying the dessert menu when I hear it. My nightmare scenario unfolding. At first, it's in the distance, far enough away that I can briefly entertain the idea that it doesn't concern me. Then, it's right next to me, and I'm no longer able to kid myself. My cheeks flame red, and I try to school my expression into one of grateful excitement.

"Happy Birthday to you. Happy Birthday to you. Happy Birthday, dear Whitney!"

Liam's voice is loudest of all. He's bellowing the notes like he's a classically trained opera singer, grinning at me with that wicked gleam in his eye, like he knows how much I hate this. I throw him daggers, trying to smile at the staff while silently communicating how much I hate him.

"Happy birthday to you!"

The staff disperse, everyone in the restaurant clapping and staring at us with wide smiles. I manage to maintain my smile as the attention draws away from us.

"Really?" I ask Liam through my teeth.

He just smiles wider. "Only the best for my wife. Come on,

dig in, we don't want to be late for part two of your birthday cele-bration," he says, pointing to the tiramisu in front of me. Rolling my eyes, I hand him one of the spoons and eat my dessert, wondering what else Liam is hiding up his tattooed sleeve.

WHEN WE GET BACK to the hotel room, we're both sufficiently drunk. If the bottle of wine at dinner didn't do it, the tequila shots definitely did.

"When she did that triple flip in mid-air, oh my God. That was crazy! Do you think they ever fall? What if they fell in the middle of a performance?"

Liam shushes me, chuckling lightly while he searches his wallet for the room key. He finally finds it and lets us in the room, the door shutting behind us.

The sight of our shared king bed sobers me instantly.

"I'll sleep on the floor," Liam offers, kicking his shoes off.

I shake my head. "Don't be silly. We'll just... stay on our sides."

He grunts in agreement, falling onto the bed and yanking his socks off. I shuffle into the bathroom before he starts taking off any more items of clothing. Wiping my makeup off, I give myself a pep talk in the mirror.

"You are not horny. You are a cold winter's day. You are made of ice!"

Liam knocks on the door. "Are you talking to yourself in there?"

"*Uhh...* no!" I turn the shower on. "I'll be out in a minute!"

I swear I hear him chuckle as I stumble out of my clothes and get into the shower. The water's still cold, which is probably for the best. It'll sober me up... among other things.

Liam is already in bed when I come out in my towel. I avoid

his eyes as I grab my pajamas out of my bag and shuffle back into the bathroom. Unfortunately, my "pajamas" are actually just an oversized t-shirt and tiny boy shorts.

Maybe he won't notice?

No such luck. Liam's eyes are on me from the second I step out of the bathroom. I bolt for my side of the bed and turn my light off, hoping to dim his view.

"What are you wearing?" he asks in a low voice.

"A Japanese Breakfast tour t-shirt. What are you wearing?" I reply sweetly.

"Let me rephrase the question. Where are your pants?"

"I didn't think we'd be sharing a bed," I tell him, flashing the hem of my tiny shorts. "They're here, don't worry."

"You knew we'd be sharing a room, *wife*," he says.

"Can you stop calling me that?"

He grumbles and turns over, pulling the comforter up to his shoulders. "I think you are wildly overestimating my restraint when it comes to you and me."

"What's that supposed to mean?"

"It means seeing you in nothing but a skimpy t-shirt and those tiny shorts is doing very bad things to my imagination, love."

I roll my eyes and shove him back to his side, but he grips his fingers around my wrist, his eyes boring into mine. I swallow, the sound echoing in the quiet room.

"Will you turn your light off, please?" I ask.

He releases my wrist and grumbles again, muttering under his breath. I swear I hear the words 'last nerves' as he turns the light off and lays against his pillow. Suppressing a giggle, I close my eyes and turn to face the wall. It's quiet for a few moments, and I focus on the steady sound of his breaths as I try to fall asleep.

"Are you still awake?" I whisper.

No answer.

"Liam?"

"What?" he growls.

I sigh into the dark room. "Why didn't you like me when we first met?" I whisper. "It seemed like right away I pissed you off somehow… you know, when you told me to fuck off."

He doesn't respond for so long I'm sure he's not going to at all. I hear the sheets rustling from his side, so I turn to face him, but his back is still to me. I can see the rise and fall of his chest as he breathes.

"It's something you said. Believe it or not, you sort of… triggered me. I know you didn't mean to. It's stupid."

"What? What did I say?" I say to his back.

He sighs. "You said 'I don't know what your last roommate dealt with, but I won't' or something."

"Oh," I whisper. "Why—"

"His name was Luke. We were roommates at uni and did our grad program together. He was… well, he was a better guy that I am, that's for sure. Funny, smart, and just a genuinely good person. He was my best friend."

The sadness in his voice shocks me. I've never heard him sound like this before, and I suddenly regret prying into his personal life.

"He killed himself six months ago."

Oh God.

Sympathy floods me. I've been judging his surly attitude and bad mood since we met, but now that I know that he's grieving… I feel awful.

"His death kind of… well, I've kind of fucked my life up. Can't really blame it on Luke, to be fair. I just can't help thinking that if he could see me now, he'd knock my teeth out for dropping out of school. Guess it doesn't really matter."

It's quiet again.

"Sorry. I dunno why... anyway, I know you didn't mean anything by it. Just kind of set me off, so I acted like a dick. Can we just forget about it?"

I clear my throat, moisture gathering in my eyes. "I'm so sorry." The urge to reach out for him consumes me, but instead, I turn back over to my side, staring at the wall.

"S'alright," he mumbles. "Thanks."

I exhale on a shaky breath and blink back the tears that are forming. "Thank you for telling me."

He hums in response.

"Goodnight, Liam."

"Happy Birthday, Whitney."

16

LIAM

I wake up feeling incredibly warm. Blinking against the bright light, I adjust to my surroundings and realize the source of the warmth is Whitney.

She's curled into me, her arms wrapped around my torso in a vice grip. Her soft thigh is draped over me and my hand strokes her skin absently. Worse than that, I've got a classic case of morning wood.

Shit.

Moving slowly, I lift her arm and try to slip out from underneath her grip. If I can just get to the bathroom before she notices the entanglement we find ourselves in, all awkwardness can be ignored. Just as I think I'm in the clear, she starts to stir. I freeze, holding my breath.

Don't wake up. Don't wake up.

Shifting further, I roll her entirely off me and onto her side of the bed. All last night, I couldn't help but grow more fascinated with her. At some point between our first glass of wine and falling asleep side-by-side, I realized how wrong I was about her. I thought she was too cheery for her own good, but the truth is that she's just an optimist. She's filled with this unexpected joy, but she will stick up for herself, biting back with an endearing stubbornness whenever I piss her off. It's a combination I find myself oddly enamored by.

Not to mention, she's gorgeous. And that kiss...

I guess I thought we'd just skip that section of the wedding. I definitely hadn't expected her to kiss me or for her lips to be soft as sin. She tasted as good as she smells — like rose petals and sweetness — and I didn't want it to end. When she pulled away, I wanted to grab her around the waist and show her what a real kiss with me is like. Though that might not have been appropriate for a chapel.

Then I went and told her about Luke. I have no clue what came over me, but something about the dim light of the room and her soft whisper had me feeling unexpectedly raw. I guess I'm just tired of carrying this shit all by myself, and telling her about it felt like a weight lifting off my shoulders.

It felt... right.

Taking a deep breath, I cross to the bathroom and close the door behind me, leaning against the wall in relief.

This is not good.

We've been married for less than twenty-four hours and I've already got a raging hard-on for the girl. Guess I'm in for a cold shower. Let's just hope it's not the first of many.

"WHAT THE HELL IS THIS? That is not a word," Whitney argues, pointing to the *Scrabble* tiles I laid out.

"Ruddy? It absolutely is a word," I point out. "Haven't you ever listened to Supertramp? *Breakfast in America?*"

"I literally have no idea what you're talking about."

I shake my head. "Your music knowledge is woefully lacking."

"You can't use British slang. That doesn't count."

"First of all, it's not slang, it's a real word. Secondly, I don't need an American to lecture me about proper English. We invented the language, you know."

"Yeah, you invented colonialism, too. You an expert on that, Liam?"

"Oh, fuck off," I say, and this time, we both laugh.

Spending time with Whitney always seems to put a smile on my face. There's just something about her that seems to both rile me up and calm me down at the same time. She's grown more comfortable with me overnight, it seems, something I both appreciate and despise, since she's currently wearing those tiny shorts again. I swear she's purposefully trying to send my mind into a tailspin.

She lays down a new word, *traitor,* and I raise my eyebrows, scanning her other words, which are *hell, lies,* and *demon.*

"Are you trying to tell me something?" I ask, waving at the board.

"I swear it's a coincidence."

"If you put down *murder* next, I'm sleeping with one eye open tonight."

She laughs again, a sweet, musical sound that has the corners of my mouth tipping upwards again.

"We've been married, what, eighteen hours? And you've had enough already?"

She laughs even more, and I want to keep it going forever. Her joy is addictive.

We play for a bit longer, and as expected, she beats me, sending me retreating to my room with a bruised ego. I pull up Luke's business plan and spend the rest of the night researching educational organizations, adding more details to the outline. Once I have a more fully formed idea, I can start reaching out to some of my old friends from school who have more experience with this type of thing. Until then, I'm on my own.

I'm bent over my desk with about twelve tabs open on my computer when I hear the shower turn on from the bathroom. The sound of it sends a jolt of awareness through my body, and suddenly the article I'm reading can't seem to keep my attention.

Who cares? Whitney is in the shower. That's completely normal. Nothing sexual about it.

Except that my mind is conjuring up all types of images. Ones of her naked body lathered in soap and hot water, her hands roaming up and down her petite figure.

Stop it. This is your roommate.

Torn between feeling like a complete creep for listening to my roommate's shower with bated breath and wanting to deal with the blood that has rushed to my cock, I groan, abandoning my laptop and falling onto my bed. I'm reaching for my headphones to blast music in my ears so loudly I'll be risking permanent damage when I hear another sound.

A moan.

Whitney's moan.

Fuck.

No way. No way is she in there touching herself right now. I'm imagining things. My horniness is making me delusional. It's been way too long since I've had sex, and this is the consequence. I'm out-of-my-mind to the point where I'm hearing fake moans that aren't there.

But then I hear it again, louder this time, and if I thought I was hard before, it's nothing compared to the throbbing I'm dealing with now. This is worse than Vegas. At least there the walls were thick enough that I could escape to the bathroom. Here, there's nowhere for me to go.

Holding my headphones in my hands, I hesitate. I should put them on. I know I should. It's a complete invasion of her privacy to listen to this. She'd hate me if she knew, and she's just starting to warm up to me. It's not worth slashing all our progress. With a sigh, I pull the headphones over my ears, drowning out the sound of Whitney's moans with the bass of the music.

It works; I can't hear anything. The only problem is that just the knowledge of what she's doing in there seems to send my thoughts to a dirty place. And if this is going to be a regular occurrence in our household, *I am so screwed.*

17

WHITNEY

I've been a married woman for two months, and it's been surprisingly uneventful. The leaves have started to turn, fall officially in full swing, my wardrobe shifting to an array of browns and reds.

Liam and I are on better terms than ever. We even eat dinner together, and our Scrabble nights have increasingly become my favorite night of the week. I spend nearly all my time working on the salon, and best of all, I finally came up with a name. Since I have my grandmother to thank for the funding, it's going to be called *All Rhodes*.

For now, I'm on a mission to speak to my mother. Before Vegas, I tried every number she's called me from, and none of them were functioning. She has a habit of using exclusively burners, and it's incredibly frustrating since she gets rid of them every few weeks. I need to tell her about grandma and the inheritance, and my last option to get in touch is through her boyfriend Chuck — if he still is her boyfriend, that is.

It rings twice before he picks up. "Yo, this is Chucky."

He's a real keeper.

"Hello. I'm trying to get in touch with Caroline Rhodes. Do you happen to have her number?"

"Sweet Caroline? Phew, that's a babe if I ever saw one."

"Charming," I reply in a low tone. "Do you have her number or not?"

"Who's askin'?"

I shake my head, searching for my inner patience. "Her daughter."

"She has a daughter? Damn. She must have been 18 when she had you."

"Just about. The number?"

There's some rustling on the other end. "You got a pen?"

He reads me the number, and I thank him before hanging up and dialing the number he gave me.

"Hello?" For the first time in months, I hear my mom's low, raspy voice. The sound of it sends an unexpected jolt of longing through me. I didn't think I missed her until I heard her voice.

"Mom? Mom, it's me."

"Whitney? Oh, baby! How are you? It's been too long, sweetheart."

"Yeah, well, if you'd just get a cellphone and keep it, we could stay in touch."

"You know I don't like those things," she says. "Government tracking you all the damn time."

I sigh. She's not wrong. "Yeah, I know. Listen, did you hear about Grandma?"

"Grandma who?"

"My grandmother. Your mom. Agnes Rhodes."

"Where the hell did you hear that name?" she snaps.

"From her lawyer."

"Why is she fuckin' contacting you? You tell her to stay away from both of us."

I take a deep breath, steeling myself. Why did I assume that

Trent had managed to contact her about the will? "I didn't talk to her, Mom. I talked to her lawyer. She passed away. She's... gone."

It's silent on the other end.

"Mom? Are you still there?"

"She's... what? No. No, she's not." She laughs, but the sound has no joy in it. "She'll never die, trust me. Not before she—"

"I'm sorry, Mom. I'm really, really sorry."

It's quiet again.

"Are you okay?" I ask. I feel awful. "You really should call her lawyer. There's a lot to settle with her estate and will. She left me a letter and a bunch of money... which, by the way, I'm married."

"You're what? What the hell is this? You call me to tell me my mom is dead and you're freakin' married?"

"You never even told me about them! Grandma told me that she tried to reach out to us. My whole life, we've had this family, this *rich* family, and I didn't know a single thing about them."

"You were better off, trust me."

"Well now I'll never know, thanks to you. I get that you want to be this free spirit, needing nothing and nobody. You've made it perfectly clear that you want nothing to do with me—"

"Hey, that's not fair—"

"You know what? Forget it.Talk to you in six months, probably."

"Whitney, baby—"

I hang up the phone and exhale a shaky breath, frustrated. I don't know what I expected, but I'm in a worse mood now than before. Maybe I shouldn't have been so harsh on the phone. I'm the one who wanted to talk, but something about her just sets me off. I hate carrying around this resentment towards her, but I don't know if she understood how hard my childhood was for me. I love her for being who she is, but I'm not a free spirit like her. I didn't want to live on the road, to be untethered all the time.

Maybe it was naive of me to think I could handle all of this by myself. Maybe this whole thing — quitting my job, getting married, chasing a pipe dream — was a total mistake. I tossed all the stability and security that I worked so hard for right out the window, and where has it left me?

It's not like this day can get any worse, so I might as well start drinking. I cross the kitchen to the freezer and take out my trusty bottle of Casamigos. A constant source of comfort for me in times of need.

Time to get drunk and wallow in self-pity.

18

LIAM

It's a Friday evening and my first night off in forever when I come home and find Whitney in the kitchen with a bottle of tequila in front of her. She's got her head resting on her arms, and Adele is blasting from the speakers.

"Hey," I say, crossing the room towards her. "You know it's only six o'clock?"

She lifts her head. "And?"

I shrug, dropping my shoulder bag on the floor and sitting in the stool beside her. "Nothing. Just wondering why you're getting pissed this early in the day."

She rolls her eyes. "I've had two shots."

I bump her shoulder. "Adele and tequila shots? I may be an idiot, but even I can tell that's a bad sign. Plus, you've got raccoon eyes."

I point to her makeup, and she wipes under her eyes with a sigh. "Can you not be mean to me tonight? Okay? I just can't handle it. Not tonight." She sighs, laying her head back onto the counter.

I swallow the lump in my throat. "I wasn't trying to be... mean. I was just kidding." I guess I thought since Vegas and our recent evenings together, we'd reached a sort of understanding. I thought she'd forgiven me. Does she still think I'm an arsehole?

"Ugh. Ignore me," she says. "I am kind of drunk."

"Do you want to... talk about it?" I stand and cross the kitchen to the cabinet, grabbing another shot glass and setting it next to hers on the counter.

"No. Yes. Maybe." She groans and lifts her head again, and I pour us both a shot of tequila. "Basically, I had a crap conversation with my mother, which may be the only conversation we have this year since she's dust in the wind at this point."

"I'm sorry."

She raises her eyebrows at me, then smirks. "Alright, don't be too nice or I'll think something weird is going on."

Fuck, she looks good two drinks deep. Her eyes aren't quite glazed over, but there's a sort of haziness there. If I didn't know any better, I'd think she was flirting with me.

"I'm always nice," I reply with a smirk.

She laughs. "When have you ever been nice?"

"I took you to dinner and a show. I play Scrabble with you." I raise my shot glass, waiting for her. "And I don't let you drink alone."

She bites her lip, and *fuck me* she looks sexy.

She lifts her glass to meet mine, then stops. "Wait! Get the limes. I'll get the salt. Let's do this right."

I slice up a lime, and we prepare our shots properly, pouring salt onto the back of our hands. Then she links our arms, lifts our glasses, and winks at me.

"To fucking it up." She smirks.

"Hear-hear."

The liquid burns going down. I pour us both another shot and slice up the lime, glancing at Whitney's drooping form. She looks like Eeyore finding out that Pooh Bear isn't coming home for Christmas this year.

Wow, what a pair we are.

I slap my hands against the counter, jolting her. "Listen, let's not mope about here. Why don't we go out?"

She lifts her head, narrowing her eyes at me. "Where?"

I shrug. "I dunno. A club or something. Anything's better than drinking 'round here like a couple of bums. You look like someone killed your puppy."

She rolls her eyes. "Let me text Abbi. Maybe she's around."

I pour her a glass of water and hand it to her while she texts Abbi. Her phone rings as soon as she sends the text, and she answers. Immediately, I hear screeching on the other line.

"Okay. Abbi, stop yelling, I can hear you fine." She pauses. "Alright, just text me the name." She hangs up. "You're in luck, big boy. Abbi's already out with Shane."

I crinkle my forehead. "Big boy?"

She chuckles, and a blush spreads across her cheeks. "Oh, shut up."

WHEN WE GET to the club, Whitney drags me to the front of the line and throws her arms around a tiny redhead in the highest heels I've ever seen. They are both squealing and giggling and talking at a pace that is unintelligible to human ears. Behind them, a ripped guy with dark hair gives me a nod and reaches out for a bro-shake.

"Hey, I'm Shane," he says.

"Liam," I reply.

"So, this is the British brute." Abbi's eyes scan me up and down in judgement. He's hotter than you said."

"He's standing right here," I mutter.

Shane clasps my shoulder. "You'll get used to it," he chuckles. We flash our IDs to the bouncer and he lets us in. The club is insanely loud and packed with people. Abbi grabs Whitney's arm and drags her towards the dance floor while Shane and I head to the bar for drinks.

We push our way to the front, and I get a beer for myself and a tequila soda for Whitney. Shane catches a table off to the side and grabs it while I settle our tabs. I carry our drinks, eyeing the crowd for Whitney. I spot her and Abbi in the middle of the dance floor as I settle into the booth. They're laughing and grinding on each other in a way that has me gripping my glass harder than necessary.

I down half of my beer in one gulp, wiping my mouth with the back of my hand as my eyes follow Whitney in the crowd. She looks so fucking sexy in that tiny pink dress and thigh-high platform boots. She throws her hands in the air, shimmying her hips and moving her body to the music. My throat feels suddenly dry.

"You wanna dance?" Shane yells from his side. "I can guard the fort."

I grip my beer tighter. Do I want to go over there and grind against Whitney until she's sweaty and panting and begging me to take her home? Fuck yes.

Should I?

Definitely not.

"I'm alright," I say to Shane and force my gaze away from Whitney. Staring down at my beer, I try to calm my racing mind. This was a huge mistake. My self-control is slipping away with every moment I spend watching her.

"Whoa, man. You might wanna reconsider that." Shane bumps my shoulder, jutting his chin towards where the girls are. I follow his gaze to see some guy grinding on Whitney, his hands around her waist.

I see red.

Before I even know what I'm doing, I push through the

crowd and cross the room to where they're standing. I grab the guy's shoulder and yank him back, shoving him backwards.

"Get your hands off my wife," I growl.

"Your wife?" He stumbles, clearly wasted. "Didn't know she was taken, man."

Whitney is staring at me in shock. I grab her left hand and flash it in his direction. "Check the ring, arsehole. Now fuck off before I put my fist through your jaw," I tell him.

"Alright, jeez. Chill out," he says before stumbling away, muttering under his breath.

Abbi has disappeared, and it's just me, Whitney, and the sea of bodies that surrounds us. I turn towards Whitney, seething. "What the hell was that?" I growl down at her.

"Me? You're the one who went completely caveman on me. Since when do you get jealous?"

"I'm not jealous," I argue.

She rolls her eyes. "Yeah, right. There was basically steam coming out of your ears."

"I don't like people touching what's mine."

She raises her eyebrows. "Yours?"

I step closer, invading her space. We're almost chest-to-chest. "Yeah. You're mine. You've got my ring on your finger, so don't fucking forget it."

Her eyes widen and she blinks up at me. Someone jostles me from behind and I end up pushed closer to Whitney. I can feel her heartbeat against mine as I stare down into her deep brown eyes. Eyes that say one thing.

Kiss me.

I lean closer, my lips at her ear. "You better not look at me like that, love. Not unless you know what you're getting yourself into."

Her breath catches, and I'm close enough that I can hear her sharp inhale. I pull back and study her expression, indecision clouding her features.

"What am I getting myself into?" she asks, her eyes sparking with a challenge.

I grumble, narrowing my eyes at her. "Don't play dumb, Whitney."

Her eyes flicker back and forth between mine, searching my expression for something. I don't know what, but she seems to find her answer. She presses impossibly closer to me, not an inch of space between us, and reaches her hand up to the back of my neck. Awareness trickles at every point our bodies touch and my brain can't seem to comprehend what's happening. That I'm about to kiss Whitney.

That I am kissing Whitney.

Her lips meet mine, soft and wanting all at once. A groan escapes me, and she pulls me further down, breathing heavily as she slides her tongue against mine. I swear I've never tasted anything as sweet as her lips. I don't know how long the kiss lasts — it could be seconds or minutes — but much too soon, she pulls back, a stricken expression clouding her features. She blinks up at me, conflicted, and I can't stand that damned look on her face, so I press my lips against hers again, taking control. It's a kiss that brands her and lets everyone in this club know one thing.

She's mine.

19

WHITNEY

I am kissing Liam.

Or rather, Liam is kissing me. He's kissing me like a dying man gasping his last breath, like he can't get enough. His lips are softer than they look, and he tastes like tequila and mint, a dangerous combination that I could easily get used to. The throng of bodies pressing against us only fuels me on, locking us into a seductive haze. I can imagine, here under the flashing lights, that I'm someone else. Someone bolder and sexier.

I can pretend.

Sliding my fingers through Liam's hair, I can't help the moan that escapes me at his touch. His hands are pressed against my skin, his thumb is rubbing circles against my hips, and the movement is making me unbelievably turned on. It's been so long since I've felt like this.

Sexy.

Wanted.

Alive.

Liam deepens the kiss as he presses against me, his hands moving upwards so that his thumbs brush the underside of my breasts. The movement sends an involuntary shiver through me. He presses closer, and I can suddenly feel *all* of him; now I know for sure he's just as turned on as I am.

Holy shit.

We're starting to cross the point of no return, and I can't find it within me to care. I don't want to stop. I *can't* stop.

Liam pulls back abruptly, both of our chests heaving. My eyes wander over to the booth where Shane and Abbi should be, but they are nowhere to be seen. He follows my gaze and seems to realize the same thing as me.

We are alone.

I open my mouth to speak, but nothing comes out. What is he thinking? His expression is completely unreadable. He's staring down at me with that blank, hard look on his face — the one that he gives me in the mornings when we're chatting over coffee. When his stubble glows golden in the morning light.

He leans down, his lips brushing against my ear again. Another shiver rocks through me, goosebumps forming all over my skin. I'm terrified for what he's going to say. Is he going to say this was a mistake? Laugh it off? Tell me that it can't happen again, that he doesn't think of me like that?

"Let me take you home," he breathes against me, and when I catch his gaze in the blinking disco lights, there's a glint of determination in his eye.

When we get back to the apartment, it's silent. We didn't speak the entire Uber ride home, both of us crowded into opposite corners in the backseat. I pressed my head against the window, watching the passing cars and pedestrians outside and trying to come up with something to say to Liam.

I've got absolutely nothing.

I blame the tequila.

The door slams behind us, the sound reverberating in the quiet, dark room. I stumble into the kitchen, keeping my back to Liam while I pour myself a glass of water. Leaning against the counter, I drink the whole thing, keeping my gaze trained on the fridge. I can't bring myself to turn around. To see the regret that must be settling over his features.

Just get it over with. Rip the band-aid off.

I'm ready to do just that when I feel it. The barely-there brush of Liam's hand against the nape of my neck, pulling my hair to one side. He presses his lips to the side of my neck, peppering soft kisses against me. I gasp at the contact and swallow a loud gulp. He stops his movements when he hears me, resting his head against my shoulder and bringing one hand to my hip, to that same spot he was touching in the club. The spot that seems to burn me from the inside out.

"What are we doing?" he groans against me.

I have no idea.

All I know is that I don't want to stop, even knowing what a mistake this is.

"I don't know," I whisper into the dark room.

He brushes his thumb against my hip, sending another flutter through me. That tiny movement, that single brush of his thumb, and clarity washes through me. I turn, pulling back slightly as he lifts his head to look at me.

"Just once," I say.

He raises his eyebrows in question, and my eyes flicker back and forth between his.

"You're drunk," he replies, shaking his head.

"Barely," I retort. "I promise. Just one time to get it out of our system. Okay?"

His brow furrows further, and he looks almost disappointed by my response. But isn't this what he wants? I can't be reading him wrong. He wants me as much as I want him. I know it. In fact, I can feel it against my thigh.

Finally, he nods in agreement. "Just once," he agrees, but he still hesitates, looking conflicted.

"Are you sure?" I ask.

"It's just... been a while. I haven't... since before Luke, I mean," he admits, biting his bottom lip. The unsure expression on his face sends a pang of affection through me, and I bring my hand up to his cheek, cupping it softly.

"We can stop whenever you want to," I say shakily, not trusting my voice.

"I think once we start, I won't be able to stop," he replies.

His lips are on mine again, and this time, I've thrown any pretense of shyness out the window. I grind against him, pressing our bodies as close together as possible. He catches on quickly, wrapping his hands around my thighs and lifting me onto the kitchen counter. I wrap my legs around him, straddling him as he moves his hands up my thighs, bunching my dress up to my hips. He pulls away from my kiss and hooks his hands around my panties.

"May I?" he asks, and I nod fervently, lifting myself up and shimmying to try to help him.

He halts me, shaking his head slightly. "Slow down. I want to take my time with you," his husky voice drawls out.

He drags my thong down my legs slowly, like I'm a gift that he's unwrapping layer by layer. He tosses them to the side, and I watch them land on the floor.

"Should we... get out of the kitchen? Go to my room?" I ask.

He shakes his head, his gaze focused on where I'm now bare for him to see. Slowly, so goddamn slowly, he moves his hands down my thighs and spreads my legs.

"Not yet. I haven't eaten, and I'm starved."

Oh my God.

I have no time to process before he drops down to his knees and drags me to the edge of the counter. Holy fuck, he looks so hot on his knees in front of me. I can't help but buck my hips slightly in anticipation, and his eyes flicker up to me, a smirk spreading across his face.

"Patience, love."

I let out a breath of frustration as he presses a kiss to the inside of my thigh, his hand wandering and caressing me everywhere except where I need him the most. He teases me like that, his breath hot against me, but he still doesn't press his lips to me.

"Liam," I breathe out, half-warning, half-begging.

His name on my lips only seems to fuel him more. He meets my eyes again, quirking an eyebrow.

"What do you want?"

I huff out another breath, this one almost a growl. "You know."

His smirk only grows. "I'd like to hear you say it. My fingers inside that dripping cunt of yours? Or do you want me to lick you until you scream my name? Hmm? I know how you can talk, Whit. Tell me what you want."

I swallow, my throat tight. Jesus, his dirty talk is making me crazy. "Your... your mouth," I whisper.

"My mouth where?"

I'm so embarrassed, I almost push him away. He must know how vulnerable this is for me, and this was just supposed to be fun. It's not supposed to be so intense. His eyes flicker up towards me, and something in my expression must give me away, because his smirk fades, his gaze softening.

"You know what? I changed my mind. I don't need you to say anything except 'yes'."

Finally, he presses his mouth against me, and *God* it's incredible. He doesn't just taste me, he devours me. I'm thrusting against him when his fingers find me, slipping one inside of me while his thumb brushes against my clit.

"Oh, God. Right there," I tell him.

He continues his movements, switching between thrusting his tongue and his fingers inside of me. The combination is driving me crazy, and his thumb circling my clit is bringing me closer and closer to the edge. I wrap my hand in his hair, needing something to clutch onto.

"Fuck, Liam. I'm close," I breathe out.

He doesn't miss a beat. I didn't think it was possible for him to give me any more, but he does. He curls his finger, pressing deeper and soon enough, I'm gasping and writhing against him. I squeeze my eyes closed as stars flash behind my eyes, an orgasm rushing through me. I bite my lip to stop from screaming, but a warbled sound still escapes me. I'm still shaking as I come down, and I look down to see Liam pull back and stare up at me with a wild grin on his face.

"Holy shit," I laugh out.

His grin only grows. "Now we can go to the bed. I think we're gonna need it." He grabs my waist and picks me up, my legs wrapped loosely around him as he carries me.

"Yours or mine?"

"Don't care."

He kicks his door open and drops me onto his bed. He's still fully clothed while I'm wearing nothing but my bunched-up dress. He seems to realize at the same time as I do as he kicks off his shoes and rips his socks off.

"Pants... off... now." I reach for his belt and start yanking it off.

He puts his hand over mine. "What did I say about patience?"

I shake my head. "Patience is overrated." I pull his pants down, and my jaw almost drops at the tent in his pants.

I can't tell for sure, but he looks... big.

He pulls his shirt over his head while I yank my dress off. His bare chest is an incredible sight. I'm about to unclasp my bra when he pushes me gently back onto the bed and crawls over me.

"Wait," he breathes against me. "I need to memorize this moment."

I roll my eyes, but he presses his lips to mine, smothering me with an intense kiss. He seems to have forgotten his own desire to take things slow as he threads his fingers through my hair, pulling me as close to him as possible. He reaches behind me and unclasps my bra, his hands immediately finding their way to my nipples. He caresses and pinches them until I'm on the edge again, and I press a palm to his chest.

"Do you have a condom?"

He blinks back at me, then nods.

"Should I... ?"

"Yes, go get it, you idiot!"

He chuckles and crosses the room. I lay back against the pillows, my head spinning. I don't know if it's from the orgasm or from the fact that I'm about to have sex with Liam, but I feel like I'm floating. He returns with the condom, pressing his lips against mine, kissing me deeply. He seems content to just kiss for a while, both of us memorizing the movements of each other's mouths. But I need more. I thrust my hips against him, moaning, and finally, he gets the hint. He rolls the condom on, hovering above me. He looks so sexy like this, his light hair tussled and messy, his lips swollen and pink. I run my hands over his abs, tracing the black tattooed lines, relishing the feel of him.

He locks eyes with me, his gaze surprisingly gentle. "You sure?"

I nod, hoping I don't look as eager as I feel. Can he tell that I need this more than I've ever needed anything?

"I'm sure."

He thrusts into me in one swoop, and it's not gentle. It's everything. I take a moment to adjust to the feeling of him, the fullness, but soon we find a rhythm. I'm so turned on I feel like I'm on fire.

"Fuck," Liam breathes against me. He thrusts against me, slow this time, building to a steady rhythm.

"I need—"

"What?"

I push against him, trying to build friction, and he seems to understand. He reaches down between us and finds my clit, teasing his fingers against me.

"You feel so good, Whit."

The sound of my nickname on Liam's lips should not be my undoing. But it is. Soon enough, I feel another orgasm building. It's intense, the swell of feeling growing within me. It's too much.

"I've been thinking about this," he groans, thrusting into me again.

"You have?"

He brings his eyes up to meet mine, his gaze intense and pained. "All the fucking time. It's better than I could have imagined."

"More. Harder," I moan.

My words unleash something in him, and he doesn't hold back. He presses into me over and over, hitting an angle I didn't know was possible. He lifts my left leg, thrusting deeper.

"I don't know... shit, Whitney. I don't know if I can last if you keep squeezing me like that."

"Oh my God," I choke out.

"You look so fucking beautiful like this," he whispers. "Taking my cock so well. It's like you were made for me."

"Oh my God," I repeat. "More. Tell me more."

He thrusts into me. "You like that? Hearing how amazing you feel? You like being a good girl for me?"

I can't. I can't take any more.

"You're dripping all over me, dirty girl. I can feel you squeezing my cock. So fucking sweet. So fucking perfect," he groans.

I'm coming. I'm coming and screaming and shaking. I've lost all sense of myself. Nothing else matters but this.

"Fuck!" Liam growls against me. "Fuck, fuck."

He's coming too. I know it. We're both pulsing against each other, incoherent. It feels like it goes on forever, until I feel him collapse against me, spent.

"Holy shit," he breathes against me, both of us sweaty and heaving tired breaths.

"I know," I reply, hoping he can't hear the emotion in my voice.

It's never been like that for me before. So... connected.

I don't have time to read too much into it. I can already feel sleep calling me, exhaustion settling into my bones. Just as my eyes are fluttering closed in a post-orgasm bliss, I swear I hear Liam mutter next to me, "I don't think once is going to be enough."

20

LIAM

I wake up in my bed.

Alone.

The sun breaks through my window, unusually bright. I normally close my blackout curtains to sleep through the morning, but last night... well, last night was different.

Unexpected. Amazing. The best sex of my fucking life.

When I watched Whitney dancing at the club, I could hardly contain my hard-on. I saw that arsehole put his hands on her, and I almost lost it; I wanted to knock him out right there on the dance floor. I could feel my heart beating out of my chest, an unexpected burst of lust rushing through me. But then I saw her face, and the way she looked up at me with such an open expression of desire and... trust.

I couldn't help myself. I needed her. Needed to possess her, to own her. To taste her.

I should've walked away. Should've walked through that door and gone straight to my room. But I couldn't. Any ounce of self-control I had left inside me has dissipated entirely. And now that I know what she tastes like? That she's sexy and sweet and everything in-between? I'm screwed.

And now... she's gone.

She did say it would be a one-time thing.

Fuck. What the hell was I thinking? In the moment, it felt like the right thing to agree with her terms. Honestly, I would have agreed to anything. I figured we'd get it out of our system, like she said, but now that I know what she tastes like, what she feels like when I'm buried deep inside her... I need it again.

And again, and again, and again.

Shit.

I crane my head, listening for any trace of her in the apartment. What if she's here? How am I supposed to act? As embarrassing as it is to admit, Whitney's the closest thing I have to a friend these days, and I don't want us sleeping together to ruin things between us. I've come to actually enjoy her company.

Suppressing a sigh, I roll out of bed. It's not like I expected her to hang around and share her innermost secrets, but I'd at least thought... I don't know. I don't know what the hell I thought would happen in the morning. I wasn't thinking that far ahead, but I sure as hell didn't think she'd just sneak off in the middle of the night like it meant nothing.

Doesn't it?

I crack open my door, glancing down the hall. Not a peep. She must be gone. I tiptoe into the kitchen, trying not to make a sound as I make my coffee.

With a sigh, I slip my phone out of my pocket and scroll down my contacts until I find Tim, an old friend of Luke's and mine from uni. Last I heard, he was working for QuestBridge, the scholarship organization. He's probably the only person I know who can help me out with Luke's foundation. Is a phone call aggressive? Nobody calls anymore, but I hate texting, and I don't want him to blow me off.

Shaking my head, I press the call button. A few rings later, Tim picks up.

"Hello?"

"Tim? It's Liam Clark, from uh… Columbia. I don't know if you remember me, but—"

"Liam! Of course I remember you, *mate*."

I suppress an eye roll. At least he remembers who I am.

"What's up? I heard you were still at Columbia getting your masters?"

I really should have thought this through before I called him. "Yeah, erm, it's a bit of a long story, but listen — are you still working at QuestBridge?"

He chuckles. "Yeah, I actually just got promoted."

"That's great." I hesitate, then take a deep breath. "Any chance you're free this week to grab a coffee or a pint? I kind of want to pick your brain about something."

"For sure. I'm free this afternoon. Want to meet me at Juniper Bar near Penn Station? It's right around the corner from my office."

"Sure, that works."

"4pm?"

"Yep," I agree easily.

"Great, see you then! Thanks for calling. You're old school, man. I like that about you."

"Sure," I say, and we chat for a bit before hanging up.

I guess that went well, all things considered. He remembered me, and he agreed to meet with me. I'm one step further than I was yesterday, and that's something. Now all I have to do is… everything.

That is if I can manage to stop thinking about the sounds my roommate — no, my *wife* — makes when she comes.

I GET to Juniper Bar at 3:50. I'm never early, but I want to give Tim a good second impression of me, since most of his first involved me chugging beers and getting into fights. Chalk it up to college, I suppose. I sit at the bar and order a Guinness while I wait. A few minutes later, Tim comes into the door in a button down and slacks. He's as tall as I remember, his blonde hair slicked back. I wave in his direction, and he smiles when he sees me, crossing to meet me at the bar.

"Liam!" He reaches in for a hug, patting me on the back before we break apart and he settles in next to me with a light smile on his face. "How are you?"

I nod, taking a sip of my beer. "Alright, yeah. You?"

"Good, good."

The bartender comes over and Tim orders a Stella, then he turns to me. "So, what's up?"

Right down to business, then.

I rub my hand down the back of my neck. "I know my call was probably a bit out of the blue. I don't know if you heard, but... my roommate, Luke... he, uh... "

Tim clasps a hand on my shoulder. "I heard. I'm so sorry, man. I couldn't make it to the funeral, but—"

"Don't worry about it." I take a generous gulp of my pint, hoping to wash down the grief along with it. "So, Luke had this whole plan that I just found out about. He wanted to start his own organization to help first generation and low-income students get access to higher education."

"Wow. I always thought he was a science nerd like you."

I slip the binder out of my backpack and hand it over to him. "He was a business double major. Here, you can look through it."

He opens the binder and flips through the pages, his eyes studying the business plan. I take another sip of my drink while I wait for him to finish.

"Looks cool," he says, handing the binder back to me.

"Yeah, well… I'm going to do it. For Luke. I'm going to start this foundation."

He nods. "Starting something like that from scratch is going to be a huge undertaking. You might be better off just finding a job with an existing organization or donating some money if this is something you care about."

I shake my head. "I don't want to just donate to some national organization. This was Luke's dream."

"But Luke is gone, man. What's your dream?"

I blink.

My dream?

Flashes from my past assault me. Eight years old, Doctor Strange comics tucked under my pillow so I could read them after my dad put me to bed. Play-chemistry sets with plastic beakers that I'd fill with water and food coloring. Late nights in the lab, feeling the rush of a new discovery. I wanted to be a scientist for as long as I could remember.

I shake my head, blinking back the memories. "That doesn't matter."

Tim shrugs. "Well, if you're committed to this, I'll try to help you out. I'm going to this gala on Friday night, lots of big wigs in the educational field. Definitely some folks you could schmooze for donations. My friend Rebecca will be there. She was the Director of Development at the Bill Gates Foundation, so she should have some advice for you."

"That would be great. Thank you."

He waves his hand. "Don't worry about it. I'll send you the info. It's black-tie."

"Great," I say, trying to keep the sarcasm out of my voice.

"You got a girlfriend? Boyfriend?"

I wrinkle my brow. "Why does that matter?"

He shrugs. "Helps to have someone on your arm at these things."

"Seriously?"

"It's mostly me being selfish. I always bring Emily, and she never has anyone to talk to."

"Well, yeah. I'm married," I say. "Just this year, actually."

"Congratulations!" He glances down at my left hand. "No ring?"

Shit.

Trying to school my expression into one of realization, I slip my hand into my pocket. I got Whitney a ring at that pawn shop, but I don't have one myself. It's never really come up before.

"I had a medical thing a few days ago, forgot to put it back on. Anyway, I'll see if she can make it."

Me and Whitney? At a black-tie gala?

This should be good.

21

WHITNEY

It's only been six hours since I slipped out of Liam's room and fled from my apartment like a thief in the night. At least I managed to shower and grab my laptop. I don't know if it's the afterglow of multiple orgasms, but I feel amazing. I'm meeting Shatar, my hairdresser, to discuss *All Rhodes* with her.

When I get to the salon, she wraps her arms around me in a warm hug. "You look great."

"I love your hair," I tell her.

"I'd love to say I cut it myself, but I didn't."

"Well, I need the number of whoever did."

She glares at me. "And ditch me? Never."

I laugh and she waves me over to the chair, but I stop her with my hand, glancing towards the hairdresser in the corner, chatting with her client. I lower my voice slightly. "I know I booked you, but can we grab a coffee around the corner? I actually just wanted to chat about something."

She raises her eyebrows at me. "Oh? Okay. Sure thing." She unties her apron and gathers her belongings, then follows me out of the shop.

When we get to the coffee shop, I turn to her. "What do you want? On me."

She asks for a cappuccino, and we settle into a booth in the corner.

"So, what's going on?" she asks me.

I take a deep breath. "I want you to come work for me. I'm opening a salon, and the first person I thought of is you."

Shatar smiles. "Well, then. Tell me more."

For the next few minutes, I explain my concept for *All Rhodes* and discuss the job expectations. We both finish our coffees, and she tells me she has to think about it, which works out because I have to focus on finding a location before I reach out to anyone else for hiring.

I'm on the train home when an idea pops in my head. On my walk back to the apartment, I call Sharon from my old office. She doesn't answer, so I leave her a voicemail asking if she wants to get together for a coffee. We were never friends, so I'm sure she'll find it a somewhat strange request, but hopefully she'll get back to me. She would make a great CFO.

When I get home, I open the door as silently as possible and glance around, holding my breath. My good luck continues as I realize Liam isn't home. I have no idea what I'm going to say for him.

Thanks for the great sex. Pass me the sugar?

Shuffling to my room, I feel my phone buzz in my pocket.

> Abbi: Want to come over tonight? I'm making lasagna.

I haven't seen Abbi since last night at the club. She texted me to say that she and Shane had left to meet up with some of his friends at another bar. I'd love to see her, but she'll know something is up with me right away, and I don't think I can stand the interrogation about Liam. But I'd be lying if I said I didn't need her advice on how the hell to handle this situation, so I shoot her a text letting her know I'm on my way.

"I KNEW IT! You owe me $100."

I groan, knowing Abbi wouldn't forget our bet. "Calm down. It was nothing."

She laughs maniacally, loading lasagna onto plates while I pour us both a glass of red wine. "Nothing, my ass. You should have seen you two at the club. You looked absolutely feral."

"You say that about everything," I remind her.

She swipes her wine from my hand. "Yeah, but this time, it actually applies. When Liam almost knocked that guy out for dancing up on you, you had that same look in your eye you get when I make my triple fudge brownies."

"Those brownies are everything."

"You know what's better than those brownies? Hate-sex with your roommate."

"It wasn't even hate-sex. I wish it was. That would probably be easier. It was much more... intimate. Intense." She slides me my lasagna and I start to dig in. "I'm freaking out, Abbi."

She grins like the Cheshire Cat. "I'm obsessed with this," she says between mouthfuls. "So, what's the plan?"

"There is no plan."

She gasps. "You? Without a plan? Unheard of."

I roll my eyes, finishing up my food. "It was a one-time thing. I'm just gonna pretend it never happened."

"But the orgasms! You need more orgasms!"

I shake my head. "It was a mistake for me to get involved with Liam. A drunken mistake. We need to keep our relationship strictly professional. Friendly."

"I think that ship has sailed, sweetheart."

I sigh, downing the rest of my wine.

Abbi pats my back. "You are the grumpiest millionaire I've ever met."

"Not a millionaire," I grumble.

After dinner, we sit on the couch and watch *She's the Man*. I end up falling asleep on Abbi's couch, and I wake up in the morning with a text from Sharon telling me she can meet me this evening. I have my first tour of potential spaces for the salon at noon, so I slip out of Abbi's apartment and call a car home, praying Liam isn't there.

I don't take the time to check, beelining for the bathroom. After I shower, I reply to Sharon to let her know I'll meet her for a drink later. Just as I'm heading out the door, I glance backwards down the hall, where I see Liam emerging from his room. He's shirtless and scratching the back of his head, clearly just waking up. I can't help but let my eyes peruse his bare chest, my mind flashing with memories of him hovering over me, his touch gentle and punishing. My eyes flicker up to his and catch his sharp, surprised gaze.

I flee, letting the door slam behind me.

The first couple of tours are total duds. The first place had mold covering the ceiling, and the second had only a tiny window that faced an alley. I'm feeling pretty defeated when I get to my last tour of the day. My feet hurt, I'm exhausted, and all I want to do is go home, but I'm terrified Liam's going to be exactly where I left him, looking grumpy and sleepy.

Why does that send butterflies to my stomach?

I'm in such a foul mood I almost don't notice the spot, too busy staring down at my Google Maps trying to navigate to the right location. But then I look up and see it. Nestled between two brick buildings with a giant A-frame window, it looks like a converted brownstone, stoop and all. A weight starts to lift off my shoulders as I take the stairs up to meet the realtor.

When she takes me inside, there's only one way to describe it: love at first sight. It's perfect. The large window lets in so much natural light that it fills the long room with the soft afternoon sun. The realtor tells me about the space and the rent, but I'm already sold. Sticking my hand into hers, I finally feel, for the first time in this whole process, that I'm exactly where I'm supposed to be.

"I'll take it."

LATER THAT NIGHT, I'm waiting for the paperwork for the rental space to hit my inbox over a bottle of champagne when I hear the sound of a key in the lock and the door opening. I don't have time to hide in my room — it's too late. Liam is already stepping into the apartment and meeting my eyes from across the room.

His gaze feels heavy on my face, just like it did this morning when he caught me rushing out the door. There's a tension in the air, as if there's an invisible thread pulled tight between us.

"Hey," he mumbles, crossing the room to toss his keys on the counter.

"Hey." I lift up my champagne flute and knock the rest of it down.

The corner of his mouth lifts up. A tiny, familiar gesture that sends a jolt through me.

"Celebrating?" he asks.

"I found a rental space for the salon, and I made some connections, hired some folks. Everything feels like it's coming together."

He smiles back at me, a slow, sexy grin that spreads across his face. "That's great, Whit. Congratulations."

My stomach warms at my nickname coming from his lips. I swallow and manage to form a word. "Thanks."

A silence settles in the space between us. What is he thinking?

"So... " he starts, and my stomach flutters with nerves.

He's going to say it was a mistake. He's going to tell me it should never have happened, and it's going to be the most uncomfortable moment of my life. I shake my head, my nerves getting the best of me.

"Let's pretend it never happened, right?"

He blinks. "What?"

"You know." I look at anywhere but him. "Last night. Let's just... it doesn't change anything between us. We're friends."

"Friends?" he echoes back at me.

Why isn't he agreeing with me?

After a moment, he seems to get his bearings, nodding along with me. "Right, friends. Yeah." His Adams apple bobs, and I can't help but stare at that spot on his neck. "Listen, I need a favor. Will you come with me to a gala on Friday night?"

A gala? That sounds an awful lot like...

"Like a date?"

He shakes his head, his dusty brows pulling together. "No, not a date. Just... two roommates who happen to be married, wearing exceptionally nice clothes, mingling in a ballroom."

I raise my eyebrows, and he sighs with a soft chuckle.

"It will help me with Luke's foundation. Tim says it will help to have someone by my side while I 'schmooze' a bunch of donors."

"What foundation?"

He plops into the kitchen stool. "I found out that Luke had a plan to open a foundation to help low-income and first-gen students get into a good uni. It's what I'm using my half of the money for — to do it in his honor."

I'm quiet in the face of his unexpected admission. Every

layer that Liam peels back is like a jolt to the chest, revealing an inner softness that I want to sink my hands into.

"That's amazing," I tell him, reaching my arm over the counter and placing my hand over his, hoping it won't spook him. He stares down at our joined hands until I pull back.

"Yeah," he finally says. "Anyway, will you come with me on Friday? It's some fancy gala QuestBridge is hosting to raise money for academic scholarships."

"Okay," I agree. "I'll go with you."

He breathes out. "Thanks."

"On one condition," I supply with a grin. He eyes me, suspicious, and I glance up at his mop of unruly hair. "Let me give you a haircut," I tell him. "You cannot go to a gala looking like that."

"Wow, thanks," he replies sarcastically. "I didn't know you cut hair."

"It's not like I can open a salon without having some skills of my own." I shrug, glancing at his face. "When's the last time you shaved, also?"

"I get it," he retorts. "Friday before the gala, you can do it."

I nod in agreement, excited to get a chance to cut hair again. I don't get to do it often, but I always enjoy it.

"Not a date?" I confirm.

"Not a date," he agrees.

But somehow... I'm not convinced.

22

___

WHITNEY

The past week has been a whirlwind. I put in the paperwork for the rental space in Williamsburg, and Sharon agreed to come on board as my CFO. Turns out she hated working for a bunch of tech bros as much as I did, and she's been looking for a new job for a while. It's overwhelming. There's so much to do, and I feel like it's all happening so fast. It's exciting, but scary.

Speaking of scary, it's the day of my not-date with Liam when I realize I have nothing to wear. I figured I had something in my closet that would work, but all I have are cocktail dresses and miniskirts, and I've got the sneaking suspicion that the event is more of a gown sort of thing.

I don't own a gown. I am gownless.

I text Abbi.

> Whitney: SOS. Going to a fancy gala with Liam and have nothing to wear.

It's a few minutes before she responds.

Abbi: A fancy gala? What happened to 'pretending it never happened'?

Whitney: It's not a date.

She sends me back the eye-roll emoji.

Abbi: I'm at work late today, but Saks is having a sale. Good luck!

Guess I'm on my own for a shopping spree.

I take the subway to Soho and go through a few different stores, not finding anything that really appeals to me. I decide that I'm being too picky, so I get my fix of caffeine and then go to a few more stores with a better attitude. Eventually, while trying on a few different dresses at Reformation, I find it. An open-backed V-neck red satin dress with a slit up the side. It hugs me in all the right places, accentuating my soft curves and making me feel beautiful in a way I haven't since...

Since I was in Liam's arms.

After I check-out, I head back home. I only have a couple of hours to do Liam's hair and get myself ready.

"Liam?" I call out as I let myself into the apartment.

"In here," he calls from his room. I find him bent over his laptop, his scruffy beard even longer than the last time I saw him.

"I swear that thing grows an inch an hour."

"Excuse me?"

"Nothing." I cough awkwardly. "Go shave and shower. Now. I'll do your hair after."

He grins. "I didn't realize you were so bossy. I think I like this side of you."

I turn away and head to my room to gather my supplies. I

haven't cut hair in a few months, but I'm excited. I've been missing it. I get set up in the living room, and a few minutes later, Liam saunters into the room.

Shirtless.

He's done as I asked, his face clean and his long, wet hair is matted against his neck. Without the beard, the sharp line of his jaw is even more clear. Avoiding his gaze, I gesture towards the chair for him to sit.

It's quiet as I get started, the air thick and awkward between us as I run my hands through his wet hair.

"Don't do it too short," he barks out as soon as I start.

I roll my eyes. "Tell me what you want."

He's quiet. "Whatever you think looks good. Just don't do it too short."

Hiding a smile, I continue cutting at pieces of hair. As I run my hand along the nape of his neck, tugging his hair upwards, he lets out a small groan, halting my movements.

"Sorry," he mutters under his breath, then clears his throat. "What got you into cutting hair?"

I hesitate for a moment, unsure how much more to reveal about my upbringing and where this dream started.

"My mom and I were really close when I was a kid. It was just the two of us, and we never really had roots anywhere. We basically lived out of our van, driving from place to place whenever my mom got bored or followed a new guy she was seeing." I slide my fingers through his hair, trimming off a few more stray pieces. "Anyway, like I told you, whenever we'd roll into a new town, she'd drop me off at some strip mall while she went to work. Eventually, I found that a lot of the salons would let me sit inside when it was hot outside. I'd watch the ladies do haircuts and nails, and I'd see the way people's faces would light up, how beautiful they felt afterwards, and I wanted to make people feel like that.

"The salons were the only place where I could forget about life for a moment, and just feel connected to other people. Being on the road was lonely for me. My mom thrived on that energy, on the spontaneity and never knowing what came next. But as I got older, I couldn't stand it. I just wanted to have roots somewhere. To have friends and feel stable. You can probably tell I'm a little obsessed with staying organized."

A low chuckle rumbles in his chest. "You? Obsessed? Never," he jokes.

I hold up the scissors. "Don't make fun of the woman who currently holds your fate in her hands."

He holds his hands up innocently. "Kidding. Please don't take it out on my scalp."

"I make no promises."

He chuckles, and it's quiet for a moment. "So," he continues, "you've wanted this for a while, then?"

"Pretty much since I was a teenager. I never thought it would be possible."

I finish the last of his hair, brushing stray strands off the back of his neck. Stepping in front of him, I lean over, holding his front pieces to compare the lengths. I feel his gaze on my face, and my eyes wander to meet his. My mouth parts slightly, my fingers brushing gently against his pulse point on his neck as my hands fall to my side. A shiver runs through me, desire sparking low in my stomach.

"You're all done," I announce, stepping back to put some much-needed distance between us. "Go look in the mirror. If you hate it, don't tell me, please."

"I'm going to love it," he tells me, standing. He squeezes my arm. "Go get ready, too. I'll meet you out here in a few minutes."

Realizing we're running low on time, I get ready quickly. I don't want to be the reason Liam is late, so I grab a clutch purse and rush out to meet him in the living room. His brown hair is tucked behind his ears, short and styled, and his suit hugs him in all the right places. His muscles strain against the tight material, and just the outline alone is enough to make me falter in my step, but I manage to stay upright as I approach him with a nervous breath.

"Hi," I breathe out.

He looks up, his eyes widening as he takes me in. He takes a slight step back, and I watch as his gaze falls down to the hem of my dress, scanning me from head to toe and sending a flush through me. His throat bobs, and I watch the muscles on his neck strain against the movement. When he meets my eyes again, his brow is furrowed and his mouth downturned.

He clears his throat, blinking. "You look... nice."

It's hard to stop my eyes from narrowing.

Nice?

The word hits me in the stomach, and I swallow the lump in my throat, keeping my expression blank. I don't know what I expected. This isn't a date. This isn't anything.

"So do you," I say, flattening my lips into a polite smile. His frown deepens, and I gesture towards the door. "Should we go?"

He nods, slipping his phone into his jacket pocket. We're quiet on the car ride over. Our banter and connectedness from the haircut seem to have evaporated into thin air. When we pull up to the venue, he slides out first, giving me a hand as I exit. As we enter the sprawling ballroom, I take in the decor and the bustle of the crowd. There's a lot more people than I was expecting.

Liam presses his palm to the base of my spine, sending another rush through me, this one filled with warmth. "Do you want a drink?" he asks.

"Sure," I say as he guides us over to the open bar and orders a beer for himself and a glass of champagne for me.

When our drinks arrive, I turn to Liam with a teasing smile, lifting my flute. "No tequila shots?"

He smirks, bringing his glass to mine. "Don't tempt me." He glances over my shoulder and waves, his smirk growing into a smile. I turn and see a couple approaching us.

"Liam! You made it." A tall blonde guy clasps Liam's shoulder and shakes his hand, turning to the woman next to him. "This is my wife, Emily."

Liam shakes her hand and nudges me closer. "I'm Liam. This is my wife, Whitney. Whitney, Tim and I went to uni together."

Emily throws her arms around me in an unexpected hug, and I manage to wrap my arms around her before she pulls back with a wide smile. I'm trying to focus on making a good impression, but I'm stuck on the word *wife* and how easily it slipped from Liam's lips. I don't know if I'll ever get used to that. Being someone's wife. It should feel wrong, but instead my body rushes with warmth as I imagine introducing Liam as my husband.

"It's so nice to meet you both," Emily says. "Tim told me about your foundation, Liam. It sounds like a wonderful idea."

Liam rubs the back of his neck, a nervous gesture I've come to recognize. I slip my hand into his without thinking and give it a soft squeeze. His eyes flash up to mine.

"Thanks," he breathes out. "It's not much so far, but I'm hoping tonight might change that."

"Absolutely," Tim agrees. "Let me find Rebecca and introduce you." Tim turns to me. "Mind if I steal your husband away?"

"He's all yours."

Liam shoots me a grin as Tim leads him towards a group of people standing by a table nearby.

Emily turns to me. "Is this your first event like this?"

"Is it totally obvious?"

She shakes her head. "Not at all. I just saw you looking around the room in interest rather than disdain. Tim only brings me around to talk to the plus ones while he schmoozes." She shrugs. "It's not so bad, I guess. Open bar, free food. It's the company I usually abhor, but you seem normal."

I can't help but laugh at her bold honesty. "Well, thanks, I guess." I lift my flute to her wine glass. "To free food and being normal."

"I will drink to that." She clinks her glass with mine and takes a sip. "How did you and Liam meet?" she asks.

I shift on my feet. We've never discussed what we would tell people. Should I lie and make up some romantic story? I decide to go with the truth. Or at least, the partial truth.

"We were roommates first, and everything sort of just went from there."

She smiles. "It's always good to be friends first."

I nod in agreement, but our conversation is interrupted by a red-haired guy stepping up next to us. "Emily, darling. You're looking stunning as always."

Emily's smile drops into a scowl as she turns to greet him. "Michael," she says icily.

He smirks, but instead of the sexy dimple that Liam usually sports, Michael's is a smarmy, arrogant one. "Babe, how many times I have told you to call me Mikey?"

She crosses her arms. "How many times have I told you not to call me *babe*?"

His smirk only grows as his sharp gaze turns to me. "Who's your friend?"

"Michael, Whitney. Whitney, Michael Sullivan. Biggest asshole in this city."

He presses his palm to his chest. "You flatter me." He reaches his hand out to shake mine. "Great to meet you. I thought Emily was the most beautiful woman in the room, but you've proven me wrong."

"Thanks," Emily mutters as I raise my eyebrows.

Wow. This guy is a dick.

"What do you do, Michael?" I ask with a polite smile.

"I'm a project manager at the Department of Education. What do you do, beautiful?"

"It's Whitney," I correct him. "I'm a business owner."

He nods like he doesn't quite care, his eyes roaming my face and lower.

"What does your job entail?" I ask.

"I oversee a variety of organizations and functions within the Department of Education."

It sounds like he could really help Liam out.

"Really?" I beam up at him, giving him a wide smile. "That's great. My husband is actually starting a foundation to expand access to higher education." Mikey's only half-listening, so I put my hand on his arm. "You must meet him. He can tell you all about it."

He smirks, bringing his arm up to touch my shoulder. "I'd rather you tell me about it in someplace more private than this."

I glance across the room to where I see Liam talking to a tall woman with long curls. She's talking animatedly, and I can almost make his expression out from here. His whole body is stiff and radiating with what appears to be anger.

"Would you excuse me for a moment?" I interrupt whatever Mikey is saying and step away from him.

"Sure thing, beautiful."

Just as I turn to find Liam and see what's wrong, a hand grips around my arm. I blink up at Liam, baffled that he managed to get over here so quickly.

"I need to borrow my wife," Liam growls at Mikey and pulls me from the group, his hand pressing at my back firmly. He nudges me, his scowl deepening.

What the hell is his problem?

He yanks me further from the ballroom, moving towards the exit, and I have a feeling I'm about to find out.

23

LIAM

I press my palm to the base of Whitney's spine, the tips of my fingers tingling against the bare skin her gown reveals. When I first saw her, I thought I was going to lose it. I wanted to rip that dress off her body and touch her everywhere. The contrast of the red silk against her pale skin, the sight of her bare neck as she turned away from me...

Fuck.

Then I saw her smiling and flirting with fucking Mikey, of all people. I only had to spend five minutes with that guy to know he was a jerk. I met him when Tim introduced me to Rebecca, but he barely glanced in my direction before making some inappropriate comment about the waitress. I would've ignored his presence completely if he hadn't crossed the room to talk to Whitney and Emily.

I leave her alone for ten minutes and she's looking at him with a smile that she's never given to me. Wide and bright and completely unguarded.

I hated it.

Now, the smile that was dancing on her face mere minutes

ago has faded into a scowl. I press her forward, gripping my hand around her arm and pulling her out of the ballroom.

"Come on," I nudge her forward, and she throws me a frustrated glare.

This night has been a total disaster. I was already thrown when I saw Whitney. I wanted nothing more than to slide my hands below that silky fabric and find her wet and ready for me. Slip my fingers inside her until she begged for my cock. Just the sight of her was making me feel out of control, but I'd managed to push it down and force myself to network. It only got worse from there; Tim had introduced me to some folks, and I managed to get a few business cards, but I spent most of my time talking to Rebecca. I pitched Luke's foundation to her, as passionately as I could, and she slashed all of it to fucking bits. Told me that I didn't have enough support or funding. That a one-man team was not enough to get started with such a large endeavor.

To her credit, I don't think she meant to tear me down completely. I suppose she's just being realistic, and if anyone knows about this stuff, it's her. If she says I can't do it, she's probably right. She'd just finished slashing me to pieces when I glanced over at Whitney to see Mikey touching her. I let out a growl at the memory.

"We're leaving," I spit, trying to control the growing rage inside of me at Rebecca's words. At the sight of Whitney touching another man.

"Stop manhandling me," she seethes, yanking her arm out of my grip. "What the hell is wrong with you?"

"Don't push me right now, Whitney," I warn her, my temper simmering. "Not when I see you flirting with Mikey fucking Sullivan."

She scoffs and rolls her eyes. "Are you kidding me? I'm getting pretty sick of this possessive boyfriend routine."

"Watch it," I growl.

"Or what? Plan to fuck the jealousy out of me again?"

The comment sizzles between us, the air taught and heavy with her words. She's broken our agreement to pretend that night never happened. She struts ahead of me, rushing out of the hotel and stepping out to the sidewalk. I order an Uber, and silence settles between us as we wait.

"Sorry I don't like watching my *wife* flirt with another man right in front of me," I growl.

She rolls her eyes as the car pulls up in front of us. I yank the door open, and she slides in, all the way to the other side.

"I wasn't flirting! And if I was, I was just trying to talk you up to him. He seems really connected, and I thought if he heard your pitch, he could help you out. I did it for you. I only came to this stupid event for you. Bought this stupid dress for you."

Her voice breaks slightly on the last word. Just the sound of it melts my icy anger. I can't see her face in the darkness of the back seat, but I reach for her hand, and she flinches at the contact, pulling back from my touch.

"I'm sorry," I breathe out, and she stiffens. "Rebecca said some shit about the foundation, how it would never work, and I was pissed off. When I saw you touching him, I lost it. I'm sorry, Whit."

She turns to me, her gaze sharp. "What did Rebecca say?"

I shake my head. "Just that the whole foundation idea is a pipe dream and that I should give up before I sink too much money into it."

"What does she know?"

"A lot. She knows a fuck ton more than I do. All I'm doing is chasing the dream of a dead man."

"So, Rebecca says it's no good, and you just believe her? I didn't know you were a quitter, Liam."

My gaze darkens. "I'm not."

She shrugs back at me, a challenge in her eyes. "Sounds like you are."

"She agreed to look at my business plan," I tell her. "Hopefully she'll have more constructive feedback."

Whitney just nods, turning away from me to look out the window. I reach for her hand again with a sigh, and this time, she lets me take it in mine. I rub my thumb on the back of her palm as some of the tension loosens from her shoulders. "For what it's worth, I think the dress was worth every penny."

"I thought I looked 'nice'."

I inhale, the scent of her surrounding the space around us. "You look fucking beautiful."

It's silent in the wake of my confession. I tighten my grip on her hand, trying to get a glimpse of her expression. "Why did you leave? In the morning?" I ask.

She glances away from me. "Don't," she says into the darkness.

"We're never going to talk about it?"

She shakes her head. "It was one-time thing. We both agreed."

I cross my arms over my chest, leaning away from her. "Well, maybe I changed my mind."

"Excuse me?" Her head snaps in my direction.

"Maybe once wasn't enough for me. Maybe I need another taste."

She scoffs, turning away from me again, and the remaining journey is the longest five minutes of my life.

"Right here okay?" the Uber driver asks cautiously from the driver's seat. I glance out the window and realize we're at the apartment.

"Great, thanks," Whitney says, shoving her door open and slamming it behind her, leaving me sitting in the backseat.

Fucking brilliant.

I open the car door and meet the driver's eyes in the mirror. "Thanks, mate. Have a good evening."

"Enjoy," he says, sarcasm seeping into his tone.

When I step into the apartment, she's already in her room. Hiding from me, I suppose.

Guess we're done with our conversation.

I peel off my jacket and loosen my tie, slipping my shoes off. I'm heading to my room when I hear Whitney call my name from her room. Her door is cracked open.

"Liam? Can you come in here for a minute?"

I hesitate outside her door, pushing it open and stepping into the room. She's standing in front of her mirror, her back to me. I meet her gaze in the reflection, and her expression is a familiar one, tinged with desire but still cautious. Guarded.

She blinks, her brown eyes shining in the warm light. "Can you unzip me?" she asks softly.

I cross the room until I'm standing behind her. I don't move at first, studying her expression for some hint of what she's feeling, what she wants. I lower my gaze to her back, swallowing. Slowly, I bring my hand up to the zipper, settling my palm against her bare skin.

Whitney takes in a sharp breath, and my gaze shoots up to hers again. Her expression is no longer cloudy. Desire, plain and clear, shines in her eyes. I can't help the slow smile that tugs at the corners of my mouth. My fingers play with the zipper as I grip it in my hand, tugging it down her body inch by painful inch. When I completely unzip her, I slide my hand to the base of her spine and step closer, pressing my body against hers.

"You trying to seduce me, Whit?" I whisper into her ear, pressing my lips to the side of her neck and sucking on the soft skin there. "What happened to a one-time thing?"

She whimpers softly, and I meet her eyes in the mirror again, my gaze darkening.

"Shut up," she says, her hands holding up the front of her dress on her shoulders.

I slip one hand around her hip to the front of her body, my fingers dancing on her stomach, teasing. "Maybe I should make you beg for it."

Her eyes flash in warning. "Don't you dare."

My smirk grows as I slip my fingers lower. "Maybe I should tease you." I breathe the words against the shell of her ear.

She presses further against me. "Liam," she groans.

"Maybe I should peel this dress off you and fuck you over this desk." I trail my hand up her arm to where the straps of her dress are still hanging. "Make you watch us in the mirror for every minute of it."

She inhales another sharp breath, her eyes closing as she settles her head against my shoulder.

"Should I? Would you like that?"

She exhales shakily but doesn't speak. I still my movements, waiting for a response, and her eyes fly open to meet my gaze head-on. "Yes," she whispers.

Slipping her dress off her shoulder, I let it fall off her arms, baring her chest to me. Her nipples harden in the cool air, and I snake my hand around her waist, trailing up her torso to the underside of her breasts. One hand still resting above her panties, I bring the other up to her nipple, massaging and rolling the peak in my fingers.

Fuck, she feels good.

The dress drops to the floor. "Step out," I breathe against her neck.

She swallows and lifts her legs, stepping out of the dress and sliding it to the side. In the mirror, I take in her naked body as she trembles slightly against my touch.

"So pretty," I murmur against her ear, slipping my hands to her panties and pulling them down. "Again."

She steps out again, now completely naked in nothing but her heels. She reaches down to remove them, but I stop her movements, gently circling her wrist.

"Leave them on."

She straightens, meeting my gaze in the mirror with a smirk. "What about you?"

"What about me?"

"Get naked."

I laugh against her spine, pulling her back against me. "Always so impatient." I reach my hand around to her inner thigh, gripping it. "You want me to take my cock out, sweetheart?" Her breath hitches as my finger teases at her entrance. "Watch yourself," I command. "Look at how wet you are." I press a finger inside her, my thumb circling her clit as I go deeper, and she groans in response.

"Take your shirt off," she breathes.

I chuckle and slip another finger inside her, thrusting against her.

"And your pants."

Chuckling, I stop my movements and unbutton my shirt as Whitney turns to face me, reaching for my belt. I yank my shirt off my shoulders, throwing it to the side, while she tugs my pants down. I press my hand against hers, settling her movements as I step out of my pants. Her eyes flicker up to mine, and a rush of heat travels through me when our gazes lock.

She reaches a hand up to my cheek, her thumb caressing my jawbone as I lower my head and press a kiss to her lips, opening her mouth to mine. She tastes just as sweet as I remember.

"Turn around. I want to see us together."

Blinking up at me, she puts her hand over mine and swallows. "I... I have an IUD, and there's no one else. There hasn't been, I mean."

The corners of my mouth tick up, and I press another kiss against her lips, slipping my tongue into hers. The thought of fucking Whitney bare has my already-hard cock thickening even more.

"Turn around," I repeat.

24

WHITNEY

Liam's command sends a rush of heat through me as I turn and meet his gaze in the mirror. He settles a palm on my hip, rubbing soft circles with his thumb while the other presses against my back, bending me slightly towards the dresser in front of us. I'm waiting for him to press inside me when I feel his hands over my ass, spreading me open. I flush with embarrassment as I watch in the mirror.

I've never done anything like this before. I'm nervous, but more than that, I'm incredibly turned on. Every sensation, every brush of his hand is setting me on fire. He drops to the ground behind me, burying his face against my center. I take in a shocked breath as he licks me from behind, bringing his fingers around to my front to tease me.

"Liam," I choke out.

He presses his tongue inside me, circling his fingers along my clit. "You taste so fucking sweet," he groans against me.

My eyes widen as waves of pleasure roll through me. Watching myself in the mirror is making me even crazier, and a blush grows on my cheek at how turned on I am by watching myself.

Just like he did in the kitchen, Liam doesn't just taste me, he *devours* me. He's a man on a mission, and that mission is to be the death of me. So far, he's succeeding.

Another tremor rocks through me as his fingers circle my clit again.

"I'm going to—" I press against him, needing relief, and he thrusts his fingers deeper inside me.

He presses off the ground, his lips finding the back of my neck, his fingers still filling me. He tugs my hair slightly, bringing my gaze to meet his.

"I want to watch you while you come," he breathes against my neck.

"I'm—" I choke out, closing my eyes.

"That's it, baby. Come for me," he growls.

I feel myself clenching against his fingers, a wave of pleasure rushing through me all at once. I think I'm saying Liam's name, but I can't be sure. My eyes fly open and lock with Liam's, the focused expression on his face sending even more tremors through me.

He slips his fingers out and grips my hips in his hands. "I need to fuck you." He drags his hand along my thigh, feeling the wetness dripping down my leg. "Can I fuck you? Please?"

I let out a shaky breath. I'd probably make some smug remark if I weren't completely overwhelmed. All I can do is nod fervently, my legs trembling in anticipation. He presses his palm to the base of my spine, bending me closer against the dresser. Slowly, more slowly than I would have expected, he sinks deep inside me. The feeling of him filling me up without anything between us is indescribable.

"Fuck," Liam breathes, pressing deeper. "You feel perfect." He pulls out before thrusting into me again, establishing a slow rhythm of his body against mine. One hand rests on my hip while his other draws up to my breast, squeezing and playing with my nipple.

"Liam." I meet his eyes in the mirror. "Don't hold back."

His gaze darkens as he pushes me down and lets go. He thrusts against me, harder now, sinking inside me with abandon. He ravages me as I arch my back against him, staring at us in the mirror.

"Talk to me," I whisper. "Give me more."

He thrusts deeper, growling against me as he does. "Does my dirty girl need it harder?"

I nod again as his hand wraps around my hair, gripping it in his hand.

"You like it like this? Me using your body however I want? Fucking you from behind until you scream?" He thrusts against me, giving me everything he has, and my eyes start to flutter close, overwhelmed by the waves of pleasure rolling through me, but he tugs at my hair. "You look at me while I'm inside you, baby," he says. "Look at how good you take it. How perfect you look."

A choked sound escapes me, somewhere between a moan and a gasp. The sound only fuels Liam on as he thrusts against me harder and harder. I don't know how long I'm going to last. His thumb finds my clit again, one hand tugging my head back while the other circles me in a torturous movement that makes me clench against him.

"You want to come?" he asks.

I nod again, unable to form words. Unable to think.

"Beg," he instructs me. "If you want to come, ask nicely."

"Please," I manage through my gasps. "Please."

He releases my hair and thrusts into me again, gentling his movements into a slower rhythm. "That's my girl," he says. "Come for me, beautiful."

Almost as soon as I feel my orgasm crash to the surface, a

groan escapes him and he collapses against me, filling me completely. We ride the wave together, both of us gasping into the quiet room.

"Oh my God." I fall onto the dresser, pressing up on my palms.

Liam breathes heavily against me, his hands resting on my hips from where he was thrusting. We stay there for a moment, our gasps filling the silent room. Finally, his weight lifts off me and he brings me up with him, tugging me into his arms in a tight hug.

"You okay?" he asks, his hand brushing softly through my hair.

I nod, still gasping for breath. "Yeah."

He presses slow kisses to my neck before pulling back to meet my eyes, tucking a stray hair behind my ear. "It was intense, wasn't it?"

I nod again, feeling a heaviness pressing in on me.

What does this mean?

He pulls me from my thoughts by bringing my palm up to his lips and pressing a kiss to the center of it. "I'll be right back," he says.

He releases my hand, grabbing his briefs off the floor and tugging them on. He slips from the room as I stumble over to my bed, grabbing his shirt off the floor and pulling it over my shoulders. I button it up and fall against the pillows, closing my eyes.

It's too much. It's not supposed to be like this.

I hear Liam come back into the room, but I can't make myself move. His weight presses into the mattress next to me and I feel a warmth against my legs. Glancing down, I see him running a damp cloth along my legs, gently cleaning me up. When he's finished, he hands me a glass of water. We drink it down in silence and he puts the empty glass on the table, settling onto the bed next to me.

"You need anything else?" he asks.

I shake my head and rest against the pillow again, my head spinning. He tugs on my hand, intertwining his fingers in mine. "You're being quiet," he says.

"I thought you'd be celebrating me finally shutting up for once," I mumble.

He chuckles and pulls me closer. "It's making me nervous," he admits. "Was it too much?"

I turn on my side to face him completely. "I'm fine, Liam."

He trails his hand along my thigh, playing with the ends of the button-down. "You look sexy in my shirt."

I blush and smirk at him, letting my hand rest on his bare chest, feeling the contours of his muscles against my fingers.

"Look even sexier out of it," he mumbles.

I chuckle against him and pull the covers up, turning over and flipping my bedside light off, engulfing us in darkness.

"Will you be gone when I wake up in the morning?" he asks, a hint of vulnerability in his voice. The sound of it tugs at my heart.

"This is my bed," I remind him with a soft smile.

He pulls me closer, his arms wrapped entirely around me. "Goodnight, Whit."

I can hardly reply before my head hits the pillow and sleep takes me completely.

THE SUN CRACKS through my curtains, bathing the room in a warm light that matches the warmth covering my body. The source of that heat? The man currently wrapped around me, his snores filling the room. Liam didn't snore in Vegas, but last night he nearly woke me up with his noise. Worst of all, I'm not even annoyed by it. I find him unbearably cute.

Liam shifts, tucking my body tighter into his and sliding his leg between mine. The movement sends a rush of heat through me, and my mind is filled with memories from last night, images of the way we looked together in the mirror.

Why does he have to be so good in bed? My ex, Christopher, was always a bit selfish when it came to sex. He didn't really like going down on me, and he wasn't that into foreplay. Meanwhile, Liam has ruined other men for me. Once the rest of my inheritance comes through and we part ways, how am I ever going to find someone who seems to understand exactly what I need? Who is as desperate to taste me, to touch me?

A pang hits me at the thought of our impending expiration date, even if it is years away.

Divorce.

Such an ugly word. When Liam and I decided to get married, I didn't think beyond *All Rhodes* and how badly I wanted to achieve my dream. I failed to grasp the reality that I'm going to have one divorce under my belt before thirty. I sigh against my pillow, my mood successfully soured. Trying to shake off thoughts of the future, I snuggle further into Liam's arms, focusing on the feeling of his body wrapped around mine. I really should get up and figure out what to say to Liam.

Does he regret it?

The night at the club was one thing. We could write it off as a drunken mistake and move on. But twice? There's an undeniable thread running between us, an attraction that I can't deny.

Liam shifts again, slipping his arms out from around me and stretching them above his head with a groan. The sound of it sends another flush of memories through me, making the room feel a few degrees warmer.

"Good morning," he murmurs, slipping his hand back to my hip.

"Morning," I whisper, my nerves building.

In the soft glow of last night, our wild sex felt bold and intimate and perfect. In the morning glow, my crusty eyes and dry mouth make it feel like a dirty secret. One that I'm scared to say out loud.

Liam tugs me closer, turning my head to face him, but he doesn't say anything. He presses his lips against mine, and I fall into the feel of him, opening my mouth with a heady moan.

We're interrupted by the sound of buzzing. I pull back from our kiss, reaching for the bedside table for my phone, but it's not mine. Liam follows my movement, sitting up and glancing around. He slips out from under the sheets and reaches for his pants, searching in the pockets for his phone. He slides back into the bed next to me, reading his screen. I avert my gaze, but when he flips his phone over with a groan, I meet his eyes again.

"Everything okay?" I ask, pulling the covers up.

He nods and exhales. "I totally forgot. My dad is coming to town next weekend, and I told him he could crash with us."

"What?" My voice pitches up. "*Here?*"

He rubs his brow and sighs. "I was going to ask you about it, but it was ages ago."

"Does he know about us?"

He shakes his head. "No, but I've got to tell him. He'll be pissed I didn't invite him to the wedding. Haven't really gotten around to telling him about me dropping out of school, either."

"Liam!" I step out of bed into my slippers and throw my hair into a bun. "Seriously?"

He shrugs and grabs his own clothes, taking the hint. "I'm gonna call him today."

"Are you sure you should tell him? About us, I mean. You definitely need to tell him about school."

He pulls on his pants and stares at me. I'm still wearing his button down from last night, the one that I slept in. He quirks an eyebrow at my guilty expression. I reach to take it off but he crosses towards me and stills my movements with his hand.

"Keep it." He smirks, his hand dragging up my arm lightly. "I'm going to speak to him. It's not like I can hide it from him forever."

"It wouldn't be forever. It'd only be three years."

His brow furrows at my response. "Right." He grabs his phone off the bed and slides it into his pocket as I turn away from him.

"I'm sorry I'm springing this on you." He crosses the room and lingers near the door. "What are you up to today?"

"Not much. I'm meeting with a contractor this afternoon to see if they're a fit for the salon."

He nods. "I've got work."

Silence settles between us.

"Listen—"

"Last night—"

We stumble over each other, and he laughs awkwardly, swiping his hand on the back of his neck.

"You go," I offer, not wanting to be the one to deal with the mess between us. My heart races in the moments before he speaks. It's a losing battle, my attraction towards Liam. He looks incredible with messy morning hair, leaning against my doorway with his brows furrowed, staring at the ground.

"I was just gonna say… "

My heart sinks.

This is it. The moment of rejection. The letting me down easy.

"It can't happen again," I hear myself say. I turn away from him and busy myself with something on my dresser, but it offers me no solace. This is the same spot from last night. It's the place where he bent me over, the mirror we stared at each other through. "It would just complicate things. We can pretend for your dad and for other people, but we can't get into all that," I say, staring at the floor. I can feel his gaze on me through the mirror, and I wonder if he's thinking about last night, too.

"You sure? Because—"

I nod my head fervently and turn back to face him, forcing a smile. "I'm sure."

He nods tightly, his expression unreadable. "If that's what you want."

"It is."

"Alright."

He turns from the doorway, leaving me standing in my room. Somehow, my heart sinks even lower, my gut twisted into pieces. I exhale a shaky breath and close my eyes, forcing back the emotions that threaten to break to the surface.

It's for the best.

But if it's for the best, why does it hurt so damn much?

25

———

LIAM

Riding the train to work, I replay the events of the last twenty-four hours, wondering where I went wrong. What I should have done differently. Maybe if I hadn't gotten so angry at Whitney after seeing her with Mikey. Maybe if I hadn't gone to her room when I heard her call out for me.

Who am I kidding? I couldn't have ignored her even if I'd tried.

Whitney is... unavoidable. She's woven herself into the fabric of my life, more and more by the day, and now she's buried somewhere deep inside my chest. If I want things to stay even remotely normal between us, I can't afford to keep her there.

Last night was everything. The sight of her coming undone in the mirror, the feel of her clenching against me. I thought I couldn't get enough after the first time, but after last night, I don't know how I'm supposed to stay away.

Even though she said to my face that she's not interested. That she doesn't want me.

Was I too much?

My stomach drops at the thought that I might have pushed Whitney too far or made her do something she didn't want to do. She seemed as into it as I was, but what if I misread something? What if she can hardly stand to be in the same room as me?

That's certainly how it felt when we first met. Hate at first sight. Still, I thought in the months since we'd returned from Vegas, something had changed with us. As bizarre as it was that we were, in fact, married, we seemed to get along well. I actually looked forward to coming back to the apartment at night, to seeing her meticulously studying her design plans for the salon or making cocktails in the kitchen.

I thought she'd started to see me — the real me.

I thought she liked what she saw.

Guess it turns out she just wanted a good time. That's all I ever am. A good time, a fun night out, but when it comes to the real shit, when it comes to real life, nobody wants me.

Just like Luke.

If I'd been a better friend, if I'd been someone he could rely on, someone who people trusted, he'd have talked to me about what he was going through. He wouldn't have felt so alone.

He wouldn't be gone.

When I get to Abe's, Darius is there taking chairs down from the tables and setting up. After I get the bar stocked and ready, he nods his head towards the backdoor as if to say *get going*. I step into the back alley behind the bar for a smoke, finding Jackson sitting on the stoop with a comic in his hands.

"Hey," I call out, and his head snaps up at my voice. "I thought you were done skipping school," I say, unable to keep the accusation out of my tone. He ignores my question, turning his gaze back down to his comic.

Inhaling my cigarette, I shake my head. "What are you reading?"

His round glasses slide down his face as he holds the comic up. *X-Men.*

"Doctor Strange is the best."

"Yep," he agrees, barely glancing in my direction.

"So... about school—"

He puts the comic down, rolling his eyes. "I finished all my homework already. Who cares if I miss sometimes?"

"Homework only counts if you're there to turn it in. What do your parents think about all this?"

"My dad doesn't care," is his empty reply.

Ambling over to his side, I sit down on the stoop next to him, then nudge his shoulder. "You know, me and your brother both think you've got a solid future ahead of you. I know it can feel like your dreams are silly or impossible, but they aren't."

He's quiet, and I can only hope that he's considering my words, that perhaps I am getting through to him as Darius hoped.

Pushing through the voice in my head telling me that this is useless, I continue on. "You still have plenty of time to submit applications, and if money is an issue, there's a lot of organizations that can help with fees and all that stuff. I can help you, if you want."

He doesn't respond, so I press on my knees and lift myself up. Glancing down at him, he meets my gaze, his expression unreadable.

"Thanks," he says eventually. "I'll think about it."

"You have my number, right? Text me anytime."

He nods, and I can sense that the conversation is over, so I head back inside. When I get back behind the bar, Darius crosses over to me, his expression hopeful.

"What did he say? Did it work, you think?"

I shrug. "He wasn't too receptive, but I think I got through to him a little bit. I hope I did."

His shoulders seem to loosen as he relaxes, leaning against the bar. "Thanks, man. I appreciate it."

"Keep me updated," I tell him.

Something about Jackson reminds me of Luke. Maybe it's that Luke's glasses always used to slip down his face during class. I'd catch his gaze during exams while he'd push them back up his nose and send me a signature smile, one that said *we got this.*

I miss that fucking smile.

THE NEXT DAY, I'm in my room avoiding my roommate when my phone rings with a call from my dad. For a moment, I consider ignoring it, terrified that he's going to ask about school and all my secrets will come tumbling out. Instead, I press the phone to my ear.

"Liam! I can't wait to see you."

Despite myself, I grin at the sound of my dad's voice. "Yeah, me too. Should be fun."

"Damn right. It's been too long. You're so busy with school, I never get to see you."

I suppress a sigh. It's time. I have to bite the bullet.

"Listen, Dad. I'm not in school anymore. I'm off it."

Silence greets me on the other line.

"Dad?"

"What do you mean?"

"I dropped out. Also, I'm married."

My dad roars with laughter for a solid minute before he settles down, chuckling lightly. "Good one, Li."

I shake my head. "I'm not joking. I know it's a dick move to tell you like this, but I knew you'd figure it out when you came to visit, and I thought it was better to tell you before."

He quiets. "You're serious?"

"Yeah."

"Well." He clears his throat. "I wish you'd told me. These are major life decisions, Liam."

"Trust me, I know."

"Who is she?"

"She... " I trail off, unsure what to say. I settle on the truth. "She's amazing. I've never met anyone like her."

He hums, and I imagine he's smiling. "Does she have anything to do with you dropping out?"

"No. I did that before I even met her."

"Li, what's going on? If you're in love, I can understand, but you're making a huge mistake quitting school—"

"Dad, please no lectures right now. Can you just respect that I need to make my own decisions, even if they end up being mistakes?"

He pauses for a moment. "As long as you're happy, I'm happy. I'm excited to meet her."

My heart skips a beat. "Me too."

"Am I still alright to stay with you? Don't want to interrupt the newlyweds."

I groan. "Yeah, you're fine. You can stay in my old room."

Yet again, Whitney and I are going to have to share a bed. As if the first time wasn't bad enough. I hardly survived waking up to her scent, to the feeling of her wrapped around me. Now that sex is entirely off the table, it's going to be pure torture sleeping next to her.

"Can't wait. I'm thrilled to meet her. Has your mum spoken to her yet?"

I shake my head, grimacing. "Haven't gotten 'round to telling Mum, either. Suppose I will when I visit for the holidays."

"Liam. Why are you keeping secrets?"

"I don't know. I'm sorry. I'm just... "

Lost?

Fucked up?

Lonely?

"I love you, Li. I'll text you when I'm headed to the city."

"Right. Love you, Dad."

I hang up, feeling like an absolute prick. It's bad enough that I've dropped out, but now I'm lying to my family about a fake marriage that has an expiration date? Maybe Whitney was right. Maybe I shouldn't have told them at all.

But somehow, telling my dad about me and Whitney has filled me with an unexpected feeling of pride. A swelling in my chest from hearing my dad congratulate me.

For a moment, it made us feel... real.

26

———

WHITNEY

It's been a week since the gala, and I've been walking on eggshells at home ever since. I don't even watch TV in the living room anymore for fear that Liam might catch me off guard. I've interacted with him twice since we had insane mirror sex that left me completely and utterly ruined. The first time was when he was heading out for work. He caught me in the kitchen cooking dinner, and he threw me a hello before storming out of the door. I spent the next thirty minutes analyzing every second of that interaction. Then, yesterday morning, I bumped into him on my way to the bathroom. His hand wrapped around my arm, steadying me from our collision, and the heat from where our skin touched seemed to warm me from head to toe.

I blinked up at him and swallowed.

"Hi," I whispered.

"Hey," he said.

We haven't spoken since.

Needless to say, I'm not handling the whole "it was a mistake" plan very well. I thought just once would be enough to get it out of our systems. Then I thought twice would be enough. But Liam is not out of my system.

In fact, he's deep in my system.

Every night, right before I've drifted off to sleep, I've listened for the sound of him across the hall. Wondered if he was thinking of me. If he, like me, was touching himself, remembering the way we came apart together.

Shaking thoughts of Liam off, I pick up my phone and see my best friend calling. Unfortunately for me, Abbi is able to sniff out when I'm avoiding her like a detection dog sniffs out drugs.

"Hey," I say into the phone.

"Come over. Shane left for preseason and I'm moping."

"I thought you were going to join him on the road?"

"Not until December. I'm stuck all alone for the next three weeks."

I roll my eyes. "Oh, life must be so hard in your two-story penthouse that your rich boyfriend pays for."

"*Whitney*," she whines. "Please come over. I'll order from your favorite Thai place?"

She's going to get the truth out of me no matter what, so I might as well face it head-on. "Alright, I'll be there in an hour."

After sending off some emails, I head to Abbi's apartment in Williamsburg. She's only a few stops away on the L. Her apartment is a waterfront suite with a gorgeous view of the city across the river. When I arrive, she opens the door and wraps her arms around me.

"I missed you," she whines.

I roll my eyes but hug her tighter. "I literally saw you last week."

She pulls me inside. Once I'm settled in, we sit on the couch, and she puts our food order in.

"How's work?" I ask.

She waves a hand. "I don't want to talk about work. How's your hubby?"

"I thought you wanted to talk about Shane."

She narrows her eyes. "We'll get to that."

"We slept together," I say reluctantly.

"I already knew that. No updates?"

"Again. We slept together *again.*"

Her mouth drops, quickly replaced by a giant grin that spreads across her face. "I knew it. You like him."

I purse my lips. "I maybe sort-of slightly have a tiny desire to keep having sex with him. That is all."

"You *like* him!"

Suppressing another eye roll, I reach for the wine between us and pour myself a glass. "I tolerate him. I like his skills in bed. There's a difference."

"Yeah, right. You don't do casual. You never have."

"Well, there's a first time for everything."

She scoffs. "The first time for you to have a friends-with-benefits is *not* with your husband."

"Stop calling him that."

Because I like it way too much.

She laughs in my face. "What else should I call him?"

"We're not... he's just—" I break off, frustrated. "It's complicated. Friends with benefits is all this can be. I told him we should just pretend it never happened."

"That's what you want?"

I shake my head, blinking furiously at the unexpected pressure behind my eyes. "I just said it because I thought it's what he was going to say, and I didn't want to be embarrassed. But now that he's actually acting like nothing ever happened? It hurts."

Abbi wraps her arms around me, hugging me tightly. "You'll figure it out. I know you will. You're the smartest, kindest, most beautiful person I know. If Liam can't see that, he's an idiot."

I let out a watery laugh, tears poking at corners of my eyes. "Thanks, Ab."

"And no more avoiding me."

"I wasn't—"

"Don't lie. Just don't box me out. It'll be hard enough when I'm on the road with Shane. Then you'll really miss me."

I wipe at my eyes. "Stop. I actually will."

"I know," she says, pulling me tighter against her.

By the time I get home, I'm exhausted and half-drunk. The wine has gone to my head as I stumble up the stairs and let myself into the apartment. I'd foolishly assumed that Liam wouldn't be home because it's a Thursday night, and he tends to be at work until the early hours of the morning.

Not tonight.

Tonight, he's standing in the kitchen, shirtless.

I try to keep my expression neutral as I kick my shoes off and toss my keys onto the counter, mumbling something close to a hello.

"Y'alright?" Liam asks, leaning against fridge with a glass of water in his giant hands.

Hands that have touched every part of me.

"Yep. How are you?"

"Good, yeah."

Great. So it's going to be awkward between us until the end of time.

"Listen, about my dad coming to visit... "

I'd almost forgotten about that. I felt too bad to turn him down, but I don't do very well with parents. I've never met my dad, and my mom comes around once a year if I'm lucky, so I don't have much of a frame of reference for how to behave.

With a jolt, I realize Liam is still talking.

"I figure I'll move my stuff into your room tomorrow and try to make mine look like a guest bedroom."

"What?" I squeak.

"My stuff. Into your room. Since my dad is staying in my room?"

"Wait, you told him?"

"Yes. I just told you that—"

"You shouldn't have told him about us." I swallow. "It's just overcomplicating things."

He frowns, the first frown I've seen in a while. "Yeah, because us getting married to fulfill your highly specific inheritance clause isn't complicated at all," he deadpans. "It'll be fine. It'll be just like Vegas."

I don't want to argue with him, and I really don't want to think about Vegas lest I spiral even more, so I nod. "Alright. I'll be around tomorrow if you need help moving your stuff."

"Okay," he says quietly. "Thanks."

Before I can say anything else, he slips out of the kitchen and down the hallway towards his room. I realize I left a pile of dishes in the sink from breakfast this morning, so I clean up a bit and start washing them. After a few minutes, Liam comes back into the room and opens the fridge, pulling a beer out.

"You want a La Croix?" he asks.

"Sure, thanks."

"Don't know how you drink that stuff. Tastes like fizzy piss."

I snort and roll my eyes, holding my hand out for the can. He hands me a lime-flavored one and his gaze falls to my hand with a scowl.

"Where's your ring?" he snaps.

My eyes widen. "Why do you care?"

His gaze darkens. "You're supposed to wear it. I got it for you."

I scoff, indignant. "It's not like you wear one. I'm sure all the girls hitting on you at the bar would back off if they saw a ring on your finger."

I realize what I've said too late, and Liam seems to realize it too.

He smirks, twisting open his beer and taking a sip. "Jealous, Mrs. Clark?"

"Oh my God. Don't call me that."

"But it sounds so *good*."

"Liam," I warn. "Stop flirting."

A flutter runs through me at the energy sparking between us. Minutes ago, it was awkward. Now, it feels like the temperature in the room has skyrocketed with the blush I'm sporting.

"I don't wear a ring because you didn't get me one," Liam says, pushing off the counter.

My smile drops.

What?

"Was I supposed to?" I turn from the sink and meet his eyes.

His Adams apple bobs as he swallows. "I'm kidding." His gaze flickers back to my hand. "But seriously," he says. "Where's yours?"

I roll my eyes and point to where the ring is sitting on the counter next to the sink. "I didn't want to wear it while doing the dishes."

Before I can blink, he crosses over to the counter, plucks the ring up, and stands in front of me. As I dry my hands with a towel, he grabs my left hand and intertwines our fingers. Slowly, he slips the ring back on, gripping my wrist lightly as he meets my gaze.

"Promise you'll never take it off again," he breathes out, a low, unexpected command.

"I promise," I reply in a daze.

Trying to shake off the intensity of the moment, I slip out of his grip and cross to the living room, settling on the couch. I turn on the TV and press play on my favorite reality TV show, forcing myself not to glance towards Liam.

"Is this *Love Island*?" he asks, his voice moving closer.

"Yeah. Season five. I'm catching up," I tell him, keeping my eyes focused on the TV.

"Why is everyone addicted to this stupid show? My dad never shuts up about it."

I smirk. "At least we'll have one thing to talk about. A shared love for head-turning and triangles."

"Is that some sort of inside joke?"

I shake my head with a laugh. "Yeah. Just funny phrases they use."

My head turns at the sound of pots and pans banging together in the kitchen. "You want cookies?" Liam shouts, hidden behind the cabinets.

"Sure?" I call back. "Why are you making cookies?"

He pops out, holding a bag of sugar. "Feeling restless."

This is the part where I would ask him if he wants to talk about it, but every time Liam peels back some layer of himself, I feel myself drawn further and further into his orbit. That's the last thing I need right now. I need to find my way out of Liam's orbit.

Out of his entire solar system.

So, I ignore his comment. "I love their accents," I say, changing the subject. "Especially Maura. She's so funny."

"You think my accent is funny?"

"No, yours is like... posh."

"Posh?" He crosses from the kitchen towards me, his hands on his hips. "Are you having me on?"

I suppress a smile, flattening my lips. "They all use slang. Like 'mugged off', 'cracking on', 'geezer'. You never say stuff like that."

"Because I'm not from Newcastle or Essex" he mutters, crossing back into the kitchen.

"Where are you from?" I ask, curious.

"London, which by the way has a lot of different accents. I moved to Brighton when I was about four and then to the States a bit later."

Liam stays in the kitchen for a few minutes while I watch my show, not offering any more commentary. After a couple of commercial breaks, he puts the cookies in the oven and settles next to me on the couch. He's scowling at the TV, shaking his head every few minutes.

"Can you stop? You're ruining the viewing experience."

He groans. "It's so stupid. It's clearly fake."

I throw my hands up. "Of course it's fake! It's amazing."

He chuckles and throws one of the pillows towards me, smacking me lightly in the face.

"Did you just throw a pillow at me?"

He grins. "Yeah."

I grip the pillow tighter and smack him with it, but the tiny thing is no match for his huge body. He shrugs me off easily, yanking it out of my hands and stuffing it behind his head. "No hitting me, or you won't get any cookies."

I gasp, pressing my hand to my chest as if mortally offended. "You'd deprive me of cookies?"

He rolls his eyes and goes to retrieve them out of the oven as the show comes back on. As I'm cheering on Molly-Mae and Tommy in one of the challenges, he drops the plate of cookies in front of me.

"They're hot," he warns me. "Don't burn your mouth."

"Thanks, *Dad.*"

I reach for one of the cookies, but he smacks my hand away with a grin. Once they're cool, he hands me one and I bite into it, closing my eyes with a moan.

"God, that's good."

When I open my eyes, Liam is staring at me, his burning gaze focused on my mouth. I clear my throat, glancing away from him. I have a sense of what he's thinking about, and it's a bad idea for us to go there right now.

He shakes his head and turns back to the TV. "Wait, so this guy's not interested in her anymore? Didn't he just ask her to be his girlfriend?"

"I thought you said the show was 'stupid'"

"It is," he grumbles. "What a prick. He's playing a game with her!"

I laugh, shaking my head. "If you don't like reality TV, what do you watch?"

"Not much of a TV guy, but I like *Star Trek*," he replies.

"Is that the one with Spock?"

He gasps in faux-horror. "You've never seen *Star Trek*?"

I shrug. "I think I saw *Star Wars* when I was a kid."

He shakes his head. "First of all: not the same. Second of all: we must fix this severe oversight."

"Fine," I reply. "You watch *Love Island* with me, and I'll give your nerdy show a chance."

"Not nerdy," he mumbles under his breath, stealing another cookie, and I can't help but laugh. There's something so simple about the two of us sitting on our couch, watching bad reality TV. It fills my chest with an unexpected warmth, and even though Liam and I are on opposite sides of the couch, ignoring the orgasm elephant in the room, I can't help but smile.

LIAM

The next day, I wake up on the couch, my body half-draped over Whitney's. Surprised that we fell asleep, I fold my arms under her body and lift her up without thinking. I carry her to her bedroom, glancing at the clock. It's not even eight yet, so I figure I'll let her sleep for a bit longer while I go get my stuff from my room. My dad's going to be here tonight, and I don't want him to suspect we've been sleeping in separate bedrooms.

As I set her on the bed, she moans, turning away from me, her arm draped over her eyes. Leaning towards her, I notice that she looks paler than usual, a clammy glow on her face. My stomach drops at the sight.

"Whitney?" I press the back of my head to her forehead, and she's burning up. "Are you okay?"

Smacking my hand away, she groans and sits up. "Migraine. Can you get my sleep mask? It's on my table."

I find the mask immediately, handing it to her. She pulls it over her eyes with another small groan, leaning back to rest her head on her pillows.

"Are you nauseous?" I ask, pulling her blanket over her.

"A little."

"Do you want me to go get some medicine from the chemist?" I ask, my voice pitching upwards.

"Quiet, please," she replies, dropping her voice. "The noise makes it worse."

"Sorry," I whisper. "How can I help?" Need is clawing its way up my throat, a desire to stop her suffering coursing through me. I feel completely helpless, and I hate it.

"I'm okay," she mumbles, curling into a ball.

My throat thickens, and I try to swallow through it. Forcing myself to leave her alone, I rush into the kitchen and get a cloth, pouring cold water over it and ringing it out. Then I grab three types of painkillers, a glass of water, and one of her La Croix cans. When I get back to her room, she's exactly how I left her.

"Here," I whisper, kneeling next to her bed. Laying the cool cloth over her forehead, I study her body movements for a sign of how she's feeling. She lets out a low exhale when the cold reaches her forehead. "Good?" I ask.

She nods, a soft smile stretching across her face. "Thanks," she manages, her words slightly slurred. I watch the rise and fall of her chest, waiting for her breathing to even out. After a few minutes, I replace her cloth with a new one and notice that she's fallen asleep.

I should check my phone to see if my dad has texted me. Instead, I lay down next to Whitney, watching her sleep, worry coursing through me. She looks okay now, but she's still pale. What if she needs to go to the doctor?

Grabbing my phone, I look up 'migraines' and spend twenty minutes researching the symptoms, causes, and possible reme-dies. A few articles suggest that weather and stress can be trig-gers. Am I stressing her out? Have I made things worse for her or inadvertently caused this somehow? Reading further, I find that caffeine can sometimes make people feel better. Without thinking, I go into the kitchen and set the Nespresso machine going. Maybe when she wakes up, she'll want to try a little bit. Unless she's still feeling nauseous?

Taking a deep breath, I try to calm my rising anxiety. Why am I freaking out? Whitney is fine. She's absolutely fine. Just in case, I go back to her room to check on her and find her sleeping still. I bring the coffee into her room and leave it on her bedside table, creeping quietly through the room. Whitney stirs and yawns, her arms reaching above her head with a groan. Immediately, I rush to the side of the bed, peeling the cloth off her head. She slips the eye mask off and meets my gaze.

"Liam?" She glances around, looking confused.

"How are you feeling? I made coffee. Do you want some? The articles said it would help."

She studies my expression then smiles, a small, coy grin. "Liam Clark," she says. "Are you fussing?"

Despite myself, a smile cracks through my nerves, relief taking over me. At least she's making jokes. She must be feeling better. Right? "I'm not fussing," I argue, if only to see her little frustrated frown, because she looks so damn cute when she's mad at me. "I'm being nice."

"You're never nice," she whispers.

"I'm always nice," I whisper back.

She grins, a sloppy, adorable smile that makes my heart skip a beat.

"I'm gonna call my dad," I tell her, still keeping my voice low. "I'll tell him not to come."

"No," she replies, sitting up completely. She winces at the low light in the room. "No, don't do that. I'll be fine by tonight, I'm sure. I just have to sleep it off."

"Okay," I agree easily, wanting her to lie back down. I don't want to stress her out any further. "Go back to sleep."

I try to make her drink the coffee, but she slaps my hand

away, taking the cup from me and taking a small sip. She pulls her mask back down over her eyes, and curls into that damned ball again, looking so small and delicate and... breakable.

My stomach lurches again.

Running my hand over her forehead and through her hair, I slowly massage her scalp. She moans, an affirmative sound that makes my whole body fill with warmth.

"Good?" I ask, confirming. She nods, so I continue caressing the top of her head, running my fingers through the strands of her hair. "Sleep," I say in a low voice, and she does. Her breathing evens out and she falls back asleep, looking like an angel despite her illness.

Working quickly, I grab my stuff from my room and clean up, trying to make it look more like a guest bedroom and less like a man cave. Once I gather everything, I bring it over to Whitney's room, unpacking silently so I don't wake her. Once I finish, I go on Amazon and order a headache hat, a migraine aromatherapy stick, and some Excedrin.

The hours pass quickly, and when I'm done prepping for Dad, I settle onto the sofa. Before I have time to relax, my phone buzzes with an email from Rebecca, responding to the proposal that I sent her a few weeks ago. I honestly thought she'd forgotten about our conversation at the gala and her promise to look over my plan. When I open her email, I almost wish I hadn't. Scanning through it quickly, I try not to panic, but it's becoming increasingly difficult to stay calm as the words flash in front of me.

Incomplete.

Missing key components.

Inadequate funding.

Some part of me hoped that despite her discouraging words at the gala, she'd change her mind when she saw my actual plan. Turns out I couldn't be more wrong. If I thought I was upset after Rebecca's comments, that was nothing compared to this detailed rejection. I don't have time to dwell on the stab of disappointment because I get a text from my dad that he's on his way, so I reply with a thumbs-up emoji.

Show time.

Not knowing what else to do and wanting to see her face again, I go back into Whitney's room and glance at her sleeping form. She rouses again, so I move to the side of the bed, reaching for her hand and intertwining our fingers. Brushing the back of her hand softly, I study her for a hint of how she's feeling. She tugs the sleep mask back again, her eyes connecting with mine.

"Hi," she whispers.

"Hi," I whisper back, pressing our palms together. "How are you feeling?"

"Good as new," she says.

"Are you sure?" I reach for the cup of coffee, which is cold. "Do you want more coffee? Or water? I brought you a La Croix."

Her nose crinkles, a smile tugging at her lips again. "You're a very good nurse, Mr. Clark."

"If you're waiting for me to be embarrassed, don't hold your breath. You scared the shit out of me, Mrs. Clark."

"It happens sometimes. It's been a while. I used to get them a lot when I was younger."

I shake my head. "Don't tell me that. I'll have an aneurysm," I joke. Well, I pretend it's a joke. The truth is every time I see her wince in pain, it feels like someone is putting a knife through me.

"Thank you for taking care of me," she whispers.

"I got you a headache hat and some other stuff that the internet said you need. I don't know why you were so ill-equipped for this. You need to take better care of yourself," I scold her, but instead of looking chastised, she just smiles.

"Okay, doctor. I promise." She grins, and despite myself, I lean over, pressing a kiss to her forehead. Rebecca's email may have put a damper on my mood, but Whitney's got color back in her face and she's smiling again. Somehow, I helped her feel better, and nothing — not even Rebecca's firm insistence that the foundation won't work — can take that away from me.

28

LIAM

"Wow! What a place. You've even got laundry? I hear that's highly coveted." My dad, Andy, slaps his hand on my back, taking in my apartment. He's grinning widely and wearing one of his overpriced shirts with awful prints on them. This one's a blue Cheetah print shirt that for medical reasons (the state of my retinas), should be burned immediately.

My dad arrived twenty minutes ago, and we've hardly made it past the foyer. He's been inspecting everything like we're at a crime scene and offering positive commentary about all of it. I think he's worried I've reached some sort of quarter-life crisis and wants to avoid talking about the whole dropping-out-school-and-getting-married thing at all costs.

"I've really got to make it up here more." He glances around. "Is that real velvet on the couch?"

"I think so."

"Apple TV? We're living in Roku City at home, but this is much fancier."

I glance down the hallway towards Whitney's room. Is she

sleeping again? Is she really feeling better, or did she just say that for my benefit?

"So, where am I sleeping? I could use a shower. Feeling a bit of the driving ick."

I don't know where my father learned the word *ick*, but I'm not going to question it. Probably from *Love Island*. I show him where the bathroom is and then guide him to my room.

"I'll be in the living room if you need me," I tell him, leaving him to settle in. Once I hear the shower start, I put the kettle on, knowing my dad would like a cup of tea when he's freshened up. I'm pouring the hot water into two cups when I hear footsteps coming down the hallway. I turn to see Whitney padding into the kitchen in her oversized t-shirt and sweats.

"Hey," she breathes out, crossing towards me. I want to reach out and wrap her in my arms, but instead, I flex my fingers at my side.

"How are you feeling?" I ask her, trying to keep my voice even.

"Like I've been run over by a truck," she replies.

I open the fridge and take out a La Croix, handing it to her. "My dad's here."

"Oh shit." She glances down the hall towards my room. "I wish I looked better."

"You look good," I tell her.

"Coming from you, that's a glowing compliment."

I scowl, frustrated that she always seems to misunderstand me. "You always look stunning, Whitney. You don't need me to tell you that. You're probably the most beautiful woman I've ever known."

What the hell did I just say?

Whitney blinks back at me, silence settling between us in the aftermath of my admission.

"Wow, that water pressure is incredible, Li. I feel like I'm getting the five-star New York experience right now," Andy calls from the hall as he enters the room... in a fluffy white robe and bunny slippers.

"Dad," I groan. "What are you wearing? Can you put some clothes on?"

"What?" He glances down at his slippers. "What's wrong with this? I'm getting comfortable."

Whitney giggles from behind me and crosses the room to my side. "Hi, I'm Whitney. It's so nice to meet you," she greets him, her expression warm. I wish she looked at me like that. No hint of wariness, no sign of skepticism. Just open friendliness.

God, what's wrong with me? I'm jealous of my own dad now?

"The missus! Thanks so much for letting me crash with you," my dad says, sticking his hand out and shaking hers. "I'd hug you, but I think my son might be right for once. I should get dressed. Didn't realize you were here."

She waves her hand. "Don't worry about it. We're family now, right?"

Family.

I swallow the sudden lump in my throat and turn away from them, fiddling with the teacups. "I made tea, Dad."

"PG Tips?"

I nod, the corner of my mouth pulling upwards. "Only the finest for your five-star New York experience."

He laughs and shuffles out of the room, his slippers smacking against the floor.

Whitney turns to me, her eyes alight and her hand covering her mouth. "Your dad is a riot," she says.

I shake my head. "He's a bit insane," I warn her.

She laughs. "I love it. How are you two total opposites?"

"Excuse me? I'm not funny? I seem to remember you holding your side in pain on Tuesday when I did my *Love Island* impressions."

"That's because you are way too good at them." She eyes the teacups in curiosity. "What kind of tea are you making?"

"The only kind my dad approves of. English breakfast with milk and sugar. You want some?"

She shrugs. "I've never tried it." She steps closer to me, lowering her voice to a whisper. "How are we supposed to act?"

I stare down at her. "Like we're married, Whitney."

"Yeah, but like... touchy?"

My eyebrows furrow. A week ago, she was begging for me to fuck her. Now she won't even touch me? What the hell did I do wrong?

"Is that a problem?" I ask.

She shakes her head. "Of course not. It's fine."

I chuckle, sliding her tea over to her. "I'm a lot better at this than you are."

Her mouth drops. "You are not."

I smirk, bringing my cup up to my lips. "I absolutely am."

"No way." She raises her eyebrows. "I wanted to be an actress when I was a kid."

"Well it's a good thing you didn't go pro because you are terrible at pretending."

"I did it at the gala."

"Yeah, and I had to drag you out of there."

Silence settles between us as we tiptoe closer to the unspoken thread that connects us: that night. Luckily, my dad comes back into the room at that moment. He's wearing a black t-shirt now, thank God. I'm about to slide his teacup over to him when I feel Whitney's arms wrapping around my torso and her lips pressed against my jawline.

I freeze.

She meets my gaze, her eyes alight with a challenge.

I'll show you acting, it says.

My lips tug into a half-smile at the realization. I didn't intend for my comment to be a challenge, but if it means I get to feel her hands on me, I'd call it a win. I slide my hands to her hips, holding her lightly. I brush my hand up to her face, tucking a stray lock of hair behind her ear.

She swallows.

"Aren't you two a pair?" My dad chimes in.

Both our heads snap up to him, as if we'd forgotten he was there. The whole reason we're wrapped up in each other.

"How did you two meet?" he asks.

I step back from Whitney and give my dad his tea. My eyes lock with hers again, a question between us. We really should have rehearsed this.

"My old roommate Olivia left suddenly, so Liam filled her spot. At first, I was worried about living with a guy, but he charmed his way into my life," Whitney answers.

"Got married pretty fast," my dad replies, a hint of judgement in his tone.

"Dad," I say in warning.

Whitney smiles. "It's okay. You're right. We did get married quickly, but I knew pretty fast that Liam was the one."

My chest flutters wildly. I know she's pretending — trying to prove she's a good actress, or whatever — but her words and the warmth in her tone sound so real.

I wish they were real.

Whitney turns to me and presses her hand on my stomach, staring up at me. "Thanks for the tea, babe. I'm going to go freshen up. What are we doing for dinner?"

I take a deep breath. I'm starting to regret teasing her, because this is not good. She can't keep looking at me like that. Like she cares about me.

"I thought we could cook here. I got stuff for burgers. Are you feeling up for eating?"

"If you're ill, Whitney, I can go off on my own," Andy says.

She shakes her head. "No, no. Burgers sounds great. I should try to eat something."

I watch her leave, my eyes drawn to the sway of her hips as she crosses the room and my chest still tingling from where her hand was resting.

"She's stunning, Li," my dad says when Whitney is out of earshot.

I nod, rubbing my hand on the back of my neck. "She is."

Before I can say anything else, my dad comes around the counter and wraps his arms around me. He's always been a hugger and a bit of a sensitive soul. Reluctantly, I wrap my arms around him, sighing into his arms.

He pulls back from our embrace, meeting my eyes. "So, you gonna tell me about school now?"

I shake out of his grip and sit in one of the kitchen stools with a sigh. "Shouldn't we at least have a pint first?"

He chuckles. "Alright. Good thing I brought a six pack, then. Figured I'd need to bribe you with Boddingtons."

"Seriously? Boddingtons? Do they even make those anymore?"

"Believe it or not, I've been storing them in the basement for years. Was waiting for a special occasion."

"I'm not drinking fifteen-year-old beer. I'll run down to the corner shop and grab some."

"But I lugged 'em all the way here!"

Shaking my head, I grab my keys and slide my shoes on.

"Don't interrogate her while I'm gone," I tell my dad.

He raises his eyebrows innocently. "Wouldn't dream of it."

I slip out of the kitchen, not quite believing him. I hope our acting skills are enough to make it through my dad's questioning. All I know is when it comes to my wife, I'm way out of my depth.

"YOU SURE YOU don't want a beer, Whitney?" my dad asks, pulling another Guinness out of the fridge.

She shakes her head. "No, thanks. I don't really like beer except for sours and the occasional Corona with lime."

My dad gasps as if Whitney's committed a horrible crime. "Corona," he says in disbelief. "Li, you should've told me your wife had such shit taste."

"Dad," I warn, but Whitney just throws her head back, laughing. She's been cracking up at everything my dad says, and my mood is swinging between thrilled admiration at the way her smile lights up her whole face and childish sourness that I'm not the one who put it there. When I got back from the bodega hours ago, I found my dad and Whitney laughing like old friends. I asked what the hell was so funny, but they just burst into another round of laughter, after which Whitney told me *I just had to be there.*

Needless to say, I'm losing my mind.

My dad reaches into his pocket with a smirk. "Well, I've got a little something else we could do." He pulls out a joint and a lighter.

"Oh my God, Dad. Seriously?"

"What? It's legal here." He turns to Whitney. "What do you think, daughter-in-law of mine. Should we toke it up?"

Something close to a snort escapes me, but when I see Whitney shrug across the table, my smile drops.

"Sure, I'm down. I haven't smoked in a while, but I'd take a hit or two." She presses up from the table, sliding her chair back. "Let's go on the balcony."

My eyes narrow. "*You're* going to smoke?"

She cocks her head, her hand on her lip. "You got a problem

with that, *babe*?" She tacks on the last word like a challenge, and my dad whistles like I'm in trouble.

It's all terribly annoying.

"You were sick today. You probably shouldn't," I reply.

"You're my husband, Liam, not my keeper." She struts ahead of my dad, and I follow. I should feel chastised, but all I can focus on is the word *husband* coming from her lips, and how badly I want to sink inside her and make her call me that over and over.

"Watch yourself, Li. She's got you by the balls," my dad whispers, grinning.

This is going to be a long weekend.

29

———

WHITNEY

I should not have smoked that joint.

I haven't smoked in years, maybe even since college. It's not something I usually do, but I thought it would help me relax. Instead, I coughed for so long that I thought I was dying. Liam was nice enough to get me a glass of water, his eyes watching me carefully. I had to wave him off and remind him that I'm not a breakable thing. I'm fine.

Besides being way too high.

And way too turned on by Liam.

We only smoked half of it before I dissolved into a fit of laughter over Andy's pronunciation of *apartment* that lasted a solid three minutes. Now, we're settled on the couch watching *Love Island.* Liam's got my feet up on his lap, his hands resting on my legs. His thumb is drawing soft circles against my calf, and the tiny motion should not be sending such an intense rush of heat through me, but it does. Every brush of his thumb on my skin feels like he's branding me.

Mine, it says.

"Don't you hate that Michael bloke? He's playing a game," Andy says from the other side of the couch.

"Yeah," I croak out. "He's the worst."

Andy glances towards us. Liam's laser-focused on the television. He hasn't looked at me once since we sat down. Even though his hands are on me, his mind is clearly elsewhere.

"Well." Andy slaps his thighs and stands. "I'm beat. Gonna call it a night."

Liam snaps out of whatever daydream he was in and looks at his dad. "You sure?"

"Yep. See you in the morning!"

Before Liam or I can respond, Andy's gone. The slam of his door rocks through the apartment, stilling Liam's movements. His hand still rests on my ankle, but neither of us moves.

I clear my throat. "I guess we should go to bed, too."

"You still stoned?" he asks, his voice deeper than usual.

I chuckle. "Only a little."

He slips my legs off my lap and immediately I miss the warmth of our contact. "I'm gonna shower," he says, crossing the room.

I turn off the TV and pour myself a glass of water before shuffling to my room. Maybe I'll get lucky and I can just fall asleep before Liam gets back to the room. No whispering in the darkness. No pillow talk.

After slipping into my PJs, I crawl into bed and turn the lights to the lowest setting. I'm snuggled under the covers when I hear the door creak and shut softly. Liam is quiet as he moves around the room. My mind flashes with images of what he might be doing behind me. Is he changing clothes? Is he naked?

I'm just about to open my eyes when I feel the bed sink next to me and the covers lifting as Liam slides into bed. I shift my weight, turning over so I'm facing him. He's shirtless — epically, beautifully shirtless — and I let my eyes fall to the ink on his chest, drawn again to the tattoo of a series of numbers on the side of his ribs.

"I thought you were asleep," he says.

I shake my head.

"Want me to turn the light off?" he asks.

"Sure," I whisper. He's reaching over to turn the light off when I speak again. "What's that tattoo? The numbers on the side of your ribs."

His movements still as he glances back at me, his expression wary.

"It's Luke's birthday."

I'm hit with a pang of sympathy at Liam's grief. He doesn't seem to want to talk about it much; I can both respect and understand that but sometimes I wish he would share more about what he's feeling.

"That's sweet," I say, not wanting to pry any further. "I like your tattoos."

Liam just stares at me, his expression hardening. "What are you doing?"

I blink. "What do you mean?"

"What are you doing? What is this? Staring up at me with those fucking endless eyes of yours in nothing but a t-shirt, telling me you like my tattoos."

Swallowing the sudden lump in my throat, I glance away, embarrassed. "Sorry," I whisper.

"You're the one who said you didn't want to sleep together again," he reminds me.

"I didn't say that I didn't want to. I said that we can't."

"Don't play games with me," he growls.

"I'm not." I turn to face him again. "I'm not trying to. I care about you. I don't want to mess with your head."

"Well, I'm fucking confused, Whit."

I shake my head and try to turn away from him again, but he reaches for my chin, making me look at him. He waits patiently for me to speak, his gaze not leaving mine.

"I'm confused, too. I just... I don't think it's a good idea."

He runs his thumb across my jawline and up to my bottom lip, pressing against it, his hazel eyes locked onto me.

"Why not? We're fucking amazing together. You know we are."

My lips part involuntarily, like my body knows how to respond to him. He presses his thumb further, slipping it inside my mouth, and I swirl my tongue around it, meeting his gaze purposefully.

I know I'm playing with fire, but I can't seem to stop.

"Whitney," he growls, his eyes widening. "I want you."

I can't help the whimper that escapes me.

"But... " I grasp at straws. "Your dad."

His other hand slides up my bare thigh to the tips of my t-shirt, fiddling with the hem. He smirks, his hand slipping under the shirt and caressing my stomach.

"You think I give a fuck? I want the whole neighborhood to hear you screaming my name."

"Liam," I whisper as his hand travels upwards, teasing closer and closer to my nipples which have hardened into peaks.

His gaze is unrelenting. "If we do this, it's not the last time. Tell me right now that you're not going to run away tomorrow, or we go to sleep right now."

I frown, indecision swirling in my gut. On one hand, I'm terrified. Abbi was right: I can't do casual. Even my random one-night stands left me checking my phone for texts, and I can't imagine a world in which I'd be sleeping with Liam and not losing myself completely in him. On the other hand, I need him. I need him like I've never needed anyone before.

"I'm scared," I admit, closing my eyes, unable to look at his face when I say it.

"Why?" He's moved closer, his breath hot on the side of my neck.

"I've never done this before."

"Done what?" he asks, pressing his lips to the side of my neck, his tongue swirling against my skin.

"No strings attached."

I open my eyes as he pulls back, studying me.

"But I want to," I say. "I want to try it with you. Casual. Just sex."

He blinks, his expression inscrutable. "No running away?"

I nod, my stomach swirling with nerves. "No running away."

Liam's mouth descends on mine, his lips meeting me with a familiar intensity. I melt into him, my whole body sagging with the relief of his lips on mine. He tastes just as sweet as I remember, minty and fresh.

His fingers finally find my nipple, caressing me softly. I moan into his mouth, slipping my tongue in between his and reaching for his bare chest, sliding my hands across the inky lines there. He tugs at my t-shirt, pulling it over my head in one swift movement, then attaches his mouth to my nipple, swirling his tongue around the bud as his other hand slips into my panties.

"Already wet for me," he groans, slipping a finger inside me. "Are you always this wet, Whitney?"

My cheeks redden at his dirty talk. I love it, but there's something embarrassing about what he brings out in me. The wild abandon that only he seems to activate.

"Answer me," he whispers, nibbling at my ear.

"Only for you," I admit as his thumb circles against my clit and my hips buck towards him.

"Take them off. I want to see you."

I waste no time, sliding my panties off. He presses me backwards and crawls on top of me, pressing my thighs open as he settles his legs in between them.

"So pretty. So ready for me." He presses soft kisses on my neck, nudging my legs open wider. "Should I get a condom?"

I shake my head, pulling him against me. "Liam. Fuck me. Now."

He chuckles and rubs his thumb against the inside of my thighs, teasing close to my entrance. He works one, two fingers inside me, and I gasp at the angle.

"So bossy," he murmurs, watching me with hooded eyes. "Are you in charge now?"

I smirk and push against his chest. "Yes," I say. "Get on your back."

He flips us over so I'm on top, my hands resting on his chest. In one swift movement, I line our bodies and lower myself onto him. He stares at the spot where we're joined together, his eyes wide. Thrusting against him, I lift myself up slightly before dropping down again, settling into a slow, torturous rhythm.

"Fuck," he moans. "That's it. Ride me."

His hands move up to cup my breasts, his thumbs running over the peaks. Sitting up, he takes one in his mouth, meeting my thrusts as he swirls his tongue around my nipple.

"Faster," he whispers, pressing against me.

I increase our speed, my breaths coming out in short bursts. He must get impatient because after a few thrusts, he flips me over so he's on top again. He slides in and out, finding the spot where I need him. His thumb finds my clit, brushing against it as he thrusts into me.

"Liam," I manage. "I'm gonna come."

He increases his movements, both of us frantic and moaning and desperate. Black spots seem to form in my vision as I throw my head back, my fingers and toes tingling.

"Me too," he says. "Fuck."

A rush of heat spreads through me as I feel Liam lose himself, both of us coming apart at the seams. The wave seems to last forever, and when I finally come down, Liam is laying on top of me, both of us spent. After a few moments, his weight shifts as he grabs one of my towels. He wipes my legs down gently before pressing a chaste kiss to my lips.

"Can we cuddle?" I ask, breathless. "Or is that too string-y? Do friends-with-benefits cuddle?"

He chuckles. "Of course we can. Pretty sure you were attached to me like a sloth last time."

I shove him away from me. "That was all you!"

He pulls me closer, wrapping his arms around my waist, our naked bodies tangled together. His warmth surrounding me, I can't help the swell in my heart. As Liam and I settle together like two perfect pieces of a puzzle, my eyes flutter closed, and for the first time in forever, I feel safe.

I WAKE up with Liam pressed against me.

All of him.

I can feel his length pressing against me, so I burrow closer, grinding my ass into him. He stirs behind me with a low groan, the sound sending a wave of heat through me. Even after last night, I find myself desperate for more. Turning over, I trace my hand down his chest, finding his hardness and wrapping my hand around him.

He inhales a sharp breath, his chest rising and falling quickly. Shifting my weight, I lift the covers and move between his thighs.

I should wake him up and make sure this is okay with him.

Just as I'm about to, I glance up and see his eyes open wide. I smile softly, then open my mouth and slide my tongue across his length, taking him into my mouth.

"Whitney," he whispers. "Fuck. What are you doing?"

His hips buck slightly against my mouth as I swirl my tongue, bobbing my head up and down.

"Do you want me to stop?" I ask, pulling back to wait for his permission.

"No," he chokes out. "Don't stop."

I smirk again, taking him deeper in my mouth, keeping my eyes trained on his blissful expression.

"Fuck, yeah. Look at me. You look so pretty like this, Whit."

I moan against him, loving his praise. Needing it. Needing to make him feel as good as he makes me feel. He rests his hand on my head, his thumb caressing my hair softly. His grip is gentle but possessive, and the feeling of it makes me want to take him deeper.

"Your mouth is so fucking sweet," he rasps. "I'm not gonna last long."

Taking him as deep as I can, I swirl my tongue against his length. Lifting off him, I take his length in my hand and stroke him, feeling bold.

"I want you to come on me. Mark me."

He moves quickly, flipping over so I'm underneath him as he replaces my hand with his own, gripping his cock in his hands. "Shit. You want that? Can I?"

I nod, licking my lips as he strokes the length of him. His other hand splays lightly across my neck, resting around my throat without any pressure.

"Fuck. Oh, fuck," he sputters as he releases onto my chest and stomach. "Oh my God."

He lowers himself onto his elbows, breathing rapidly. The only sound in the room is our breaths, in-sync and labored.

He glances up at me, a satisfied grin across his face. "Good morning," he whispers. He lifts off me to grab the towel off the ground and wipe me off, as gentle as he was last night.

I laugh. "Morning."

"I wish every morning started this way. I'd be in much better spirits."

"Who knew orgasms would be the best way to tame your grumpy attitude?" I smirk at him, sitting up. Liam wraps his hand around the back of my neck, bringing his lips down to mine.

"You look so pretty covered in my cum," he whispers, causing goosebumps to rise on my flesh. "I want to see you tied up and covered in it."

His words send another wave of desire through me, so I push him lightly and slide out of bed to get dressed. If I keep listening to him, we'll never leave this bed. Not that I'm entirely opposed to that.

"Sorry," his gravelly voice says from behind me. "I don't want to make you uncomfortable. Will you please tell me if I am?"

I whip my head back to him, his gaze steady but unsure.

Vulnerable.

Crossing back to him, I wrap my arms around his neck, stepping in between his thighs as he looks up at me.

"I love your dirty mouth. You haven't made me uncomfortable at all," I tell him, swiping my hand across his hair and tucking it behind his ear.

"Okay," he says, his eyes flicking back and forth between mine. "Are you sure?"

"I'm positive. I feel safe with you."

No strings attached. No strings attached.

Liam takes my hand and presses a soft kiss at the center of my palm, his molten eyes staring up at me, the flecks of gold somehow brighter in the morning light.

"Come on," he says, tugging on my hand. "I'll make you breakfast."

I'm a goner.

30

WHITNEY

Liam and I spend the rest of the weekend entertaining Andy. He's got major tourist energy, and even though he's been to New York a few times, he's never been to the Statue of Liberty, so on Saturday we get dumplings in Chinatown before catching the ferry. After that, we get pizza and see a Broadway show.

Liam can't keep his hands off me, and I am not complaining.

I don't know if it's because we're in front of his dad and he wants to keep up the pretense, or if it's from our agreement last night, but his hands keep finding mine as we walk. On the ferry, he wrapped his arms around me and held me against his chest, resting his head over mine. While we watched the show, he held my hand for the entire performance.

I can't get enough.

I've also learned that Andy is a great listener. He spends all weekend asking me about myself. Even when I try to skirt a question or toss the attention onto Liam, Andy is relentless, genuinely interested in *All Rhodes*, my family, my friends, where I went to college, and most importantly, which couple I'm rooting for on *Love Island*. Liam interjects occasionally with follow-up questions.

Outside of the theater on Saturday night, Liam tugged on my arm and pulled me close to him.

"I've learned so much about you today. I didn't realize that I don't ask you many questions about yourself."

I shrugged, brushing him off, but he brought his hand up to my cheek, cupping it.

"I'll be better about that. I want to know everything about you."

Needless to say, between Liam's soft touches and thoughtful words, the phrase *no strings attached* has been ringing in my head all weekend like a taunt.

"What a day," Andy says on Sunday night when we get back to the apartment. "I'm exhausted."

Liam beelines for the bathroom while I grab a La Croix from the fridge. I put the kettle on, assuming that Liam and his dad will want tea.

"What was your favorite part of the weekend, Andy?" I ask as I prepare their drinks.

"I think it's a tie between one-dollar pizza and those dumplings... or maybe that Ethiopian brunch we got today."

"So, just the food, then?"

He chuckles, then his gaze turns serious. "Truthfully, the best part of the trip has been getting to know you. It's wonderful to see Liam happy. I'm proud to call you my daughter-in-law."

I'm hit with a pang of longing. I never knew my own father, so hearing Andy say that he's proud to call me his daughter-in-law, well... it has tears forming at the corners of my eyes.

"Thank you," I say, gratitude shining in my voice. "That means a lot, Andy."

Liam comes back into the room. Perhaps sensing the energy

in the room, he glances from me to his dad with vague suspicion. "Everything okay?"

I nod and slide his tea over to him. "Yep."

"I was just telling Whitney how lovely it's been getting to know her and how excited I am for you two. Young, in love, the whole world at your fingertips."

Liam doesn't reply, but he locks eyes with me as I cross the room to give Andy his tea, his expression unreadable.

"I don't feel like cooking, so I was gonna order takeout. How does sushi sound?" Liam asks.

"Good with me," I croak out.

The food arrives almost an hour later, and we settle in the dining room with a bottle of white wine as Liam pulls out enough sushi to feed a small army.

"Liam," I groan, pouring Andy some wine. "How much did you get?"

He shrugs. "Didn't know what everyone liked."

Liam reaches for the spicy salmon rolls, about to pop one in his mouth, when Andy stills his movements.

"Before we eat, I just wanted to say thank you Whitney for letting me stay with you and for putting up with my son."

"Thanks for the glowing praise," Liam deadpans.

Andy pushes on. "Just feeling a bit grateful right now. I know things have been hard, Li, and I'm sorry I can't make that better for you, but you know what? I've never seen you look at anyone the way you look at Whitney, and I think that's something to celebrate."

He lifts his glass to cheers, and I follow suit, willing my hand to stop shaking. Andy's sentimentality is a crushing pressure on our fragile dynamic; Liam and I are dancing on a line that is disappearing beneath our feet, and it's terrifying.

"To Whitney and Liam, and your new life together. I only wish Luke were here to see it."

Liam swallows, the sound seeming to echo in the silence following Andy's words. I study him, worry crashing through me. Liam lifts his glass, then knocks it back, finishing half in one gulp.

"Thank you, Andy," I manage, taking a sip of my own wine.

We're about to dig in when the door buzzer goes off, indicating someone is downstairs. My gaze flickers to the door.

"We expecting someone?" Liam asks, looking at me.

I shake my head. "Not that I know of."

I cross over to the front door to look at the camera. When I see the person tapping their foot impatiently, my heart drops.

My mother.

What is she doing here?

The buzzer sounds again, jolting me.

"Who is it?" Liam asks from the dining room.

My throat tightens. She's done this before. Showed up out of the blue and crashed on my couch. We usually end up arguing the whole time and then she'll ask me for money and slip out in the middle of the night.

How do I play this? It's not like I can just ignore her or send her away.

"It's my mom," I hear myself say.

"What?" Liam responds.

"Wow, our first joint family meal!" Andy exclaims.

"I'll go down and get her," I say, reaching for my shoes.

Liam crosses the room and stands in front of me. He lowers his head, dropping his voice. "What's going on?"

"I don't know," I whisper. "She's a wildcard. Sometimes she just shows up like this. Shit."

Liam drops his hand over mine, bringing my eyes up to his. "Hey, it's alright. Take a deep breath."

I do as he says, inhaling and exhaling, reveling in the feeling of us breathing together. It reminds me of our flight to Vegas

"I'll be right back," I say, squeezing his hand in gratitude.

As I descend the stairs, I try to figure out what to say to my mom. What the hell is she even doing here? I should be used to her showing up like this by now, but her timing could not be worse. I open the door to the building, finding her leaning against the wall, smoking a cigarette.

"Mom. What are you doing here?"

"Peanut!" She drops the cigarette on the floor and throws her arms around me. "I had to come. You drop the bomb that you're married and don't expect me to come?" She eyes the stairwell. "You gonna let me in or what?"

Sighing, I hold the door open and lead her upstairs. "We're right in the middle of dinner. Liam's dad is here," I tell her.

"Who's Liam?"

I swallow. "My husband. Liam."

The words still feel strange on my lips, like they can't be real. Somewhere though, underneath that strange feeling, there's a warmth at the way it feels to claim Liam as mine.

I bring Caroline upstairs, and the next few minutes involve awkward introductions and forced laughter. I'm almost thankful that Andy is here because his positive attitude and chattiness seems to be keeping this conversation alive. Liam is cordial but quiet as the four of us eat sushi together.

It doesn't take long for my mom to start drinking. She's telling Andy stories about being on the road, and they aren't the most dinner-table appropriate. Every time I try to direct the conversation to something safe, my mom ignores me. Liam is no help. He's more reserved than usual, staring down at his plate, his jaw locked.

When my mom spills her soy sauce on Andy's pants and offers to "clean it up", it's the final straw. Unable to take it any longer, I push my chair back and stand. "Mom, can I talk to you for a minute in the other room?"

She turns to me, surprised. "Sure thing, peanut."

"Excuse us for one minute," I say, avoiding Liam's gaze. I can feel his eyes on me as I stomp down the hall to my room, my mom trailing behind me. I let her in and take a deep breath, closing the door.

"What are you doing?"

She blinks at me. "What? What's wrong, nut?"

I shake my head. "You're being flirty and inappropriate. Andy is married, mom,"

She shrugs, rolling her eyes at me. "Lots of supposedly married people 'round here. Pretty silly if you ask me."

I will myself to stay calm, not wanting to get into a full-on screaming match with Liam and his father right down the hall. "If you're talking about me and Liam, just leave it alone."

"Come on, baby. You can do better than a bartender. I know my taste in men is shit, but I thought you had high standards."

"Since when do you care about my love life? Or about me at all, for that matter?"

She shakes her head. "Of course I care about you. If you hadn't hung up on me last time we talked, you'd know that."

Here it comes. The guilt trip. Everything is my fault and nothing is her fault. That's always how it goes, and worst of all, I used to fall for it when I was younger. I would have done anything to please her.

Now, I couldn't care less.

"That *boy* in there has barely said a word since I walked in. He didn't even ask my permission to marry you!"

"Permission?" I scoff. "What is this, 1955?"

My mom crosses her arms. "My point is this whole thing is so rushed, and I don't want you to make the same mistakes I did—"

"Mom! Stop, okay? Just stop. Liam is my husband. He is kind and considerate and thoughtful. He respects my boundaries, and he *listens* to me. You don't have to like him, but if you continue to criticize our relationship, I will ask you to leave."

My mom stills, shock coloring her features at my words. "Fine." She smacks her lips. "Just don't come crying to me when it all blows up in your face. Trust me, it always does."

The hurt in my mom's voice almost breaks through my armor, my wall between us that keeps me safe. I know she's only coming at me because of her own romantic insecurities, but it doesn't mean I have to stand here and take it.

"Don't worry about that. When have I ever been able to come to you when I needed help?"

Silence settles in the room, the emptiness swallowing my whole.

My mom pushes past me and opens the door to reveal Liam standing in the doorway. She storms out, not bothering with an apology. Liam doesn't follow her movements. His gaze is locked onto me. Turning away from him, I let out a shaky breath, the fight coming out of me. I sit on the edge of my bed and the tears start strolling down my face before I can stop them. Liam crosses towards me, coming down to the floor in front of me. I squeeze my eyes closed, trying to stop the tears, but I can't.

"Whit," he says, sounding pained. He presses the pads of his thumbs to my cheeks, wiping my tears. "Please don't cry."

I open my eyes, meeting his steady gaze. "Did you hear all of that?"

"Most of it, yeah."

I sniffle and let out a watery laugh. "I'm sorry she said all that about you. She's always been like that. Just... judgmental."

He thumbs my cheeks again, cupping my face with both his hands. "Thank you for defending me," he whispers. "You didn't have to do that."

I don't know what it is. Maybe it's the expression on his face or the soft caress of his fingers on my skin, but something about this moment makes me want to forget that wall. Forget the protections built up around my heart. Forget our no-strings bullshit.

"I meant every word."

He brushes his thumb across my lip, his gaze flickering down to my mouth. I'm sure he's going to kiss me, but instead, he lets his hand drop. I try to hide my disappointment, wiping my face with the back of my sleeve.

"Come on," he nudges me. "Let's go back out there. We can deal with it together."

He wraps his hand in mine and pulls me forward, back to our dysfunctional family dinner.

Together.

31

LIAM

I didn't have hosting my father and mother-in-law under one roof on my bingo card for this year, yet here we are. Caroline didn't say a word to me as I set up the pull-out couch for my dad, who insisted that she take the guest bedroom in his place. I don't know how long she plans to stay, but for Whitney's sake, I'm hoping it's not very long. Whitney hasn't told me much about her mother, but from what I overheard, I get the sense that their relationship is... strained.

My throat bobs, remembering the way that Whitney defended me earlier tonight. The things she said about me. She said I was kind. Considerate. Thoughtful.

Is that really what she thinks of me?

"Thanks for this, Li," my dad says, gesturing towards the makeshift bed in the center of the living room. "Looks grand."

Whitney pads into the room, pulling her hair into a bun as she crosses over to us. "I think my mom went to sleep," she says, her eyes darting around the room. "Andy, I'm sorry—"

My dad waves his hand, cutting her off. "None of that. I'm glad we got the weekend together. It was fun, yeah?"

Whitney nods. "It really was. It was so great to meet you."

He opens his arms, gesturing for a hug, and Whitney wraps her arms around him with a laugh. He pulls back, patting her shoulder. "You'll be meeting Charlotte and Simon for Christmas, yeah? I'm glad you'll get to see where Li grew up. I'm sure they're gonna love you."

Whitney turns to me, her eyes wide with questions.

Shit.

Yet another thing I forgot to mention to her: my trip to England to see my mum and Simon. A trip they will certainly be expecting my wife to tag along with since I'm sure my dad will have put photos of us all up on Facebook by the end of the week. The worst thing about having amicably divorced parents? When they start a Facebook group with themselves and their partners called *Team Liam.*

"You'll make sure he's nice to Simon, yeah?" My dad continues, oblivious. "I'm sure you know how sensitive he gets, but Simon's a great lad and Liam knows it."

I glance over at Whitney, who still looks as confused as ever. "Whitney doesn't like to fly, so I'm going to just go alone for a few days. Be back for New Years together."

He frowns, glancing between us. "You can't spend Christmas apart, Liam. It's *Christmas.*"

Another thing about my family — they absolutely love Christmas. For my parents, spending Christmas apart from the ones you love is akin to murder.

Whitney narrows her eyes at me, and I clear my throat, choking under the pressure of his moment. "Yeah, Liam. It's *Christmas,*" she says with a biting smile.

"Dad," I reach my arm around his shoulder for a side-hug. "Thanks for coming. See you in the morning?"

"I'm gonna hit the road first thing. I'll just let myself out, if that's alright."

"Sure thing."

Whitney hugs him again and retreats to our room while I linger with my dad, feeling like there's more I want to say but not sure what.

He clasps my shoulder and looks at me, perhaps sensing my mood. "I meant what I said, Li. I'm real proud of you, and I love you so much. I know you like to handle things your own way, but if you ever want to talk, I'm just a phone call away, and if it's really dire, just a-hop, skip, and a-jump down to Philly."

I offer my dad a grateful smile. "Thanks, Dad. Love you too."

I shuffle down the hallway towards our room feeling exposed, like a raw nerve sticking out. When I press open the door, I find Whitney in her PJs, sitting on the bed with her arms crossed.

"England? Christmas?" Whitney shakes her head. "What the hell, Liam?"

"I know, I know." I sigh and cross to the bed, settling down next to her. "It's been a long night. I'm exhausted. Can we please just talk tomorrow?"

Whitney quiets as I pull my shirt over my head and slip my pants off, sliding under the covers next to her.

"Okay," she murmurs. "We can talk tomorrow."

She leans over and turns the bedside lamp off, shrouding the room in darkness. Pulling the covers closer to her side, she turns over and lays down next to me. I reach for her, joining our bodies together so my arms are draped lightly around her waist.

"What are you doing?" she whispers.

"We agreed on cuddling," I remind her.

"But I'm mad at you," she says. Then, after a moment: "Kind of."

I chuckle against the back of her neck and pull her closer. "Alright. You're mad at me, then."

She sighs, silence settling between us. Even though she

hasn't moved from my arms, there's a stiffness in her body that isn't usually there. Pressure clamps around my chest as I try to figure out what to say. How to be good enough for her.

"I'm sorry," I say into the darkness. It's easier without her looking at me. It reminds me of Vegas, the way the darkness in the room felt like an opening. A safety net. "I know it seems like I'm keeping secrets and just throwing shit at you, but that's not been my intention at all. I'm just... I've been avoiding my family because I'm worried about their reaction to me dropping out and us getting married. I planned this trip home a while ago, but I haven't even booked my flights 'cause I've just been pretending it's not happening."

For a while, Whitney says nothing, but then she settles into my arms, the tension rolling off her as she exhales. "It's fine. It's not like we're really together or anything. I just don't like being taken off-guard or looking stupid."

I squeeze her arm. "You never look stupid. Even if we aren't... real, we're still in this together, Whit. We're a team."

She turns over, our noses almost touching as we lay side-by-side.

"Okay," she whispers. "I like that. Team Whit-lee."

The corners of my mouth tick up. "Whitley? What is that?"

"Our couple name, obviously." She grins. "It could be Lianey or Whitam."

Chuckling, I nuzzle my head into her neck and inhale her scent. "Team Clark. Mr. and Mrs. Clark."

She shoves me playfully, turning back over to her side. "You're obsessed."

Tucking her against me again, I close my eyes and settle into the darkness. I can't help the smile that spreads across my face at Whitney's words. She might be joking, but she's hinting at a truth I'm trying to ignore.

After a few moments, Whitney speaks again. "Do you want me to come with you?"

I hesitate, taken off-guard by her question. "I just assumed you wouldn't want to or that you had plans for the holidays..."

I'm hit suddenly with the realization that I *do* want her to come. Whitney and I haven't really spent any time apart since we got married, and the thought of spending a week away from her...

One thing I know for sure is that I'd miss her.

A lot.

"Never mind," she says, pulling away. "It was just an idea."

I pull her back against my chest. "No. I want you to."

"Really?"

"Absolutely. I'll be terribly bored without you. Please come."

I'm begging. I'm officially becoming pathetic.

"Okay," she whispers. "We can book our flights tomorrow."

"Okay," I reply, and I fall asleep with a smile on my face.

IN THE MORNING, I find Caroline in the kitchen, her feet kicked up on the counter as she drinks a glass of orange juice.

"Good morning," I offer.

She just nods her head at me and picks up a book on the counter, opening to a bookmarked page. I pull Whitney's oat milk out of the fridge and fiddle with our Nespresso machine.

"Did you sleep well?" I ask, trying to make polite conversation. Hopefully, I can make a better impression this morning, now that I'm feeling less like a pressure cooker turned up to the highest setting.

"Yep," she answers.

"That's good," I reply, setting Whit's cup to the side while I prepare my own drink. "So, do you plan on staying for a while?" I ask.

She cocks her head at me. "Trying to get rid of me already?"

"Not at all. You're welcome to stay as long as you like. With Whitney's blessing, of course."

She clicks her tongue, her gaze dropping back to her book.

"What are you reading?" I ask.

She eyes me from above the book. "It's a thriller. I like all that stuff. True crime, serial killers. Real gory, fucked up stuff. Reminds me to keep sharp." She taps her forehead with a grin.

Great. My mother-in-law is obsessed with violent murder.

"Cool," I manage, my throat dry. "I'm gonna bring Whitney her coffee."

"I'm here," Whitney interrupts from behind me.

I turn to see her shuffling into the room with a yawn, and I can't help but smile. She looks adorable in the mornings. Hair strewn everywhere, all sleepy-eyed and tired.

"Morning," I murmur, handing her a coffee and pressing a soft kiss to the top of her head. Her eyes jump up to mine in surprise, but she covers it quickly, muttering her thanks as she sits at the counter next to Caroline.

"You hungry?" I ask, pulling a carton of eggs out of the fridge.

"Sure. Whatever you're making is fine," Whitney answers, then sips her coffee with a soft moan that sends a jolt straight to my cock.

Jesus. How does she make drinking coffee seem sexy?

"Caroline? Would you like anything?" I ask, trying to distract myself.

"Nah. I've got stuff to do." Caroline stands and closes her book.

"Like what?" Whitney asks, turning to her mom.

"Just meeting up with some old friends..."

"So, you're meeting up with a guy."

Caroline rolls her eyes. "So what if I am? I'm a grown woman. Your *mother*. I can do what I want."

"You always do," Whitney mutters under her breath.

"You better quit it with that passive aggression. You got something to say? Say it."

"I think we said everything we needed to last night." Whitney sighs. "How long are you staying here?"

"Don't worry. I can see when I'm not wanted. I'll be out of your hair tomorrow," Caroline says with a bite.

I see the moment when Whitney's face falls and the careful way she tries to put it back together.

"Mom—"

"I'll be back later. You got a spare key for me?"

Whitney sighs but grabs her keys and hands them to Caroline. Before Whitney can say anything else, Caroline struts out, slamming the door behind her. Whitney sits down at the counter, dropping her head into her hands.

Shit. This is just like last night. She's upset, and as usual I'm ill-equipped to handle the situation.

"I can't believe we got stoned with my dad," I say with a smirk, hoping to lighten her mood.

It works. She lifts her head with a soft smile. "Never let me smoke like that again."

I turn to the stove, cracking a couple eggs into the pan. "That's nothing compared to you after a few tequila shots."

She scoffs. "Excuse me? I handle my liquor very well."

I laugh, throwing my head back.

"Why are you laughing? I'm serious!"

At that, I just laugh even harder, my shoulders shaking. Eventually, Whitney starts laughing too, until we're both just cracking up in the kitchen.

"I'll take you out to the pub in Surrey, then we'll see how well you can handle your drinks."

"You're on. That reminds me, we need to buy our tickets today."

I slide her plate over and sit next to her, digging into my own food. "You sure you want to come?"

She throws a death glare in my direction. "I said I would."

"Just making sure," I grunt in response, stuck on the fact that in a few weeks Whitney will be coming home with me. "What are you up to today?"

"Meeting with an interior designer for the salon. Construction has started, so I need to go check on how everything is going. What about you?"

"Not much. Probably go to the gym."

She nods, and silence settles between us as we eat. Once I finish, I leave my plate in the sink and glance in her direction. I find her watching me, a look in her eyes that is starting to feel quite familiar, one mirrored now in my own expression: desire.

"When do you have to leave for your meeting?" I ask, my gruff voice betraying the heat coursing through me.

She bites her lip with a small smirk. "Not for an hour, at least." She licks her lips, an invitation.

Crossing the room, I slam my lips against hers and lift her off the stool. I carry her back to the bedroom, depositing her onto her bed and crawling on top of her.

"Let's be quick," she manages through our kisses. "I don't want to be late."

I grunt in agreement, but underneath it, that feeling in my chest seems to swell and grow. The one that seems to lodge itself there when Whitney is around. When I feel her body wrapped around mine. When she looks at me like she wants me.

The bottom line is that when it comes to me and Whitney, there isn't enough time in the world. That thought alone should scare me. I should be running for the hills. Shutting it down. But I can't.

I need this.

I need her.

But with an expiration date on this... how long will I have her for?

32
___

WHITNEY

By the time Liam and I finish round three, it's time for me to meet my interior designer, Monique. She meets me at the building, where the construction crew is busy at work. After exploring the space, we spend about an hour on Pinterest, Monique showing me some pieces that she likes. She doesn't stay for much longer; she has another meeting in Brooklyn, but she agrees to purchase the pieces we discussed. I check in with the foreman that everything is set with the construction calendar, and I'm about to head back home when I hear a knocking on the front window. I glance towards the sound to find Shatar waving wildly at me. I didn't expect to see her today. She gestures for me to come outside, so I wrap up my conversation and grab my coat.

When I get outside, Shatar throws her arms around me.

"What are you doing here?"

She pulls back and smiles. "Thought I'd come check out the space, and let you know... I'm in."

My jaw drops. "What? Are you serious?"

She nods, grinning. "I just let my boss know I'd be wrapping up in the next couple of months and moving on. He was kind of pissed because he knows I'll be taking, like, all of my clients with me, but whatever."

I let out a squeal of excitement. "Oh my God! What swayed you?"

"Time for a change, you know?"

I know exactly what she means.

On my way home, I swing by AT&T to get my mom a cheap flip phone. If she's going to stay in the city, I want to be able to get in contact with her. All I can hope is that she doesn't throw it away like she normally does.

When I get home later that afternoon, I'm feeling pretty good. *All Rhodes* is really starting to take shape and having Shatar on the team is exciting. Unfortunately, that good mood is dashed as soon as I walk into my apartment to find Caroline halfway out the door.

"Hey," she says, eyeing me cautiously.

"You're leaving?" I already know the answer, but I ask anyway.

"Yep," she replies, popping the *p* with her lips.

"You were just going to take off without saying goodbye? Again?" I can't help the anger that seeps into my voice. It's the same old routine with her, and I'm sick of it.

"I thought you'd prefer it. You obviously want me out of your hair," she mutters.

"Why did you even come here?"

"I told you. Had to see this husband business in person after I talked to that lawyer and learned the truth. That your sudden love match is a big fuckin' scam."

I suck in a sharp breath.

She knows.

She knows about the marriage clause, about the inheritance.

"He told you?" I ask, my shaky voice betraying my nerves. "Isn't that confidential?"

"It's in the will." She shrugs. "So, how long are you gonna keep up the charade?"

"It's not—" I feel suddenly protective, knowing that my mom knows the truth about me and Liam. "What do you want?"

She shrugs. "A cut of the cash couldn't hurt. After all, my ever-so-generous mother left me nothing even though you got a nice little handout."

My stomach drops. She's asked me for money before, but never like this. Never in a threatening manner.

She waves her hand, brushing me off as usual. "Don't be so dramatic. Do you know how it feels when your own parents leave you *nothing* and you have to watch the girl you raised on your own get all of it?"

I shake my head, empathy clouding my decision-making. When she puts it like that, it does sound really unfair.

"I'm sorry, Mom, but that's not my fault."

"Yeah, but you aren't doing shit to fix it, are you?"

My chest rises and falls, agitation seeping into every part of me. "Why did you keep them from me? Grandma and Grandpa?"

"I told you, we were better off," she scoffs.

"Better off?" I yell. "We slept in a barn, Mom! I got my first period with a stranger in an abandoned warehouse because you left me there to go off with some guy you'd just met. I'm terrified to fly because I never got on a plane until I turned eighteen, and you told me that they randomly fall out of the sky."

"That is true," she interjects, and I don't bother to correct her. If we get into conspiracies that she believes in, we'll go around in circles for hours.

I take a deep breath, trying to steady my emotions. "I know you want me to be like you, but I'm not. I'm not like you."

"Trust me, I know that. I know you don't want to be like me. I hardly want to be like me," my mom yells back, stunning me into silence. "I did the best I could," she says, brushing a sudden tear away. "You don't know what it was like. When I left home, my parents told me I was dead to them. They disowned me. They were *ashamed* of me, but when they found out I had a kid, they tried to come after you. I knew they wanted to get their claws into you just like they did with me, and I was trying to protect you from that. Don't you get that everything I ever did I did to protect you?"

I want to argue, to point out every time she abandoned me to hang out with her boyfriend of the month, but I can't.

I'm just... sad.

"That's why I'm trying to protect you from this boy. You're just gonna get yourself hurt. Do yourself a favor and get a divorce. This was a huge mistake, Whitney."

My anger rears its head again as she attacks Liam. "How will you get your precious payout if I get a divorce, huh?"

I don't wait for her response.

"Get out, Mom. Just go." Suddenly, I remember the phone that I got for her. Shaking my head, I pull it out of my bag and thrust it into her hands. I cross the room to the front door and yank it open, gesturing to the hallway.

"Take the phone. It's programmed with my number. Next time you decide to ride into town and fuck with my head, call me first."

She stares at me, tears swimming in her eyes. She looks like she wants to say more, but she doesn't. Tucking the phone into her pocket, she grabs her bag off the floor, and walks out the door.

She doesn't look back.

I don't let myself cry after my argument with my mom. I know that if I think about it too much, I'm going to turn into a puddle of tears on the floor. Instead, I throw myself into work. After signing up for an online marketing class and spending a few hours working on a website for *All Rhodes,* I've successfully avoided all emotions related to my mom. I've channeled all that rage and sadness into preparing my salon for a killer launch. According to the contractors, they only need a couple of months to finish everything. By my calculations, I should be able to schedule the grand opening by early spring. I can't wait.

My phone buzzes with a text from Liam.

Liam: You free tonight?

Whitney: Yeah, why?

Liam: It's a surprise. Be ready at 7. Wear something sexy, wife.

My mouth drops open as I read Liam's message. Of everything I was expecting him to say, that was not it. After three rounds this morning, I figured he'd be tired of me, especially after spending basically the entire weekend attached at the hip. But now he's planning a surprise? one that involves me wearing something sexy?

I type a response, trying to cool the heat rising in me as I guess what he's planned for tonight.

Whitney: That sounds awfully string-y, husband.

He just sends back the shrugging emoji. I toss my phone onto the bed, falling backwards with a groan. The mystery of what Liam has planned is sending a thrill of excitement through me. I just hope it involves his dirty mouth.

The next few hours are a whirlwind of outfit changes and a very lengthy FaceTime with Abbi in which she comes up with three different nicknames for Liam's dick. Eventually, I settle on a blue dress and my black platform boots. I haven't heard from Liam, so I text him and ask what the plan is.

Liam: Be home in 10.

True to his word, Liam bustles through the front door after ten minutes. I hear him from my room as I stand nervously in front of the mirror, touching up my lipstick.

"Hey!" he yells from the hallway. "I gotta shower, but we'll leave in a bit."

"Where are we going?"

His only response is a door slamming and the running water of the shower.

Great.

Bracing myself for The Return of the Grump, I grab my purse and head to the kitchen. I scroll on my phone for a few minutes, waiting for Liam. After a few minutes, he pads into the kitchen, barefoot.

My heart seems to skip a beat at the sight of him. His wet curls fall gently around his face, his tattoos peeking out from his t-shirt. I try not to gape at him as he crosses the room. My eyes widen as he braces his arms on either side of me, his mouth descending onto mine. I barely have time to react, but my body seems to respond to him instinctively, melting into his embrace easily.

"You look beautiful," he murmurs against my lips. "As always."

He pulls back and smiles that secret, subdued smile that

feels like it's just for me, and my stomach swoops impossibly lower.

Liam grabs his keys and wallet off the counter, then gestures to the door. "Shall we?"

"Are you going to tell me what this is?"

He just grins. "Patience, love."

We stumble out of our building, and he leads me down the sidewalk, taking my arm in an exaggeratedly gallant gesture. This is the part where I would make a joke about how much this feels like a date, but I hold my tongue. I don't want to burst this bubble between us. On the train, Liam asks me about my day and lets me rant about the salon. After we exit the station and head down the street, I feel Liam tug lightly on my arm and nod towards the building next to us.

"Sorry to interrupt," he says with his signature grin. "We're here."

I glance up to a sign that says *Mel's*. It's an upscale restaurant that I read an article about around two weeks ago; I was making dinner in the kitchen while Liam sat at the counter doing work on his computer, and I went on and on about how I've been dying to go here but I can never get a reservation. I had no idea he was actually listening to me.

Turning to face Liam, my brows furrow in confusion.

"I remembered..." He rubs the back of his neck with his hand, another gesture I've come to know. A pink hue grows on his cheeks as he glances away from me.

My stomach flutters. Is Liam... nervous?

"You mentioned that you wanted to try this place, right? I thought you did, so I got us a reservation."

I nod, my confusion melting away. "I did. I can't believe..." I'm caught off-guard by an unexpected wave of emotion. "Let's go in."

Blinking back tears, I let Liam press his palm to my lower

back as he guides me inside. He gives the hostess his name, and she brings us to a table in the corner. I glance around at the decor with a smile. When we settle into our seats, I flash Liam a wide smile.

"This is so thoughtful. Thank you."

He nods, his gaze unsure. "I just... yeah. I'm glad you like it. It's not much of a surprise. Probably should've just told you what it was."

I reach across the table, setting my hand over his. "It's the best surprise. I love it." I flip the menu open with a smile. "Let's split a whole bottle of wine and order the escargot."

Liam crinkles his nose. "Snails? No way."

"Don't knock it 'til you try it, Clark. After all, I have exquisite taste."

He locks his eyes on me, his gaze darkening. "Yes, you do, sweetheart."

I nearly choke on my water, but thankfully we're interrupted by the waiter. We order some appetizers, a bottle of wine, and decide to split the duck confit.

When the plate of escargots arrives, Liam eyes it like it's a foreign object, and I can't help but laugh.

"Come on," I chuckle, sipping my wine. "Just try it. Don't be a baby."

He rolls his eyes. "Fine. If it will get you to stop bullying me."

Now it's my turn to roll my eyes. Smiling despite myself, I show him how to spread it onto the bread and watch as he takes a bite.

"So? What's the verdict?"

He chews, swallows, and glances up at me. "It's not terrible," he says, taking another bite.

Laughing, I refill my wine glass. "I knew it. You like it. Admit it. You *love* it."

"Wow." He smirks. "Very mature. Next you'll be chanting and spelling out the word kissing."

"K-I-S-S—"

"Alright, I like it. Thank you for pushing me outside my comfort zone. You are a genius, you're always right, and you win," Liam says, his voice dry.

I clap my hands together, cheering in delight. "Cheers to that." Clinking my glass against his, I take another sip.

My eyes flicker up to see Liam reaching across the table. He swipes his thumb against the corner of my lips, smearing off a droplet of wine, then brings his thumb up to his mouth and sucks. His gaze doesn't leave mine.

"Don't drink too much," he says, his voice deceptively soft. "I want you sober for what I'm going to do to you tonight."

I don't respond, because I have no idea what to say. I squeeze my legs together, my whole body reacting to his words. God, how is it possible this man can turn me on so much with just a few syllables?

Our food arrives, and we both dig in, an involuntary moan leaving my mouth as soon as it hits my tongue. We're both stuffing our faces like animals when a young woman around my age approaches our table with a smile on her face.

"How is everything?" she asks.

"So good," I reply.

"I'm thrilled to hear it. I'm Quinn, the owner. If you need anything at all, let me know."

My mouth drops. *This* is Quinn Marks? One of the youngest restaurant owners in the city, according to the article I read. She's already opening a companion restaurant to *Mel's*, even though the place has only been open for a year and a half. Liam must be able to tell that I'm slightly awestruck by the culinary genius in front of me, because he reaches his hand out to shake Quinn's and gestures towards me.

"I'm Liam, and this is my wife, Whitney."

Again, his casual use of the word *wife* sends a jolt of awareness through my spine, warmth trickling through me.

"Lovely to meet you both. Bon appetit!"

Quinn walks away, heading to a nearby table, and I throw Liam a megawatt smile. "Best night ever," I whisper, and he chuckles, the rough sound scraping against his throat.

By the time we get back to the apartment, I'm sufficiently tipsy and totally full. I tried to split the bill with Liam, but he insisted that he was paying, which made the night seem even more date-y. Yet, I didn't seem to mind. I go straight to my room to put on sweatpants. As cute as I look, I cannot spend another minute in this tight dress. When I pad back into the living room, Liam is settled on the couch.

"Want to watch *Love Island?*" he asks.

I smirk. "I thought you hated it."

He shrugs. "You like it."

I open the fridge to get a La Croix, but Liam's voice interrupts me. "I already have one for you over here," he says.

Perking up, I close the fridge and walk over to him. Sure enough, he's sitting on the couch, an unopened La Croix sitting in front of him. He reaches for my legs and lifts them to rest on his lap. He looks at me, his gaze softening. "Your mom left?"

I swallow, emotion welling in my throat. "Yeah," I manage. "She's gone."

He squeezes my calf. "I'm sorry."

I shrug, a pathetic lift of my shoulders that does nothing to hide my disappointment. Part of me is glad she's gone. Part of me misses her. It's a confusing mess of conflicting emotions, and most of all, I'm upset with myself over how we left things. I worry about her, despite everything.

"Do you want to talk about it?" Liam asks, his voice as soft as velvet, his thumb lightly stroking my ankle.

"It's a long story," I reply.

"Come here," he says, patting his lap. He turns me around so that my head is resting across his thighs. "Tell me about it."

So I do.

I tell him about my days on the road with my mom: the good, the bad, and the ugly. I tell him that tulips are my favorite flowers and I've never been to the top of the Empire State. We argue about which ice cream flavor is the best and agree on which cartoon character is objectively the hottest (Jessica Rabbit, of course). He talks to me about his childhood in England, how he was so angry after his parents' divorce that he got into fights all the time and ended up in jail once or twice.

Liam Clark peels back layers of himself with my head in his lap and his fingers splayed across my hair.

By the time we finish talking, my voice is hoarse and it's almost three in the morning. Eventually, my eyes flutter closed and I let myself drift. I'm floating somewhere between sleep and consciousness when I feel myself being lifted off the couch. Dimly, I register that I am being carried. That I am in my room. In my bed. Liam releases me onto my bed as I squint into the room. I feel his breath against my neck, his voice a soft, soothing murmur. Stirring, I try to blink, my mouth dry.

"Good night."

He goes to release me, his arms unraveling from around me, but I tighten my grip on him.

"Stay," I whisper.

His whole body stiffens, and he pulls back, his eyes searching mine.

"Stay," I repeat, blinking up at him, waiting.

I don't know why this moment feels so important. I feel that invisible string between us tighten and pulse with energy. Heat coils low in my stomach, my heart thumping with nerves. His deep green eyes sear me with an intensity as he brings his hand up to the side of my neck, his thumb brushing against the curve of my neck and down to my collarbone.

Finally, he speaks, his voice soft and low, a shade deeper than usual.

"Okay," he murmurs. "I'll stay."

33

LIAM

"Goddamn." Darius comes storming into Abe's bar, letting out a string of curses. He crosses the room, anger written all over him, and ducks behind the bar without a glance in my direction.

"You alright?" I ask cautiously, and Darius snaps his gaze to me.

"Fine," he barks out, even though he seems anything but.

I don't say anything else as we set up the station, instead letting my thoughts wander to where they always do these days.

My wife.

Since my date with Whitney, I've been trying and failing to keep my distance. Failing because we live exactly three feet away from each other and no matter how I try to stop myself, I find myself knocking at her door in the late hours of the night. I've probably spent more time in her bed than my own at this point. Not that I'm complaining. The past few months feel like a dream, one that I don't ever want to wake up from. But more and more I feel the cool glow of morning creeping up on me, warning me that this dream won't last — that we've been doomed from the start.

I've been so caught up in Whitney that I've hardly thought about Luke's foundation. To be honest, ever since the gala, I've been avoiding thinking about it. Between Tim's hesitations and Rebecca's rejection, I'm feeling pretty disheartened. The truth is that it's hard to chase someone else's dream, especially when it feels out of reach. Yet again, I wonder what Luke would think if he could see me now. Would he thank me for following along on his path, or would he be disappointed by my pace?

"It's my dad," Darius interrupts my spiraling from beside me. "He's an asshole."

I glance towards him. "What happened?"

He shakes his head, rubbing his hand on the back of his neck. For a moment, I think he's not going to respond at all, but then a slew of words start tumbling from him. "I don't care if he comes at me, but when he starts ragging on Jackson, it sets me off. He's always poking fun at him for being into comics and studying all the time. Jackson actually listens to my dad, so now he's rethinking applying for college since my dad said it's a bad idea."

"Has he talked to any of the counselors at his school?"

"I've been caught up in my own shit... my girlfriend thought she might be pregnant. She's not, but I haven't really been there for him the last few months. I'm supposed to be his big brother, but I fucked up," he says, a slight tremor in his voice that makes the hairs on my arm stand up straight.

Clasping a hand on his shoulder, I study his blank expression, which I recognize for the mask it is. "You haven't fucked up, man. You're doing the best you can. You even asked *me* for help." That earns a slight chuckle. "I don't want to overstep, but if I can help you guys out somehow, I want to."

"Thanks, Liam. I appreciate it."

I step back and grab two shot glasses and a bottle of Don Julio, setting them on top of the counter. Glancing over my shoulder to make sure Abe isn't around, I line up the glasses and pour two shots.

"Jackson reminds me of someone I used to know," I tell him. "Someone who I let down. I want to do things differently this time. Offer help instead of ignoring the problem."

I slide one of the shots over to Darius, who knocks it back with me. He coughs, and I slap his back, chuckling. I grab my jacket and slip out to the back door, spotting Jackson sitting in that same spot on the stoop, a comic book in his hands. It's a mirror image of our scene a few weeks ago.

"Hey," I call out.

His head shoots up and he scowls at me. "What do you want?"

"Nothing. Just saying hello."

Dipping his head back into his comic, Jackson ignores me.

"Which one are you reading this time?"

He lifts up the cover towards me with a small smile. "X of Swords."

"Where do you get your comics from?"

Eyeing me warily, Jackson shifts. "Mostly from the library. I can get free ones there."

"Cool," I reply, struggling to find footing in this conversation. "How's school going?"

Jackson sighs, putting his comic down. "It's Thanksgiving break, so I'm not even missing."

"You gotta graduate."

"You gotta chill."

I shrug, crossing the alley to crouch down next to him. "I'm cool as a cucumber."

He rolls his eyes. "Wow, that is lame. Did my brother talk to you?"

"Yeah. Pretty sure you both like me even though you try not to. That happens a lot."

Jackson laughs despite himself, shaking his head.

"Is it too late? Have you missed too much school?" I push.

"No. My teacher keeps calling me. She's annoying," he says, kicking a rock with his shoe.

I nudge his shoulder. "Have Darius call her back. Come on. I know you like school, so don't pretend you don't."

He glares at me. "How do you know?"

"Because you're fucking *reading,* dude. You're a nerd."

I realize my mistake a second too late. His expression darkens, shutting down. "Fuck you," he spits out.

"Hey, I meant that in a good way. I'm a nerd, too. My idea of a good time is being in a lab looking at slides of bacteria. My buddy and I used to memorize the periodic table with a song we wrote to the tune of a Drake song."

He's quiet for a moment, then throws me a glare. "Seriously?"

"Listen, man. Just ask yourself: WWIMD?"

He stares at me, his brow furrowed. "What?"

"What would Iron Man do?"

"That's the dumbest thing I've ever heard," he says, deadpan.

"Yeah, but it works," I tell him with a wink. "Trust me."

WHEN I GOT HOME from work last night, I started compiling spreadsheets and resources for Jackson to look at. Whenever there was a lull in business, I talked to Darius about affordable colleges in the city and scholarships. I know how much he wants this, and I want to help in any way I can.

Quite selfishly, all the research gave me a rest from thinking about other things. Other things I've been thinking about a lot. Other things that smell incredible and feel even better...

I get home from the store and find Whitney in the kitchen

with an apron around her waist and headphones on. The room is a total mess, ingredients covering the counter and a pile of open cookbooks in the corner. She turns and sees me in the doorway, relief and excitement settling into her features.

Pulling her earbud out, she smiles at me. "Thank God you're home. I need help."

I glance around with a sardonic smile. "That much is clear. It looks like a hurricane came through here."

She sighs, turning to stir some sauce. "It's for Friendsgiving. I've never cooked a turkey before, and I think I'm doing it wrong."

"Friendsgiving?"

"Thanksgiving with friends. You must know this."

I shrug. "Not American, remember?"

She turns and raises her eyebrows. "Didn't you celebrate during college?"

Memories of a warm fireplace and cranberry sauce hit me unexpectedly. I usually spent Thanksgiving with Luke's family. He always invited me to come home with him during breaks since he knew my family wouldn't be celebrating. His house was full of warmth. Just like him.

"Once or twice," I reply after a moment.

Whitney studies me with those big, brown eyes. Her gaze on me always makes my skin pulse with awareness. It's not just looking... it's something close to seeing. It's terrifying and liberating all at once.

"Do you have plans tonight?"

I shake my head. "No plans."

She grins wickedly. "Perfect. Then you're totally free to help me tackle this turkey."

I roll my eyes, joining her at the counter. "Who's coming over?"

"Abbi, Shatar, and Shatar's friend, Lauryn. You haven't met all of them, but they're nice."

"I don't want to crash your girls night."

"It wouldn't be very husbandly of you to miss Friendsgiving," she says sweetly, and I step closer to her without thinking.

"Hmm, husbandly." Brushing her hair away from her neck, I press a soft kiss to the exposed skin. "I've never once been described that way, but you do look awfully wifely right now." Trailing my fingers along the back of her neck, I inhale, breathing in her sweet scent. Blood rushes through me, my body stirring with desire. "Who knew such a domestic scene could be such a turn-on?" I whisper against her skin.

She shudders slightly before pulling back and pressing her palm to my chest. "No distractions. It's turkey time."

SOUNDS of boisterous laughter and soft chatter float down the hallway towards my room. I know Abbi is here because I heard her witchlike screech of a hello a few minutes ago. After helping Whitney prepare dinner, I retreated to my room, trying to keep myself from marching into the kitchen and laying Whitney out on the table for my own Thanksgiving feast. Showing her how thankful I am.

"Girl, you are in so much trouble. If I didn't know any better, I'd think you were falling..." Abbi's voice trails off as I enter the kitchen, her eyes widening. "Liam!" she exclaims. "You're here!"

The door buzzes and a few more women arrive, so I let Whitney mingle with them while I make a salad, tossing ingredients into a large wooden bowl. Opening the oven, I check on the turkey and side dishes. As I'm moving around the kitchen, I feel a soft hand rest in the space between my shoulder blades.

"Thank you." Whitney lowers her voice so only I can hear it. "Come meet the others."

She tugs me along to the group and introduces me to everyone. Shatar, one of Whitney's friends from her salon, hands me a bottle of wine while they settle at the table, which is already set with plates and silverware.

I open one of the bottles and bring it over to the table. "Wine, anyone?" I ask.

Lauryn, another woman in the group, raises her eyebrows. "Whitney, is your husband our waiter for tonight?"

Whitney smiles at me, her gaze teasing.

"My wife already knows that I live to serve," I say with a wink, my voice deepening.

Shatar fans her face with her hand. "Damn, girl. Where'd you get him? They sell that at Target? Hinge?"

Whitney shakes her head and laughs as I pour her a glass of wine. "No way. He's one of a kind."

I'm so taken off-guard by her words I almost spill the wine. My throat bobs, an unexpected lump gathering.

One of a kind.

Turning to face Whitney, I give her a questioning tip of my chin, searching her expression for a clue of how she's feeling, whether her words are meant to keep up the ruse with her friends or reveal an unspoken truth. Her eyes meet mine, bright and open. I don't know if she can read the question in my gaze, but she reaches her hand up and strokes the length of my back, her fingers brushing along the line of my spine. A shiver runs through me, quickly followed by a wave of frustration.

I'm sick of constantly questioning what's real. Tired of wondering if I'm alone on this island, or if the woman I want is standing beside me.

"I'll have the red," Lauryn says, a welcome interruption.

I bolt to the kitchen, trying to breathe. My heart is racing, and my blood feels like it's stirring beneath my skin. Shaking my head, I open the bottle of Pinot Noir and pour two glasses, bringing them over. I avoid Whitney's gaze as I rush back and forth between the kitchen and dining room table with the food.

"Liam, are you sure you don't need help?" Abbi asks, calling out to me.

I finish slicing the turkey and bring the remainder of the dishes out to the group with an accommodating smile. "No, I've got it." I set everything down and step back with a smile. "That's everything. Whitney cooked, so I claim no credit."

"That's not true. You did the turkey," Whitney argues with a grin.

I shake my head. "We did it together," I concede.

"Well, I don't care who cooked it, it looks amazing," Abbi says.

We eat quietly, everyone too busy stuffing their faces to engage in polite conversation. When everyone is finished and picking at bits left over, Lauryn, Shatar, and Whitney talk about *All Rhodes* while Abbi tries to grill me about my five-year plan.

"What are you guys doing for the holidays?" Shatar asks.

"We're going to London to visit Liam's mom and stepdad," Whitney says before I can answer.

Abbi raises her eyebrows, shock coloring her expression, but nobody seems to notice besides me. Lauryn and Shatar are fawning over the announcement and listing off must-sees in London, a few a bit touristy for my liking, but if Whitney wants to see Big Ben and ride a double decker, we'll do it.

I glance again at Abbi's concerned expression, but she quickly schools it into one of excitement as she lays her hand over Whitney's with a soft smile. "That'll be fun. I'll miss you."

"You have to take a million pics and send them to us," Shatar announces. "We'll make a group chat."

"Do you get to visit home often, Liam?" Lauryn asks.

I shake my head. "Not really. Bit far."

Lauryn nods and the group settles into an awkward silence.

Nerves spiking, I grab my plate and reach for Whitney's. "What do we think? Dessert time?" I reach for Abbi's plate. "I'll wash up and put the pie in the oven."

Whitney pulls on my sleeve, her brow furrowed. "Leave them. I'll do them."

Without thinking, I press a soft kiss to the top of her head. "Hang with your friends. I got it." Carrying the rest of the dishes into the kitchen, I take a deep breath. I try not to eavesdrop as the group moves to the couch, but I definitely hear my name once or twice. Once I'm finished cleaning, I take the apple pie out of the oven. When I get to the living room, Shatar and Lauryn are chatting on the couch.

"Where's Whitney and Abbi?" I ask, setting the plates down.

Shatar shrugs. "I think Whitney went to her room. Abbi's in the bathroom."

"This looks so good," Lauryn says, grabbing a plate.

I slip down the hallway towards our bedrooms, finding Whitney's door ajar. Knocking lightly, I press the door open, finding Whitney and Abbi standing near the bed, hugging. Their heads snap up at the knock and immediately, I notice that moisture is glistening on Whitney's eyes. I'm hit with a jolt of panic.

Abbi steps back. "I'll give you two a minute," she whispers to Whitney, squeezing her arm. As she brushes past me, her gaze flickers to mine, a hint of warning in her expression.

Shaking it off, I cross the room to Whitney, lowering myself to wrap my arms around her. "What's wrong? What happened?"

She shakes her head, wiping at her eyes. "Nothing."

She tries to pull back from my hold, but I don't let her. "Tell me—"

"Liam," she mutters. "I'm fine, really. It was just... the stuff with my mom. It's still weighing on me."

I don't know how I can tell, but she's lying. I guess after months of living together, I've come to know her well enough to know that something in the tone of her voice rings false.

"Baby," I whisper, the endearment tumbling from my lips. I brush my thumbs under her eyes, wiping at a stray tear. "Can't you tell me?"

She stares back at me, her brown eyes filled with so much anguish that it takes my breath away. I feel like I've been kicked in the gut. My grip on her tightens, another wave of panic rolling through me.

"The tulips..." she trails off on a whisper, her gaze studying mine.

I furrow my brow. "Tulips?"

"In the living room. You got them for me. When?"

Is this why she's upset? Have I crossed a boundary somehow?

I blink heavily and shake my head. "Yesterday. You said they were your favorite, so I thought... what, you don't like them?"

"I love them," she whispers. She closes her eyes, confusing me further, and when she opens them, any trace of anguish is gone. Her beautiful brown eyes are back to their usual brightness and warmth. She sets her hand against mine, pressing at it softly.

"Come on," she says. "Let's go get some pie."

34

WHITNEY

I always thought falling in love would feel like, well... falling.

A sharp swoop, all at once. The force of gravity pushing rapidly against an object. I thought it would happen suddenly and swiftly. That I'd snap into a sort of clarity, a moment of assuredness. I'd know, all at once, that I was in love. I'd be certain.

It turned out that I was right.

It was sitting at the dining room table as my husband pressed his soft lips to my head that I knew, without a doubt, that I was in love. Liam had spent the day side-by-side with me in the kitchen, patiently answering all of my questions, and then he'd been so perfectly attentive all evening, so sweet and caring in every tiny gesture that my heart couldn't take it. He only lingered for a moment before I lost his warmth, a realization hitting me so strongly that I'd lost all sense of time.

But it was what happened afterwards that really cinched it.

I was sitting in the living room, glass of wine in hand, one thought swirling in my mind — *I love him, I love him, I love him* — when I heard Lauryn's voice.

"Wow, these are beautiful. I love tulips."

Her words jolted me from my eureka moment as my gaze tugged to where hers had landed, at the small vase in the living room and the bundle of pink tulips sitting inside. How could I have missed them before then?

"They're my favorite," I murmured, my mind spinning.

I love him, I love him, I love him, I thought, over, and over.

"Whitney?" Abbi glanced at me, too perceptive for her own good. I felt myself standing, my feet moving without my control.

"Excuse me for a moment," I managed before fleeing the room.

When I collapsed onto my bed, I tried and failed to keep my emotions in check, a wave of tears threatening to break through. As soon as those thoughts settled in me, that inherent truth that I now know I cannot escape no matter how hard I try, another settled right there next to it.

I'm scared, I'm scared, I'm scared.

This feels exactly like falling.

Now, Liam knows something is off. Since he found me in my room, I've managed to evade his concerned gaze. I don't know how, because staring at his stricken expression felt like swallowing barbed wire. He clutched me with such gentleness, such care, that it sent more waves of unwanted emotion through me.

"Can't you tell me?"

No, I couldn't tell him. He was the one person I couldn't tell because it would change everything. Ruin everything. I was the one who'd insisted that this was casual. For me to tell him... it would probably just confuse him.

I feel like such an idiot. My mom was right; I'm falling for this guy, and our entire relationship is fake.

But what if it isn't?

"I'm going to explode," Shatar interrupts my spiral from the couch, clutching her stomach.

Lauryn chuckles. "I knew you shouldn't have had two slices."

Liam is silent, staring down at his plate of pie like it might give him answers to a very confusing puzzle.

"It's not Thanksgiving if you don't eat until you want to die," I manage, forcing a tone much lighter than I feel.

"True," Lauryn agrees. "Thanks so much for inviting us over, Whitney. I know we just met, but I have a feeling this is a start to a very beautiful friendship."

"We should probably go," Shatar says with a groan. "Let's call an Uber. I can't walk to the train right now."

Realizing that Liam and I are going to be alone, I'm filled with a sudden flurry of nerves. I'm going to have to figure out what to say to him, because my lie about my mother didn't fool anyone.

Abbi hugs me tightly, her lips close to my ear. "It's gonna be okay," she says so only I can hear, squeezing me for reassurance. "I promise."

I send her a watery smile as she follows Shatar and Lauryn out of the apartment and down the stairs, Liam closing the door behind them. He turns to me, his presence seeming to take up the whole room. When did I become so acutely aware of every part of him? Every movement of his body and micro expression on his face?

He crosses the room to me, then lifts me up by the back of my thighs and sets me on the counter. I take in a shocked breath, peering up at him. His eyes study my face, fierce with emotion, before he settles his mouth against mine. He tugs at my lip with his teeth, nipping and licking until he coaxes my mouth open completely.

"I've been wanting to do this all night," he murmurs, brushing his thumb against the side of my neck, up towards my jawline. "Been staring at those pretty lips, wanting to taste them."

He kisses me again, this one deeper than the last, his tongue exploring my mouth with a mounting pressure that sends waves of heat through me. Brushing my hair off my shoulder, he ducks his head, pressing lines of languid kisses along my neck.

"I missed you," he sighs. "How the hell can I miss you when I'm sitting right across from you?"

His sweet words are my undoing, tears prickling at the backs of my eyes. I wrap my hands in his hair, tugging him up to me, pressing my body against his. I need him like I've never needed him before. I feel frantic, out of control, desperate for him. I reach for his pants, tugging at his belt and yanking it free from his jeans, throwing it to the side.

"Impatient tonight?" He grins against my lips.

"I need it. Now."

My hands pull at the sides of his jeans, but he settles his hand against mine, stilling my movements softly. "What's the rush?" he asks, titling my chin up with his other hand, forcing me to look at him.

I swallow, hoping he can't see the moisture gathering at the corners of my eyes. "Please, Liam. Please."

He studies my expression, his green eyes seeming darker than usual. Then he nods slowly and steps out of his pants, stripping down slowly to free himself. His eyes never leaving mine, he reaches under the hem of my dress and pulls my panties down my legs.

Tugging my ankles so that I'm at the edge of the counter, he lines us up and slides into me with excruciating slowness. A moan escapes me as I try to wiggle closer to him, to take him as fast as possible. He doesn't let me, pressing deeper and deeper until he settles against me. Then he does it again, thrusting at a punishingly slow pace.

"More," I whine, wrapping my arms around his neck.

He reaches for the straps of my dress, pulling them down to

free my breasts, his gaze laser-focused on my hardening nipples. Taking one into his mouth, he licks and bites at it until I can feel a wave of pleasure building low in my stomach. Unable to speak, I let out another moan as he quickens our pace, thrusting into me with a perfect rhythm. The room seems to sharpen and brighten as Liam grunts against me, muttering praises under his breath. The sound of him, the feel of him, the inky lines of his broad chest pressing against me, all of it seems to shatter me.

He pulls back, his gaze catching mine. His green eyes are filled with desire, an expression so intense that I want to look away.

"Look at me," he commands as he slows our rhythm, bringing us back to an incredibly torturous pace.

Something seems to shift and morph in the space between us as we stare at each other, as he presses into me with such sweet strokes.

"Whitney, I... " He breaks off, a flash of fear in his eyes. "I —I—"

He spills into me with a groan, his hands tightening around my back, pulling me somehow closer to him. The feeling of it triggers my own orgasm, a heavy rush of emotion pulsing through me. I clamp my hands around his neck, pleasure coursing from my fingertips to my toes.

Something seems to pass between us in the silent moments following our climaxes. The air between us is heavy, mixed with our sweat and gasping breaths.

"It's so good," he whispers into my neck. "You're everything."

My heart soars, tripping in my chest.

Everything.

A smile spreads across my face, a warm and tranquil feeling settling inside me. That's the way Liam makes me feel all the time: at peace. It's like he sees me. Like I am worth something.

Like I am worth everything.

35

LIAM

"Your ticket, please?"

The flight attendant glances at my phone, then gestures towards the first-class seats that I booked for Whitney and me. I figured that since Whitney was willing to confront her fear of flying just to come home with me for the holidays, the least I could do is try to make the experience somewhat bearable.

"First class? Is that why you insisted on buying the tickets?" Whitney groans.

I turn to meet her challenging gaze. "If I let you buy them, you'd have me up at the crack of dawn like a drill sergeant again."

She laughs and her eyes sparkle, the sound bringing a smile to my own lips. I could watch her laugh forever.

It's been almost a month since the night in the kitchen when those damned words almost spilled from my lips.

I love you.

I'd almost said it. I was ready to, ready for the pressure in my chest to cease, to free myself from this torment once and for all.

But I didn't, and every night since, as I lose myself in the indescribable feeling of her, I've had to bite down on my tongue to stop the words from escaping.

"These must have cost a fortune. You shouldn't have," she says as the flight attendant takes her bag.

"Don't tell anyone, but... " I lower my voice to a whisper, smirking, "my wife is loaded."

She shoves against me, and we slide into our seats, which are more like pods than actual seats.

"Abbi gave me a Xanax, so I think I'll be fine," she says, tapping her foot as she straps in. I rest my hand on her knee, stilling the jerky movement. Brushing my thumb lightly against the inside of her thigh, a sly grin spreads across my face.

"You'll be fine. I've thought of the perfect way to keep you distracted."

She glowers at me, but the bob of her throat as she swallows gives her away. "Liam," she says in a scolding tone, but the sound of my name on her lips only fuels my excitement.

The flight attendant comes over and asks if we'd like anything to drink, so I ask for two sparkling waters. I draw soft circles against Whitney's inner thigh while we wait, my hand slipping higher up her leg. Her eyes dart down to the movement, and she swallows again, but she says nothing. As the flight attendant starts the safety presentation, I leave my hand on her thigh. Soon enough, the plane is nearing takeoff, and I can feel her tightening beneath my grip.

"I should've taken the Xanax before we boarded. Shit," she says, a hint of desperate trepidation in her tone.

Slipping my hand higher, I brush another circle with my thumb and lower my head towards her ear.

"I bet if I slid my hand into your leggings I'd find you wet right now, wouldn't I?" I drop my voice to a low murmur, breathing against the shell of her ear. "Nobody on this plane knows how needy you are for me."

"Liam," she breathes, her eyes fluttering closed.

I slide my hand half an inch higher, tightening my grip on her thigh. "Maybe I'll have to find out." I inch higher. "Maybe I'll let you ride my fingers if you can be quiet." I smile as her breath hitches. "Maybe I'll have to take you into that tiny bathroom and fuck you against the wall. See how quiet my good girl can be."

She lets out a quiet moan, her face flushing with desire. The sight of her lips parting and her chest rising and falling in quick breaths sets my own pulse racing. Abruptly, I pull my hand away, sitting up straight. Her eyes fly open, and a flush of pink travels up her face as her shocked gaze meets mine.

"Look at that," I say casually, glancing around at our surroundings. "We've taken off."

She heaves a heavy breath and swallows, blinking. "You... you—"

"I think I'll watch *Die Hard* on my flight. What about you?"

She smacks my arm lightly, then huffs out a breath, her gaze softening. She slips her hand into mine and squeezes it.

"Thank you," she says quietly. "Even though I'm all worked up now."

"I think you mean horny like a cat in heat."

That earns me another smack. "Shut up," she groans, then turns to her TV. "I'm gonna watch *Notting Hill*. I need to practice my British accent."

"Please don't."

She just grins and turns her movie on. A few minutes later, I feel the brush of her fingers against the knuckles on my left hand. My eyes flicker up to her face in surprise, but she doesn't glance my way, her gaze locked onto her screen. The corners of my mouth tugging upwards, I slip my fingers into hers, our hands intertwined.

When we land at Heathrow, I'm exhausted. Whitney took the Xanax after watching her movie and slept for a few hours. I have to rouse her awake and keep her droopy figure upright as we find our way to our rental car. By the time we pull up to my mum's house, Whitney's previous tiredness is nowhere to be found. She's bouncing up and down in her seat, her eyes darting all around.

"Can you chill out? You're making me anxious," I tell her.

She shakes her head. "I'm nervous! I want your mom to like me," she confesses, looking out the window. "Wow, is this it? It's so pretty. I love the garden."

I reach for her hand, undeterred by her attempts distract me. "Of course she's going to like you. She's going to love you."

Just like I do.

"I wouldn't be so sure about that. I don't know if you noticed, but I am not great with moms."

"Stop it." I reach for her chin, turning her to meet my gaze. "That says much more about your mom than you. You know that, right?"

She shrugs and reaches for her bag. "Come on, let's go in."

I pull the key from the ignition and round the car to grab our suitcases from the boot. Whitney hops out of the car, stretching her arms above her head and inhaling deeply. Before I can unload the cases, I hear my mum's voice.

"You're here! Simon, they're here!"

I glance up to see my mum bounding down the steps of the house with her arms outstretched. She's headed straight for Whitney with a wide smile on her face.

"You must be Whitney. It's so lovely to meet you." My mum wraps her arms around Whitney, who hugs her back with a dazed expression. "I'm Charlotte."

"It's great to meet you," Whitney replies. "Thank you so much for inviting us."

My mum waves her off and runs towards me, squealing. "Darling!" she exclaims. "I missed you so much."

She hugs me, gripping my shoulders tighter than expected. I drop our bags and wrap my arms around her small body, my eyes prickling. When I pull back, she's wiping at her tear-stained face and laughing.

"Mum," I groan. "Crying already?"

She waves me off. "I'm a mother." Skipping over to Whitney, she locks arms with her. "Let me show you inside. Liam can get the bags."

They go inside without another glance in my direction. Shaking my head in laughter, I grab the bags and follow them into the house. Simon greets me in the doorway, taking Whitney's suitcase off my hands and clasping my shoulder.

"Liam," he says softly. "Great to see you."

I slap his back lightly. "You too, mate."

"Good flight?"

"Yeah, not too bad."

We both nod in silence. I hear my mum's laughter floating from the kitchen as Simon helps me bring our stuff upstairs to the guest bedroom. We fill the silence with meaningless small talk then meet my mum and Whitney back downstairs.

"Shall we go for a walk down to the beach?" my mum asks when we get to the living room.

Whitney glances at me, and I slip my arms around her waist, wanting her closer. "Do you want to?" she asks, her head tilted up to meet my gaze.

I don't want to go for a walk. I want to take her to the bedroom right now and stay there for the rest of the day, exploring every inch of her body.

"It's not far, but it is nippy," my mum says. "We've got extra hats and gloves."

"Sure," I murmur against Whitney's head. "You're not tired from the journey?"

She shakes her head. "Stretching my legs would be good."

After we all add about three more layers, covering ourselves with scarves, hats, and gloves, the four of us ramble down the lane towards the pebbly beach. Simon and my mom clasp hands a few feet in front of us, and Whitney snuggles close to me, burying her face in my chest for warmth as the wind picks up. While we stroll down the sparse, unpopulated beach, Whitney shivers against me.

"Do you want to go back?" I ask, tucking an arm around her.

She shakes her head, her teeth chattering.

"You're freezing."

"It's s-s-so pretty," she manages with a smile, looking out at the waves on the horizon. "It's like a p-painting."

I watch her expression as she takes in the view, the reality of her being here with me settling in. She came all the way to England for me. She braved her fears just to stand beside me and meet my family.

Those three little words, always so present these days, hang on the edge of my tongue. This is as perfect a moment as I'm going to get — Whitney's blonde hair whipping in the wind, the light blues of the sky fading into a wide-sweeping mélange of pink and orange, the soft sound of children's laughter floating from a few yards away.

I tug her to a halt, meeting her eyes with a fierce intensity. "Whitney, I—"

"Look!" my mum shouts, flailing towards the ocean. Both of us glance up and in the direction of her pointing in time to see a dolphin head peeking out of the water.

"Oh my God," Whitney exclaims, running ahead towards the shoreline. "Liam, did you see?"

I nod and follow after her, trying to hide my disappointment.

I'm sure there will be another moment soon. I don't know if I can keep this in for much longer. It's eating me up, the desire to hear her say those words back to me.

What if she doesn't say it back?

She has to.

She came here for me.

That has to mean something, right?

36

WHITNEY

It's official: I love England.

It's Christmas Eve, and Charlotte is showing me her sticky toffee pudding recipe while Liam and Simon sit by the fireplace, drinking spiked eggnog. We're both wearing festive colors; I'm in a red dress and Santa hat, and Charlotte's wearing a gold blouse with reindeer ears on her head. I even managed to wrangle Liam into an emerald sweater that looks painfully good on him, bringing out the green of his speckled eyes.

Simon's boisterous laugh travels to our spot in the kitchen and Charlotte rolls her eyes, nudging me conspiratorially. "My husband is the silliest man in all of England, I swear," she says. "Let's join them. I need a drink."

After washing my hands, I follow Charlotte into the living room. She's sitting on the couch next to Simon, her arms draped around his shoulders. Liam is pouring us both drinks, a glass of white wine for me and an eggnog for his mom.

"Let's play Charades," Simon announces, slapping his thighs.

I glance around the room, unsure where to sit, but before I can move, Liam settles into the available armchair and pulls me down to sit in his lap. I glance at him with a soft smile, and he tugs at the white ball at the end of my Santa hat, bringing my head closer to his. He presses a soft kiss to my cheek, rubbing his thumb against my jawline. The motion tugs at my heart-strings, the memory of our night on the kitchen counter flashing through my mind.

"I'll start, then!" Simon whirls around to face the group, the fire illuminating him from behind.

Liam shifts so that he can see Simon, settling his hands on my thighs. We watch as Simon flails about, making wild gestures that neither Liam nor I can decipher. We're both laughing and making terrible guesses while Charlotte just sits in silence, watching her husband thoughtfully.

"*The Princess Bride!*" she yells, and Simon claps his hands together, nodding. She squeals and jumps up to hug him.

"How the hell did you get that?" Liam asks in a baffled tone.

Charlotte shrugs. "When you're married for a long time, your minds sync. You two will experience that eventually."

Silence settles in the aftermath of her words, a knot forming in my stomach. The idea that Liam and I will be together for long enough that we can read each other's mind fills me with a hopeful warmth. I feel Liam shift, and I want so badly to turn and meet his expression. To know what he's thinking.

We play a few more rounds, and Charlotte and Simon wipe the floor with us. All Liam and I can do is laugh at how competitive they are — that and how utterly terrible at this game we are. Then, just as I'm thinking things can't possibly get more ridiculous, it's Simon's turn again; he moves his hips, shoulders, pelvis — everything. It's like he's trying to run and have sex at the same time.

Liam's face is a picture of horror while Charlotte yells maniacally.

"Running... you're running. Oh, Blade Runner! Secretariat!"

"My God," Liam says, grimacing, "this is painful."

"What am I watching?" I say into his ear in sheer disbelief, too stunned to laugh.

As Simon continues his bizarrely erotic movements with more intensity, Liam leans into me and groans, nuzzling his face into my shoulder. "Nothing that we can unsee."

"Forrest Gump! Back to the Future!"

Liam nuzzles closer. "Oh, God... "

Finally, even Charlotte is stumped, opening and closing her mouth as ideas come and go.

Then it hits me.

"Oh my God," I say, totally entertained. "Oh my God, I've got it. It's Baywatch!"

"Yes!"

I squeal, jumping up to give Simon a high five.

"That was brilliant, darling," Charlotte says. "I don't know how I missed that. It was so obviously Baywatch."

Liam looks around the room like he's looking for signs of intelligent life. "In what world was that obvious?" he says, his voice high pitched and frantic. "I almost called an ambulance."

For a moment, we all look at each other in silence. Then, we fall into a pit of hysterics.

Best night ever.

"Well, I think I sufficiently entertained our guests," Simon says, placing a kiss on Charlotte's head. "I'll get dinner ready now."

"Entertained, scarred..." Liam mutters.

Simon slips out of the room, and the three of us expel the last of our giggles as we settle back on the sofa, Liam placing his warm hand back on my thigh.

I have no plans to move it anytime soon.

Charlotte turns to us, leaning forward. "So, Liam. Why did you drop out of school?"

"Jesus, Mum." Liam stiffens beneath me. "Already?"

She shrugs. "I let you have a couple of drinks and some fun first. That should count for something." She grins a little, but her eyes remain serious. "Now before you say 'I don't want to talk about it', remember that I'm not going to let it go for the next three days if you don't tell me."

He sighs from behind me, and I shift my weight.

"Maybe I should let you two talk alone," I suggest, but Liam clamps his hand down on my thigh, stilling my movements.

He shifts me so that he can look at Charlotte directly. "You know why," he says in a low voice.

Charlotte blinks into the dim light. "Darling." She reaches her hand out towards his. "You should talk to somebody. This isn't the right way to handle things."

"It is what it is."

"You could always change your mind about school. It's never too late," she argues.

Liam shakes his head, his expression resigned. "I don't even think I'm that person anymore."

My heart aches watching his chest rise and fall with ragged breaths, his walls lower than usual in the presence of his mother.

"It's not just about Luke. It was at first. Just didn't see the point in school anymore. Didn't feel like going to class. Didn't feel like doing anything. I realized that I was failing half my classes and it would be nearly impossible to catch up with all the sessions I'd missed. Then I just... shut down, I guess. Started working at the bar to fill my time with something. Everything was just... gray all the time. Just running on autopilot until..."

He trails off, his fingers reaching towards my hand. I don't realize I'm crying until I feel a tear stroll down my cheek. I don't wipe at it, not wanting to draw attention to myself. To hear him talk like this, to know that he's been struggling so much and hasn't talked to me about it...

He doesn't trust you.

I hate myself for making this moment about me, for twisting his honesty into some fault against myself or some flaw in our relationship.

Fake relationship, you mean.

"Darling," I hear Charlotte say. Glancing in her direction, I realize her eyes are coated with moisture, too. "You should have called me."

Liam shrugs. "I'm figuring it out," he says evasively. "It's Christmas. We're not supposed to talk about depressing shit."

Charlotte shakes her head. "We're supposed to talk about whatever we want to, and right now, your poor mother who never gets to see you anymore wants to talk about loss."

"Mum," he groans.

"You didn't just lose Luke, Liam. You lost your dream. *Your* dream, love. Remember? I certainly do." She smiles sadly. "You used to talk my ear off about whatever experiment you were working on, what paper you were writing. You loved it, and you were great at it."

"Yeah," he mutters, his hand finding mine. He presses his fingertips against mine, intertwining our hands without looking in my direction.

"What do you think, Whitney?" Caroline asks, looking at me curiously.

I swallow and my eyes flicker to Liam's. This is new territory for us, and I'm not sure if he even wants to hear what I think about his life choices. It's certainly not my place to pass judgement on them. He hasn't spoken to me much about what his life was like before we met. I know that he was in graduate school and that he dropped out. That he's focused on Luke's project and trying to do a lot.

"I think... that sometimes we need time, and that's okay. Sometimes just getting out of bed is enough, and everything else we can figure out as it comes..." I ramble on, unsure of what I want to say. "Liam is smart and brave, and he's got an amazing heart, so if he needs to lock the door and throw away the key sometimes, I trust that he's going to come back stronger than ever."

Silence fills the room.

Charlotte lifts her glass, her smile deepening. "Cheers to that."

When I finally work up the nerve to look at Liam, he's staring at me as if he's just remembered something or solved some puzzle he's been stuck on for ages. He studies me with an intensity that sizzles through me.

Charlotte shifts, standing and brushing her skirt. "I'm going to help Simon," she announces, then slips out of the room.

"Is that really what you think of me?" he finally asks, his voice low and controlled. "You think I'm brave?"

I swallow again, but nod. "Of course," I whisper.

He brings a hand up to brush his thumb against my cheek, his intensity fading to a sweet softness as he presses his lips to the side of my neck. He places his hands on either side of my face and lowers his lips to mine. I feel him shake his head lightly.

"I'm not," he admits, his breath playing against my face. "I'm terrified."

I inhale a shaky breath, feeling the energy pulsing and shifting between us. Liam pulls back and meets my gaze again, his eyes filled with longing.

"This is real," he murmurs. "It's real, right?"

My stomach drops in one fell swoop. Swallowing, I take in everything about this moment. The low crackle of the fire, the sound of Christmas music floating softly from the kitchen, and Liam, his green eyes locked onto mine.

"It's real," I whisper.

Liam's entire face lights up, a smile spreading across his face. He presses his lips to mine again and warmth spreads through my body, sending tingles down my spine. He nudges my shoulder, and that tiny motion makes me want to spill those three words more than I ever have before.

Say it, say it, say it.

"Come on," I say instead. "Let's go eat our weight in sticky pudding."

37

———

LIAM

I'm in love with my wife.

I think deep down, I've always felt it. This current, this thread between us. Maybe it started when I saw her standing in our kitchen in nothing but a t-shirt, or when she came to my defense with her mother. I don't know. But somewhere between saying *I do* and smoking a joint with my dad, Whitney has become a part of me. An essential part.

After we finish dinner with Simon and my mum, we get ready for bed, both of us exhausted. I'm nervous to be alone with Whitney again after my confessions in the firelight, so I try to keep things light as I watch her crawl into bed.

"Do you want your gift now, or in the morning?" I ask.

Whitney smiles as she pulls the covers up over her chest. "We have to wait until tomorrow."

I glance at the clock, then pull my sweater and t-shirt off. "It's after midnight, so technically it is Christmas."

"Okay, fine, let's do them now."

I perk up, a spike of nerves hitting me in the chest. "Really?"

She nods, then crosses the room and reaches for a small bag. I reach into my backpack and get the small box tucked in there.

The room feels warmer as she settles back into bed with me, a soft smile on her face.

"You first," I say quickly.

She scoffs. "No way! You're the one who insisted we do it now."

Taking a deep breath, I hold my gift out to her. "It's not much," I say softly. "I didn't know what you'd like, or... "

She opens the small box, lifting the top off to reveal the tiny gold necklace I got for her. She studies it, her eyes drawing on the small pendant at the end.

"Scissors?" she says, her brow furrowed as she lifts it, studying the tiny golden scissors at the end of the chain.

"Since you're a hair stylist. I mean, because of your salon. If you don't like it, I can take it back," I reply, reaching for the box, but she pulls it out of my reach.

"No. I love it," she says. She looks up at me, her eyes swimming with moisture. "Really, Liam. It's amazing."

A wave of emotion surges through me, and my hand reaches for hers without thinking, my fingers playing at her palm.

"Here. I'll put it on," I tell her, reaching for the chain.

She lifts her hair, displaying the back of her slender neck. I unclasp the chain and reach around her, putting the necklace on. She turns back to me, and I finger the small pendant, placing it against her chest. Crossing the room to the mirror, she stares at her reflection, her hand reaching up to her chest.

"I love it," she repeats with a smile. "Thank you."

"My turn." I smirk, putting my hand out expectedly.

She crosses back to the bed and hands me the tiny bag. "It's not really a gift so much as... something I probably owe you," she says. "It's not as good as yours. Now I wish I had gone first."

"Hush," I tell her, opening the bag to find a small box that looks like a ring box. I open it to see a simple gold band.

It's a wedding ring. For me.

I'm speechless. Out of everything, I was not expecting this. I pick up the ring and hold it up in the light before slipping it onto my left hand. It fits perfectly on my finger.

"Sorry it took me so long," Whitney whispers.

"Whitney," I manage, overtaken by emotion. "God, Whitney."

"Do you like it?"

My reply is pressing my mouth to hers like it's a drug I can't get enough of. Sliding my hands to the side of her face, I groan against her lips as she opens her mouth to me, kissing me with ardor.

"It's perfect," I say against her. "You're perfect."

I pull back to stare at the ring on my finger, marveling in how right it feels. I love the way our hands look intertwined, both of us wearing the symbol of our bond. Now the whole world is going to know that she's mine and I'm hers.

Totally and completely hers.

A FEW DAYS LATER, we say goodbye to Simon and my mum, heading back to London to go sightseeing before we go home. Our goodbyes are an emotional affair, my mum crying and hugging me for a solid five minutes. It makes me feel guilty for not coming home more often, but Whitney promises that we will visit again soon.

We climb into the car as Simon loads our bags into the boot. My mum clasps Whitney's hand from the passenger window, the two of them whispering in hushed, emotional tones.

"I love you," my mum says at last.

"I love you, too. I'll text you updates of our time in London."

Everyone yells goodbyes through the window as I pull the car from the driveway. Whitney sighs, settling into the seat next to me, so I reach over the gearstick and grasp her hand in mine.

"Should I say I told you so?" I ask.

She narrows her eyes at me. "For what?"

"My mum. She absolutely adores you, as I knew she would. Simon, too. You were a nervous wreck on the way here and now you're a picture of contentment."

"I was not a nervous wreck." She rubs her thumb on the back of my hand. "It was a great trip. This is such a beautiful town, and I love their house."

"Would you ever consider moving here?" I ask her.

She blinks. "Would you want to move back?"

I shrug. "I don't think so. I've never really thought about it. I'm a dual citizen, so I could come back."

She gazes out the window. "I love New York, and I've never lived outside the United States. Hardly even travelled in Europe, even though I've always wanted to."

It's quiet for a moment.

"I think I would move. If you wanted to," she says eventually.

I love you.

Whitney releases my hand and slips her phone out, fiddling with the Bluetooth and putting on a playlist she likes, which turns out to be entirely Taylor Swift songs. Not that I'm too mad about it. My wife's habits have somehow rubbed off on me. Last month, I found myself singing *Lover* in the shower.

We hit traffic when we get to London but eventually check into the hotel. It's a brand new Hyatt Marks Hotel, the first of its kind in London. Whitney is eager to hit the ground running and has a list of activities to do and places to go. In classic Whitney fashion, it's incredibly organized, everything planned out down to the hour. We've only got two days before we head back to New York, so she's really crammed it in.

The first thing we do is head to Tower Bridge, which

Whitney mistakenly calls London Bridge. She argues with me about it for fifteen minutes before eventually Googling it and realizing that I am right. After that, we walk through Borough Market and pop into a pub for a drink.

"You have to drink beer," I tell her when we stumble upon a corner pub.

She wrinkles her nose. "Fine. When in Rome, I guess."

After a pint each, we go to the London eye and ride the Ferris wheel, watching the sunset over the river. It's a perfect moment. Whitney has probably taken a hundred photos since we've arrived in England, but when she snaps a selfie of us at the top, I know it's going to be my favorite. My heart fills with warmth as I wrap my arms around her, feeling more at peace than I have since Luke died. This woman has come into my life and somehow, without me even realizing, has healed me. I don't know if I'll ever be who I once was, if I'll ever stop missing him and the life I had, but right now, with my wife in my arms, all I feel is gratitude.

Gratitude, awe, and most of all... love.

38

LIAM

"Pass me that rag," Darius calls from the other side of the bar.

It's been two weeks since Whitney and I got back from our trip to England. It's been fairly quiet at Abe's since New Years, and I haven't seen Jackson around much either. He texted me a couple of times to ask for advice on tutoring jobs, but other than that, it's been mostly radio silence. I've chalked it up to the holiday break, but now that the new year is in full swing, I wonder where he's been.

"Where's your brother?" I ask Darius, tossing the towel in his direction. "Haven't heard from him much."

"He's been busy. Trying to catch up on all the work he missed last semester. Plus, he's working on this scholarship thing. I guess you got through to him, so, thanks."

"No problem," I reply.

"I just don't want him to be crushed if we can't figure out the money shit. College is expensive."

He's not wrong. I was lucky enough to get financial aid and scholarships, but I'm still paying off student loans. I guess it's a good thing I don't have to worry about those costs anymore, now that I'm done with school.

"I know," I tell him. "But there are options."

Darius hesitates. "He wants to apply to Columbia. My dad told him that was the dumbest thing he's ever heard."

"I went to Columbia."

He raises his eyebrows at me, surprised. "Yet again... what the fuck are you doing working here?"

I chuckle, shaking my head. "Long story."

He gestures around to the empty room. We closed up twenty minutes ago, pushing out the last stragglers who refused to move on. "I got time. Besides, all ever I do is talk about myself. I wanna get to know the guy I'm working side-by-side with every day."

Taking in a deep breath, I lean against the bar and start talking. I tell Darius about Luke, about our adventures during undergrad and the two of us going to Columbia together. How we bonded over video games and a mutual love of *Star Trek*. How he fell in love, and it didn't work out, and it sent him into a spiral that I didn't notice. Darius listened to all of it thoughtfully, without interjecting with questions.

Then I tell him about Whitney, about how I needed a place to stay and she needed a roommate. My plan for the money. How slowly I stopped caring about my half-baked plan and focused more and more on the woman in my life. How she broke through my walls and became the best thing I have.

"So now, I'm in love with my wife, and I still haven't told her. I've got all this money that I don't know what to do with. I feel guilty as hell for even thinking about abandoning Luke's quest and the promise that I made to him — to myself. But I just feel... I don't know. I see Whitney and she's so full of life, so full of dreams that she's chasing, and it's like she's just glowing with it. I wish I could be more like that, but I still just feel so... lost."

When I finish my monologuing, it's quiet for a moment.

"Damn," Darius says eventually, shaking his head. "That's a lot."

I bark out a weak laugh, nodding. "Yeah, it is."

He shrugs. "You'll get there. When you know, you know. Shit always works itself out."

"Wow, you're chock full of inspirational quotes. You an optimist, Darius?"

"You gotta be."

We're both quiet for a few minutes as I consider my situation. It's time for a change. For something. I can feel it in my bones, in my chest, the desire for something new. Maybe it's the new year that has me itching for an opportunity to start fresh. To figure out my path instead of just wandering around, waiting for something to happen. I'm not sure what it is yet, but Darius' words ring through my mind, like a buoy to hold onto, something to keep me treading water as I navigate these changing tides.

When you know, you know.

THE NEXT DAY, I get back from the gym to find Whitney clad in an apron and fuzzy socks. The apartment is warm and inviting, a scented candle burning in the corner. It's another frigid January day, and I'm starving, so the sight of my wife dancing around our cozy kitchen sends my mouth watering for more than one reason.

"Hey, baby," I say, crossing towards her.

Say it.

I love you. I love you so much. Please be mine forever.

"Hi," Whitney replies, her eyes filled with warmth.

I wrap my arms around her waist, hugging her against me.

"Missed you," I mumble against her, feeling drunk on the sight of her in our home. She grips me tighter, perhaps sensing that I need her embrace right now.

Always.

She nudges me. "You're in a good mood."

I love you.

"How was your day?" she asks.

"Good." I sit at the counter, watching her. "Darius and I went to the gym together."

"Who is that?"

"My coworker at Abe's. We ended up talking for a while last night after our shift ended. He's a good friend... I think."

Stirring what appears to be a curry on the stove, Whitney smiles over her shoulder. "I'm glad you have a new friend. God knows you need to hang out with someone besides me," she teases.

"But I like hanging out with you," I shoot back. "How was your day?"

She turns off the stove and gets two bowls from the cabinet. "It was great. *All Rhodes* looks amazing. I can't believe how close I am. Busy as hell, but close. It feels good."

I smile. "You deserve it."

Whitney crosses over to me with two bowls of rice and curry, setting one in front of me. "Thank you," she says.

"Thank *you*." I point to the bowl of food. "This looks amazing."

"What did you and Darius talk about?" Whitney asks.

"Luke," I reply. We both chew quietly for a moment. She glances at me curiously, giving me the space to go on or change the subject.

"It's been a weird few months," I start. "I've been thinking a lot about what my mum said. Maybe I made a mistake dropping out so quickly. I can't help but have regrets. Can't help wondering what might have happened if I'd stayed.

"I don't know what I would have done without you these past few months. I got into all this because I wanted to honor Luke, to fulfill his life's plan, but the truth is I wasn't living for myself. I loved Luke, I really did, but I'm starting to think that he wouldn't want this for me. He'd want me to do my own thing, forge my own path."

"I think you're right," Whitney says softly.

"I guess I just wanted to make a difference. Change the world. Maybe that's stupid."

She reaches out, placing her hand over mine. "It's not. You have so much to give. Maybe it's not about changing the world. It's just about changing one person's world. I think that can be enough. With my salon, it's not like I'm really making a difference in the grand scheme of things. But if just one person who comes through our doors leaves feeling better about themselves, it's a win. That's important, too, and Liam... you've changed my world. Completely."

The warmth of her words settles deep into my bones. Into every part of me. I want to wrap my arms around her and never let go.

It's just about changing one person's world.

I'm reminded of Luke's original mission statement. Of the importance of effecting individual changes as well as structural ones. An idea flashes through my mind as clear as day. The answer, so obvious and so simple that I don't know how I didn't see it before.

I suddenly remember Darius' words from the previous day: *when you know, you know.*

"I have to make a call," I tell Whitney, pushing out of my chair, my mind spinning.

Rushing out of the room, I slip my phone out of my pocket and dial Darius' number. He doesn't answer, so I shoot him a text, and then send one to Jackson, too. Amped up, I glance at my phone to see a text back.

Darius: What's up?

Liam: Can I come over

Darius: Bro are you booty-calling me?

Darius: Where's your wife?

Darius: Lol

Liam: Shut up. Have an idea. Wanna talk in person.

Darius: Ur being weird.

Liam: Can I come over or not?

Darius: Yeah, come through.

He sends me his address, and luckily it's only a short bus ride away. I go back into the living room where Whitney is still sitting at the counter. She glances in my direction as I pull on my fleece.

"I have to go," I tell her. "I'll be back later."

"Is everything okay?" she asks, turning to face me. "You just got home."

"Everything is fine." Staring at the woman in front of me, I realize that yet again, Whitney has been my guiding light. Her words, her advice has given me the realization I've been waiting for. I cross the room to her, my heart racing. "You're amazing."

I drop my head to hers, kissing her.

"I—"

Now isn't the time. I'm junked up on adrenaline and halfway out the door. She's eating curry in her fuzzy socks. But I can't contain it. I can't go another moment without telling Whitney how I feel about her.

"I love you," I hear myself say, the words spilling out of me.

She blinks up at me, her expression one of total shock. A million emotions seem to flash across her face as she processes what I've said. I bring my hands to the side of her face, my thumbs caressing her cheeks.

"I love you," I repeat, because it sounds so damn good hearing it. Feels so damn good to say it. "I'm in love with you."

I close my eyes for a moment just to savor this moment. The rightness of it. When I open my eyes again, Whitney stares back at me, her mouth opened slightly. She closes it and swallows, her brown eyes searching mine.

That's when I realize something.

She's not going to say it back.

I feel it pass between us, the moment where she would have said it. Where she'd throw her arms around me and say *I love you, too.* Instead, it's silent. Another beat passes. Another opportunity. The pressure of it bares down on me, impossible to avoid.

"You don't have to say it back," I choke out, hating the words as they fall from me. "I just... I've been wanting to say it. For a while."

She shakes her head, seeming to break out of whatever trance she was in. "Liam—"

"It's okay. Really. I'll be back later, and we can talk," I manage, pressing a soft kiss to her forehead and turning on my heels.

I have to get out of here. Grabbing my coat and my keys, I turn to her for one last moment before opening the door. I wait for another beat to give her another chance.

She could say it now.

We lock eyes, a breath passing between us as I wait for the words that I want so badly to hear. The three little words that aren't coming.

"I'll see you later," I whisper into the silence, then I turn on my heels, heading out into the cold.

39

WHITNEY

I blink into the empty room, tremors rocking through my body, cold blanketing me like a winter shadow.

I love you.

The words are still lodged in my throat. I'd been waiting for days for this moment. To finally tell Liam how I feel. To hear him say the same. To know, once and for all, that our marriage was real. That somehow, in this crazy mess, we'd found each other.

Instead, I just stood there. Silent. Frozen.

I said nothing.

Did nothing.

I tried to push away the memories that threatened to break through again, those images swirling through my head the second Liam's words registered in brain. My mom, three whiskeys deep, sobs wracking through her chest as she cried over another guy who walked out on her. Walked out on us.

"Never trust a man," she'd said. *"They bring nothing but heartache."*

Moisture pricks at the corners of my eyes. My hands shaking, I reach for my phone. I should call Liam, beg him to come back and try to explain. Get him to understand the fear clawing its way up my throat, the cruel voice in my head telling me I wasn't enough. That he wouldn't stay no matter what he said. No matter what he promised.

I wrap my arms around myself, trying to ease the tremors rocking through my body.

Am I in shock? Is that what's happening right now?

Flexing my fingers, I try to focus on the sensations in the room, what I can feel, hear, smell, and touch; the pads of my fingertips pressing against my arms, my knees digging into my chin, the soft crackling of the candle. Once I feel the shaking subside, I take a deep breath and reach for my phone, dialing Abbi's number instinctively. As soon as I hear her voice, the tears that have been threatening to break through since Liam left finally come.

"Whit? What's wrong? Are you okay?"

I shake my head, willing my chest to stop shaking with sobs. "Liam told me he loves me," I manage through my tears.

"Babe," Abbi replies. "That's amazing! Why are you crying? Happy tears?"

"No," I gasp. "I-I didn't say it back. I just stood there, and then he left."

"Like, he left? Or he *left?*"

Another sob rocks through me. "I don't know. He said he would see me later."

"Okay, then he's coming back. When he gets back, talk to him."

"I feel so bad." My voice drops to a whisper. "I couldn't stop thinking about all my issues. About my mom. I just felt completely out of control."

"That's okay," Abbi says, her voice strong and reassuring. "It's okay that you didn't say it right away. It doesn't mean you don't love him. It just means you need time."

I nod, my shoulders no longer shaking. Sniffling, I wipe at my face and take in a few steadying breaths. Abbi is right; I know she is. All I have to do is wait for Liam to come back, and we can talk.

"You're right," I say to Abbi. My phone buzzes and I glance down. "Hey, I have to go. I'm getting another call."

"You sure you're okay? Want to call me back?"

I sniffle again. "I'm okay. Thanks for being there."

"Always," she says.

I hang up and switch to my incoming call. "Hello?"

"Hey, peanut."

Just what I needed in this moment. Caroline to drop back in and check on me. She must have some sixth sense, knowing that I was thinking of her. Thinking of the trust issues she drilled into my brain.

"Hi," I reply numbly.

"I'm in the city. I'm staying with a friend, so don't worry about me crashing again."

This whole night has been a whirlwind. Ever since Liam came thundering through the door, everything has been off-balance.

"Can I come over?" she asks, a hint of urgency in her voice.

"Sure." I hesitate for a moment before continuing. "Is everything okay?"

"It will be," she says. "Be there soon."

Hanging up, I glance around the room, wondering how the hell I got here. Caroline sounded... off. Maybe it's because of my emotional state right now, but I feel uneasy, like I'm waiting for the other shoe to drop.

"Yeah, so, listen. I need some money," Caroline says.

There it is.

I turn to face my mother, sat on the other end of my couch, and run my eyes over her pale skin and the pronounced bags under her eyes. "What happened?"

She avoids my gaze. "Just someone I owe some cash. It's not a big deal."

"It seems like it is a big deal, if you came to me about it. I thought you had a job at that auto shop?"

"Not anymore," she mutters. "Besides, that won't cover this."

"How much do you need?"

"Ten thousand."

I blink, sure I must be hearing her wrong. There is no way my mom just told me she needs ten thousand dollars.

Dread creeps up my chest. "What's going on? What did you do?"

She makes a noise of disapproval. "Do you have it or not? I know you got the first part of your inheritance. Ten G's is hardly any of it."

I shake my head, disbelieving. "You think I'm just gonna give you ten thousand dollars?"

She shrugs, a familiar callousness seeping into her tone. "Call it paying me back for eighteen years' worth of meals, clothes... the whole shebang."

"Paying you back?" I manage, my head pounding. A wave of nausea rolls through me, but I breathe through it. "I can't believe you."

"Whitney," she says, her tone serious. "I need that money, peanut."

"What's going on, mom?" My voice shakes with fear. I'm starting to get worried. I know my mom has always been a bit of a player in the game of Life, but if she's gotten herself mixed up in the wrong crowd or something...

Her gaze shoots to mine. "You got the cash or not?"

"Not right now," I reply. The weight of his conversation, the fear of what my mom has gotten herself involved in, the longing for Liam to come back, all of it is pulling down on me, drowning me.

"What about the money from the will?"

"Most of mine is tied up in the salon right now."

"Bullshit," my mom growls. "Let me guess, you're giving money to that husband of yours."

"Mom," I sigh. "Don't start."

"Sorry, I meant *fake* husband, since you only married him for the cash."

I can't listen to this anymore. Her words are pressing on a fresh wound, one that I need to tend to before it grows and festers even worse. Liam and I are okay. We're fine.

"I told you I don't need your opinion when it comes to my marriage."

"Marriage? Yeah, right," she scoffs. "You mean that pretend scam you're pulling? If you had any sense, you'd be divorced by now."

"He loves me," I nearly shout. "He told me he loves me, and I didn't say it back, but I'm going to. We're in love."

Her gaze turns pitiful. "Oh, peanut—"

"I'll get you the money, okay? Just give me a couple of days to move some things around." I press the backs of my hands to my eyes, the pressure building. "I feel awful."

"Is it a migraine?" she asks, her expression concerned.

I open my eyes, meeting her gaze warily. "Yeah," I reply. "I think so."

"You should go lie down."

Not bothering to protest, I drag myself to my room and collapse onto my bed, light flashing behind my eyes. I hear a rustling and manage to open one eye to see my mom bringing me a glass of water and a damp cloth.

"Thanks," I rasp as she presses the cloth to my forehead.

"I'll see myself out," she says, her voice a low murmur. "We can talk later. We have a lot to discuss."

I can't parse through what she's saying or decipher her tone, too overwhelmed by the throbbing in my skull. I roll over, squeezing my eyes closed, hardly noticing when my mom slips from the room. Reaching into my nightstand, I grab my sleep mask and curl into a ball, willing the pain to subside.

40

LIAM

Adrenaline courses through my veins as Darius and Jackson stare at me with twin expressions of bewilderment. I practically ran here to meet them, forcing myself not to think about what just happened. Thrusting the memory of Whitney's gutting silence out of my mind.

"What did you just say?" Darius asks, even though I'm pretty sure he heard me the first time.

"I want to pay for Jackson's college tuition," I repeat. "I want to give him a scholarship. The Luke Monroe STEM Scholarship."

"Did you just make that up?" Darius asks.

I shrug, smirking slightly. "Yeah, but it sounds legit, right?"

Jackson hasn't said a word. He's just sitting on the bench beside Darius, his expression thoughtful.

"What do you think?" I ask him.

He shifts. "I don't even know if I'm going to college. I don't even know if I'm gonna get in."

"You've submitted, right?"

"Yeah, but I still have to finish my Columbia and NYU applications."

I go to speak, but Darius cuts me off. "You can't just pay for all our shit, Liam."

How can I explain this feeling? This clarity.

"I know it's unexpected, but I have to do this. This is what I'm supposed to do with the money. I know it."

Darius shakes his head, glancing over at Jackson. Then he sighs, sounding somewhat resigned. "If this is what you want to do, I'm all for it, but we're not the ones you gotta convince. It's our dad you have to win over, and I have a feeling he's going to toss you out on your ass when he hears this plan of yours."

I rub the back of my neck, my nerves spiking. I'd anticipated that their father might be apprehensive about the idea. He doesn't know me at all. If some stranger showed up at my house and told me he wanted to pay for my kid's education, I'd probably take it as an affront to my pride or an indictment of my parenting skills. I don't want him to feel like I'm judging them, even if I am sticking my nose into their business.

"It'll be a challenge, but if you guys are with me, I think your dad will see this as a good thing... eventually. There are absolutely no strings attached. Neither of you owe me a single thing. He might be resistant, but I hope he's on board, and if he's not... " I hesitate, unsure if I should say this next part. "Jackson, you're almost eighteen. It won't necessarily be his decision."

Darius shakes his head. "If we go behind his back about this, he'll be livid."

"I don't want to lie to my dad," Jackson mutters. "I want to talk to him." He stands up, patting his thighs. "Come on."

I blink. "You want to go talk to him... now?"

He shrugs, glancing at Darius. "Why not?"

"Alright." I stand up, clasping Jackson on the shoulder. "Let's do it."

THE TENSION in this room is so intense, it's almost unbearable.

To start off with, Mr. Cooper and I did not get off on the best foot. It started when I reached in to shake his hand and instead spilled his beer all over his shoes, and it only got worse when I accidentally stepped on the tail of Lulu, their dog, who emitted a yelp so sharp and heart-wrenching that I wanted to shrivel up and die on the spot.

It didn't get much better once I opened my mouth; after I explained that I recently came into a large of sum of money and wanted to fund Jackson's undergraduate education with it, Mr. Cooper had one thing to say:

"We don't take handouts."

His tone left no room for arguments. Luckily for me, I've been dealing with Darius long enough to know that his sharp tone is likely a front for deeper feelings.

Now, I'm sitting across from Mr. Cooper while Jackson and Darius float around the kitchen nearby.

"Sir, please let me explain before you say no."

He nods and crosses his arms, his expression betraying nothing. He might be a tougher nut than his kids to crack. So I start talking. I tell him about Luke, about the kind of person he was, and how I've spent the better part of last year trying to carry out his life's wishes, only to realize that what Luke would have really wanted was for me to be happy.

After I finish my speech about both the intellectual and fiscal value of higher education, Mr. Cooper uncrosses his arms and stares at me. Jackson and Darius have joined us in the living room, eyeing their dad with curiosity.

He glances at Jackson. "You want this?"

Jackson hesitates, but then he purses his lips and nods. "Yeah, Dad. I do."

He tilts his chin down, his expression thoughtful. He looks at Darius, his jaw set. "What do you think?"

"Me?" Darius echoes.

"Yeah, dipshit. Who else?"

Darius smirks. "Never turn down a check," he jokes, but then his gaze turns serious. "Jackson's got a shot, Dad. He's got a real shot."

Mr. Cooper nods and meets my eyes, his gaze unwavering. "Alright," he says eventually. "I have conditions, though."

For the next hour, the four of us discuss the scholarship. Mr. Cooper insists that part of the deal means that I can't just cut the check and run. Not that I was planning to, but it's nice to know that they actually want me to stick around. Mr. Cooper also tells Jackson that he has to get a part-time job to support himself during school. I guess he doesn't want him getting too comfortable. I don't peg Jackson as the type to slide by and take the easy route, but I respect that his father wants him to have a good work ethic. It's late when I finally decide to leave, satisfied that everyone is on-board and happy with the decision. At the door, Jackson gives me a tight, quick hug, barely giving me a chance to reciprocate, while Darius just punches my shoulder with a smile.

I head back to the apartment, buzzing. My skin feels like there's an electrical current running through it. Energy and excitement pulses through me. My mind is a swirling jumble of thoughts.

What now? What's next for me?

Whitney.

Her name drifts through my mind like a siren calling out to the sea. I can't wait to see her face when I tell her about all of this. I owe everything to her. Everything good in my life comes back to her.

My wife.

By the time I get back to the apartment, I feel like I'm high. I've got a woman who I love and a life that is finally starting to feel like it's mine again. I turn my key into the lock and let myself into the apartment, which is silent. I glance around for a sign that Whitney is home, finding nothing. As I cross to the kitchen, my eyes catch on a stack of papers sitting on the counter.

Glancing down at them, I blink. Once, twice. My mind whirs and slows, as if unable to accept what I'm seeing.

Petition for dissolution of marriage.

No.

This can't be right.

There must be some mistake. Whitney wouldn't do this. Even if she decided that things were moving too quickly or that she didn't want to see me anymore, she wouldn't do it like this. She'd talk to me. She'd tell me.

"She didn't want to be here for it."

My head snaps to the couch, where Caroline sits with a pitying frown on her face, her hands pulled together in her lap. My gaze flickers back down to the divorce papers, disbelief filling every part of me.

"Where is she? Whitney!"

"She's not here. She thought it was better this way," Caroline says.

I shake my head. "I don't believe you. Whitney wouldn't do that."

"I'm so sorry, Liam. I really thought you two might make it work, but she's more like me than she wants to admit. She wanted me to give you this and to tell you that she's sorry she can't say it back."

Caroline holds out her palm, and when I see what she's

holding, my hand comes up to my chest, as if bracing for a physical blow. The excitement that was just rushing through me is nowhere to be found. Instead, all I can feel is an emptiness that threatens to swallow me whole.

Whitney's wedding ring. She took it off.

This isn't happening. This isn't real.

My mind flashes back to that night in the kitchen, the feeling of her hand in mine as I slid the ring back over her finger.

"Promise you'll never take it off again."

"I promise."

My heart seems to go cold. Numb.

Hollow.

Of course she doesn't want to be with me. It's taken me months, *months,* just to figure my shit out. I've been moping around here with no direction, no clue what I wanted. From her, from myself. It was stupid of me to think that someone would rely on me. She's got her salon. That's what she wanted all along from this arrangement, and now that I've sorted everything with Jackson, I suppose I have, too. Except not really. Because all I want now is to hold my wife in my arms one last time. I'll beg if I have to. Get down on my knees and plead with her not to leave me. To let me be a better man for her.

What kind of woman wants a husband like me? I don't know why I thought...

My hands tremble as I stare down at the reality in front of me. The knowledge that my marriage is over. That this is what Whitney wants. Nausea churns deep in my gut and for a moment, and I'm sure that I'm going to throw up. Instead, I take a deep breath and force myself to glance around at the apartment. At my home.

Not my home.

Not anymore.

I can feel it. The shutting down. My teeth clamp shut, a

shudder running through me. Blinking back tears that threaten to break through the surface, I squeeze my hands into fists. My body feels all wrong. Out of place.

"I'll give you a minute," Caroline says before placing the ring into my shaking hand and slipping down the hallway.

I can't let myself stay in this apartment for a second longer. I glance at the stack of papers again, my chest cracking open, my heart nothing but an empty shell. Forcing my hands to move, I pick up the pen, flip to the final page, and close my eyes. The image of our names side-by-side on that damned piece of paper burns through me like a bolt of lightning. The weight of the world pressing down on me, I have no choice but to click the pen, take a deep breath, and sign my name on the dotted line.

41

WHITNEY

When I wake up, my migraine is mercifully gone. I'm still groggy, my eyes adjusting to the light of my room as I pull my sleep mask off. I have no idea how long I've slept. Sometimes, migraines can knock me out for hours. My first thought is of Liam, remembering how he took care of me last time. Remembering the expression on his face when he told me he loved me.

Rubbing my eyes, I drag myself to the kitchen, finding my mom sitting at the counter, a grim expression on her face. "How long was I out?" I ask her.

She meets my eyes with a fierce expression, a mixture of pity and sadness on her face. "Long enough," she says, sliding a stack of papers towards me.

"What is it?" I ask.

She shakes her head, gesturing towards the papers again. I glance down and when I see the words shining up at me, I rub my forehead, my anger and confusion growing.

"What is this? I told you already that I don't want you sticking your nose into my relationship."

"They're not from me," she says with a frown. "They're from

him." Reaching across the counter, she flips to the last page, where my eyes are drawn to the bottom.

To the two dotted lines, side-by-side.

To Liam's signature staring up at me.

Blinking, I swallow the lump growing in my throat, only to glance to my right and see a bronze ring next to the stack of papers.

Liam's ring. The ring I gave him.

No.

No, no, no, no.

"What?" I croak out. "When?"

"Just now."

"You talked to him?" I manage. "What did he say?"

She purses her lips. "Just that this was for the best, and that he was sorry. He thought it was better this way, easier to make it a clean break."

A clean break? Is that what this sharp pain inside me is?

He's gone.

Is it because I didn't say it back? My hands shake, tremors working their way up my arms and rocking through my whole body. I manage to blink back tears, pressing my hand to my chest in an effort to stay calm. To think this through.

He left you.

No, that can't be right. Because he said he loved me. *Loves* me. He wouldn't... he wouldn't just leave. Not without talking to me. Not without fighting for me. For us.

But he did. He left.

I shake my head, not believing her. "He wouldn't do that. He wouldn't."

Hands shaking, I grab my phone and find his contact frantically, anxiety churning in my gut. If I can just hear his voice, if I can just talk to him, everything will be okay.

I press call.

It rings.

And rings and rings and rings.

I try again, but this time it rings only once before I get sent to voicemail. I stare down at my phone in disbelief. The tears that I've been holding back suddenly break through, rolling down my face in steady, painful streams. I stare down at my phone, shaking my head, still not quite comprehending this new reality. That my husband has left. That my husband has signed divorce papers.

He doesn't want you.

I stumble towards the bathroom, barely making it to the toilet before I drop to my knees and hurl up the contents of my stomach. I press my forehead to the cool ceramic of the toilet bowl, tears streaming down my face.

He left you. He told you he loved you, and then he left. Just like you knew he would.

"Shh, it's okay." Vaguely, I register the feeling of Caroline's hands rubbing soft circles on my back. The gesture should be comforting, but all I can think about is Liam's hands, holding me, keeping me safe, protecting me.

"It's all for the best. You'll see," my mom says in a low voice.

I don't know how long I sit slumped over the toilet. Thankfully, I don't throw up again. Instead, I hug my knees to my chest, rocking back and forth. Emotions pass through me in waves, crashing against me relentlessly. Eventually, I drop my knees and lean against the wall, steadying my breath.

Only one emotion remains.

Anger.

"Get out," I tell Caroline.

"But, peanut—"

"I need to be alone. Please," I reply, almost begging.

"I'll make you a cup of tea," she says, and my heart lurches at yet another reminder of Liam.

Once my mom slips out of the bathroom, I reach for my phone and dial Liam's number. It goes straight to voicemail again, and this time, I inhale a deep breath before I speak, words tumbling out of me.

"Fuck you, Liam. *Fuck you.* I thought you saw me. I thought this was real. You told me this was real. You told me you *loved* me—"

I break off, a sob gathering in my throat. I force myself to be steady, to say what I have to say.

"—and then you leave divorce papers for me without a word? Without even giving me the chance to say it back, you're done? I was going to say it back. Thank God I didn't, because if this is your version of love, I don't want it. You're a coward, and I never want to see you again."

I inhale a shaky breath, my heart cleaving in two. Something irreparable is breaking inside of me. Something I can never get back.

Somehow, I manage to hang up the phone and push myself off the bathroom floor. I meet my own gaze in the mirror, noting my pale skin, dead eyes, and tear-stained face.

It's just you and me now, my reflection says.

Just like it always has been, I call back.

ONCE I DRAG myself out of the bathroom, I crawl into bed and gulp down a glass of water. I find a note from my mom on the kitchen counter, right next to the divorce papers.

I'll give you space, but we need to talk soon.

Exhausted and emotionally drained, I can't bring myself to think about Caroline and her money problems. I feel steady enough to call Abbi, who I'm hoping will make me feel better, even though the thought of our last phone call, of her hopeful, encouraging attitude, sends a stab of pain through me.

She picks up after one ring. "Babe! How did it go? Did you talk to him? Did you tell him?"

My mouth dries up. I open my mouth to reply but nothing comes out.

"Whitney?"

I take a deep breath, blinking rapidly. "He's gone. It's over."

"What do you mean?"

"He left divorce papers for me. With his signature on them."

Silence greets me on the other line. It's rare for Abbi to be shocked into silence, but I think this qualifies as a jaw-dropping moment.

"No," she says. "No way."

"Yep," I reply.

"Do you want me to come home? I'll book a flight right now."

"No." I shake my head, wiping at my eyes. "I'll be fine."

"Whit," she says, sympathy in her voice. "It's going to be okay."

Another swell of pain rises in my chest, my heart aching with despair and longing. "He ignored my calls. I left him a horrible voicemail. I was so angry."

"Just keep trying. Keep calling him. He cares about you so much. I know he does," Abbi replies.

"Obviously not, since he wants a divorce," I snap, anger seeping into my voice.

Abbi hums. "Something isn't adding up. A man doesn't tell you he loves you and then ask for a divorce the same day. It just doesn't make sense."

"I don't know. I worry that it was codependent. He's gone, and I feel like I'm dying. Nobody should have that type of power over me. He was going through so much with Luke, and it felt like he was so focused on me, on us, and not on his own path. I want what's best for him, and now I'm worried that I was holding him back. That he's better off without me."

"First of all, nobody is better off without you, so get that out of your head," Abbi interrupts. "Secondly, you are the most independent, driven person I know. There's nothing wrong with letting yourself rely on somebody."

"Yeah, well, look at where it got me." I let out a humorless laugh, hating the coldness of it.

"Why don't you come here? Fly out to meet me," Abbi suggests. "We can drown your sorrows in cheap liquor and hot basketball players. I'll hook you up with one of Shane's teammates."

"I'll be okay," I reply, unsure if I'm trying to convince her or myself. "I'll let you go. I should shower or something."

"Okay," Abbi says, hesitation clear in her tone. She probably knows I won't listen to her advice. "Call me whenever. Seriously. I'll come back to the city if you need me to."

"It's really okay. I'll call you."

"Love you," she says, and the words cause a swell in my chest. Will it ever not hurt to hear those words?

"I love you, too," I reply despite the lump growing in my throat.

After I hang up, I sit in silence, trying to adjust to this feeling of emptiness. I almost laugh, remembering how badly I wanted Liam out of the apartment when he first arrived. Now that he's gone, I hate that I ever wished it into existence. Glancing around at the empty room, I close my eyes, trying to ward off the reality of this moment and how it crystallizes inside of me, but it's no use. One truth remains.

I have never been more alone.

42

LIAM

I didn't think the suburbs of Philadelphia would be my solace from a broken heart.

Yet here I am, doing what I do best: running away.

I considered returning to Darius and Jackson's house and asking Mr. Cooper to let me stay with them for a while, but I thought better of it. I don't want them to feel beholden to me, as if they have to let me crash on their couch just because I'm setting Jackson up with this scholarship.

Instead, I dragged my suitcase to Penn Station and bought a ticket for the next Amtrak to Philly. I called my dad on the way, keeping the conversation brief and avoiding any details. If he was surprised by my abrupt visit, he didn't let on. He just encouraged me to come on by and told me that he'd make up the spare bedroom for me.

On the ride over, I called the Columbia Admissions office. The best way to distract myself from my shattered heart is to focus on what I *can* control. If Jackson can follow his dreams, so can I. Maybe there's a chance, somehow, that I can still finish my degree. That I can find my way back to the idea of having a career. A job that I actually get excited about when I wake up in the morning.

When I finally got connected to someone with my transcripts on hand, the words poured out of me. I told her about my time at Columbia, about Luke and how I dropped out after he died. How I've been getting my life back on track and realizing that finishing my degree is what I really want. Once I finished explaining, she said the last thing I expected to hear. "Hmm, that's strange. We actually don't have any record of an official withdrawal."

"What do you mean? I stopped showing up. I moved out of the dorms."

"Right," she said. "According to your transcripts, you do have four incompletes from that semester. However, you are technically still enrolled at the school. You'd have to connect with your department head, but it's my understanding that if you want to complete your degree, that is still possible."

"Wow," I replied, reeling. "I don't know what to say."

I guess it's true that I never officially submitted any paperwork withdrawing, but I assumed that the whole me-not-showing-up thing was enough for them to get the picture. My professors emailed me over and over, and I ignored all of it. I was so shut down, I didn't care what happened. But if there's even the tiniest possibility that I could finish my degree, I'm taking it.

I stomped toward the house with that determination in my bones, but as I stepped through the threshold of my dad's front door, all zeal in me evaporated. Since, my dad has been alternating between glee at having me here and vague concern for my surly mood. I think he can sense that this isn't your typical father-son bonding time. If my expression is any indication of how I'm feeling, I probably look downright murderous.

"So," Andy says from his spot on the couch, interrupting my train of thought. "You plan on staying a while?"

I try and fail to suppress a sigh. I should have known he'd start asking questions as soon as I arrived. At least he gave me a solid ten minutes to settle in before starting the interrogation.

"Don't know," I reply, a hint of warning in my voice.

He frowns, a wrinkle forming between his eyebrows. "Did something happen with Whitney?"

Again, her name sends a stab of pain through me, my gut churning with a mixture of longing and anxiety. I can't think about her. Can't think about that dotted line.

"Yeah," I mutter, not wanting to lie to my dad. I'm sure he'll manage to pry the truth out of me somehow, especially if I end up staying here for a few days. I glance around the room. "Where's Stacy?"

"She's on a work trip. It's just us boys." He grins and wags his eyebrows. "What shall we get into?"

I shake my head. "I think I'll just go to bed. I'm pretty beat from the journey over."

He scoffs. "Journey? It's an hour on the Amtrak," he points out.

"Fine," I say through my teeth. "Let's just get it out of the way. Whitney and I... we're separating."

"Oh, Liam," Andy says, his tone sympathetic.

"There's nothing else to say. She doesn't want me anymore, and that's it. It's over."

Her message was crystal clear. It doesn't get more clear than divorce papers.

"What happened?"

My hand closes into an involuntary fist. If I let myself think about the events of the past few days, I'm going to lose it completely. Besides, the last thing I want to do is burden my dad with my tales of woe. It feels like I've had enough of those to last a lifetime.

"It doesn't matter," I answer, my voice hard.

My dad gives me a look that I'm quite familiar with by now. It's a *stop bullshitting me* look. I falter under his gaze and shake my head with a sigh, trying to figure out how to explain everything in a way that makes sense when my head is still reeling.

"She wants a divorce," is what I manage to get out.

Despite my hope that he'll let it go and accept my half-hearted response, he presses on. "She told you that?"

I grimace. "She left me divorce papers. I guess she didn't think it warranted a conversation."

My dad frowns, his brow furrowing in confusion. His expression is a mirror of mine when I stared down at those damned papers. While my brain tried to compute the words and story unfolding in front of me. The gut-wrenching truth that my marriage was over. Before I can stop myself, my shoulders sag, and I let go.

"It was fake. All of it," I blurt out.

"What do you mean?" he asks.

"I mean our marriage was a sham. We only got married because she needed to get her inheritance. We barely knew each other when we flew to Vegas and got the marriage certificate. It was all a lie."

My dad leans back, sinking into the couch thoughtfully. "You can't fake what I saw," is his response.

I shrug. "Well, we did. We got pretty good at it, I guess. So good that I had myself convinced that she felt the same way I did. But I was wrong. I told her how I felt, and she threw it back in my face like none of it meant anything to her. I guess it didn't."

"I can't believe it. You two really looked like you were in love. I would have sworn on it."

"Please, don't remind me," I murmur. I close my eyes, trying to ward off the memories that break through. Whitney's fingers threaded through mine. Her soft smile. The feel of her skin against mine.

"I'm so sorry, Li," my dad says, then hesitates before speaking again. "I bet it's not too late to talk to her. Maybe—"

"I know you want to make me feel better and fix things, but some things are too broken to fix. This is one of them."

It's the truth. Maybe if she hadn't done it so callously, so cruelly, I could have found it in my heart to forgive her and give us another chance. But to break things off like that? The idea that she cared so little about me burns through me, setting my heart on fire.

How could I have been so stupid? Was I deluding myself, thinking the love in her eyes was real?

"Okay," my dad says, sounding far away. "I won't mention it again."

I nod sharply, my stomach churning. I should feel relieved, but instead it feels like the final nail in the coffin. Without my dad's nagging voice in my head encouraging me to talk to her, all I'm left with is a crushing sense of defeat. Shaking my head, I rub my chest, trying to ease some of the pain building there, but it's no use. There's nothing I can do. Nothing except face the reality that Whitney is no longer mine, and maybe... maybe she never was.

"I just need a place to chill out for a bit while I figure shit out. I'm thinking of going back to school, so that's my focus now," I say, pivoting the conversation.

His face lights up, and fuck if that hopeful expression on his face doesn't make me feel like shit.

"Really?"

"Yeah. I talked to someone in the admissions office, and it turns out I wasn't officially withdrawn, so there's a chance I can start back up."

His smile grows. "That's amazing, Li."

I rub the back of my neck, faltering under his praise. I never would have found the conviction to go back to school and give it another shot if it weren't for Whitney. She's the one who inspired me to help Jackson and gave me the confidence to go after the future I really want.

A future that I always envisioned with her by my side.

The dull ache in my chest intensifies with the realization that the future I've been imagining isn't happening. Not with her. Maybe I'll finally finish my degree, but I'll be standing up on that graduation stage alone.

No Luke. No Whitney.

Just me.

When I wake up the next morning, it takes me a few minutes to get my bearings. Waking up in an unfamiliar room sends a flash of panic through me, but then I remember the last twenty-four hours. I remember that I'm not in New York. I remember that my marriage is over.

Rolling over in bed, I reach for my phone, and my heart sinks when I see what's on the screen.

A voicemail from Whitney. Missed calls from Whitney.

My chest tightens, and suddenly the corners of my vision blur, a sensation of panic taking over. I feel myself trying to inhale, gasping for breath, but it doesn't seem to do anything.

I can't breathe. I can't breathe.

She needed you. She needed you to pick up, and you didn't. She needed you to answer her, and you weren't there. You left her.

Just like you left Luke.

My hands shaking, I press to listen to the voicemail immediately. What if she was in an accident? What if she's in the hospital? Oh God. She wouldn't... she wouldn't hurt herself. No, she wouldn't do that. Right?

You didn't think Luke would, either.

I need to hear her voice. Need to make sure that she's okay. That she's safe. My stomach lurches, and for a second, I'm sure that I'm going to throw up. Forcing myself to take another steady breath, I press the phone to my ear, and listen to the voicemail, fear overtaking me. My whole body shakes, my jaw clenched so tight I rub my hand against it, trying to ease some of the tension. But when I finally hear her voice, when I compute the words she's saying, the fear in my body dissipates, the vice grip around my heart loosening.

Only to be replaced with a single, clear thought, a rush of guilt and mortification accompanying it:

I've made a huge mistake.

43

WHITNEY

"Did you sign them yet?"

Caroline sits across from me at the diner, her arms crossed. The bags under her eyes more pronounced than usual, probably a mirror of my own. Since Liam left a few days ago, I feel like I'm in a waking nightmare. One that never seems to end.

"I will," I reply unsteadily, unsure who I'm trying to convince more: her, or myself.

She frowns. "What are you waiting for?"

"Why do you care?" I snap, my patience thinning.

Avoiding my gaze, she picks at her napkin, tearing small pieces off and flicking them onto the table. The past few days have been an absolute nightmare. Between my mother's constant badgering and my cold, empty apartment, I feel completely defeated. I don't know why she won't leave me alone about it, but Caroline has taken to texting me twice a day to ask if I signed the divorce papers.

"I don't understand what's taking you so long. The relationship was fake—"

I shake my head. "I already told you it wasn't fake. My feelings for him were real."

She meets my gaze, her expression unreadable. "Really?"

I nod, swallowing the lump in my throat. "I think he's the only person I've ever really loved." Tears gather at the corners of my eyes, and I blink furiously, wishing them away.

"I thought—"

"We're not here to talk about me. I can get you the money by tomorrow."

"Oh." She blinks then coughs, and for a while she just sits there looking more through me than at me. "Don't worry about it," she says eventually. "I figured it out."

Why the lack of reaction? All she's done since Liam left is go on about the damn money, and now it's *figured out*? Before I can reply, she starts sliding out of the booth.

I grab her arm, confused. "You just got here."

"I have to go." Avoiding my gaze, she flees from the diner like a thief in the night.

I shake my head, baffled by her actions but too tired to worry about it any longer.

"More coffee?" the waitress asks, holding up a steaming pot. I shake my head and ask for the check. After I finish paying, I stumble out onto the sidewalk. Glancing around, I can't help but see all the happy couples passing by, their hands intertwined, their heads turned towards each other like they have a secret language away from the world.

A pang of longing hits me in the gut.

Reaching into my pocket, I dial Mr. Wilson, the attorney in charge of my grandmother's estate. I figure I should inform him about the divorce and see what's going to happen with the remainder of my inheritance.

"Trent Wilson," he answers immediately.

"Hi, it's Whitney Rhodes," I say, trying to keep the sadness out of my voice. "Agnes Rhodes' granddaughter?"

"Ah, yes! Ms. Rhodes, how are you?"

I shake my head. "I'm fine, thank you. I just wanted to inform you that... my marriage is... well, I'm getting a divorce."

It's quiet for a moment before he responds. "I'm very sorry to hear that."

"What happens with my inheritance now?" I ask him.

"Give me just one moment." I hear papers shuffling on his end. "Okay, so in the case that you did not meet the requirements laid out in the will, your inheritance would defer to Agnes' last living kin, which would be your mother, Caroline."

I'm shocked into silence.

If I get a divorce, my mom gets the money.

Suddenly, everything seems to crystallize and click into place. No wonder she's been showing up again. Pushing me so hard to sign the papers. Just when I thought I couldn't possibly be any more disappointed in Caroline, this happens. I always knew she cared about her herself more than she cared about me, but I never expected she'd...

"Ms. Rhodes? Are you still there?" Trent interrupts my spiraling.

"Yeah, um, thanks for letting me know. I guess... yeah. I guess that's what is happening."

"I can wait a few days to start processing it," Trent suggests, his tone sympathetic. "If you'd like?"

I sigh. "That would be great. Thanks."

"No problem, Ms. Rhodes. You take care."

I hang up the phone, my mind reeling. Then, because of course it does, it starts raining. Big, fat raindrops that drip down my forehead as I glance up at the sky with an exasperated smirk. Covering my head, I pick up my pace, jogging back to my apartment. When I get there, I see a familiar figure sitting on the stoop with his head in his hands, the rain pouring over his messy, golden hair.

My heart drops.

Liam.

What is he doing here?

The image of his ring sitting on the kitchen counter flashes through my mind like a taunt. Without thinking, I turn on my heels and run. I don't know if he's seen me, but I can't take the chance. My feet carry me down the street, my body moving on autopilot. I run, and run, and run until I'm out of breath. By the time I stop, I'm blocks away from home and soaked through my clothes. I slip my phone out of my pocket and dial Abbi, but it goes to voicemail. She immediately sends me a text.

> Abbi: Can't talk. Everything okay?

I reply telling her that everything is fine, even though my heart is racing. Sweat drips from my brow down my forehead. Checking my texts and calls again, I notice that Liam hasn't tried to reach out to me at all, which makes no sense. Why was he waiting for me outside my place?

Feeling overwhelmed, I spot a dive bar across the street and make my way inside. The place is mostly empty since it's the late afternoon, but I grab a seat at the bar and order a tequila soda. Exhaustion hits me all at once, an overwhelming feeling of loss spreading through me. I can't keep running forever. If Liam wants to talk, I should just get it out of the way so that I can move on. But the thought of what he might say... I don't know if I can handle hearing that it's over straight from his lips. Lips that once pressed against mine in a way that felt like forever. As much as it hurt to see his signature on that page, it might hurt more to see the look on his face as we say goodbye for the last time.

Chugging the remainder of my drink, I signal the bartender for another one. I guess this is my plan for the rest of the day: drink and wallow. I have a meeting with Sharon tomorrow to go over finances, and I'm scheduled to do a final check with the construction crew later in the evening. All I can do is throw myself into work and ignore that the rest of my life is falling apart. If I can focus on the salon opening, I don't have to think about the fact that I'm going to have a divorce under my belt before thirty. I can ignore everything falling apart in my life and just spend every waking moment on *All Rhodes.*

Just as long as I don't find Liam on my stoop again.

44

LIAM

"*If this is your version of love, I don't want it.*"

I press play on the voicemail again. By now, I've lost count of how many times I've listened to it. The first time I was so consumed with fear and regret, all I could focus on was that she was alive. She was okay. Physically, she was going to be fine. Eventually, sometime after the third or fourth listen, her actual words seemed to register.

"*I thought you saw me. I thought this was real.*"

It only took me five minutes to pack all my stuff and run out of my dad's apartment. Getting back to the city took a bit longer, but I was rushing through Penn Station like my life depended on it. The train ride from Philadelphia was only about an hour, but I must have listened to Whitney's message at least twenty times.

There's just one sentence that I can't seem to get out of my head.

"*I was going to say it back.*"

She was going to say it back.

My heart leaps in my chest, a confusing mixture of hope and guilt swirling through me. The thought of hearing those words from Whitney's mouth after thinking that she wanted me out of her life fills me with a hopeful warmth. I'm scared to let myself latch onto that feeling, so instead, as I sit on our stoop and rub my hands together, I focus on the guilt.

I press play on the voicemail again, my head in my hands.

"I never want to see you again."

The sound of her heartbroken voice sends a wave of nausea through me. Closing my eyes, I can almost picture her angry, tearstained face. My strong, beautiful girl was crying because of me. Because I failed her. Because I let my insecurities take over and imagined the worst. Because I believed Caroline.

What kind of mother does this to her own daughter? How the hell did she get Whitney's ring? Anger pulses through my chest. If I ever see Whitney's mother again...

I'm an idiot. I should have trusted Whitney. I should have given her a chance to explain. Instead, I ran from my problems like I always do. Here I thought I'd finally made some strides in figuring my life out, but yet again I fucked things up. When she needed me be to be there for her, I left her.

I glance down the sidewalk, searching for Whitney. I've been sitting here for hours, and she still hasn't come home. It's getting late, and I need to figure out where I'm going to sleep tonight. Feeling desperate, I scroll through my texts to find Abbi's number. I'm sure she's about to tear into me, but I'm feeling pretty masochistic right now. It rings for so long I'm sure it's going to go to voicemail, but then she picks up.

"What the hell do you want?" Abbi barks out.

"I just want to talk to her. Can you please tell her to come home?"

"Oh, *now* you want to talk to her? Last I heard, you were ditching her without a word."

"Listen, Abbi, I know you probably hate me — and trust me,

I hate myself a lot right now too — but can you please, *please*, just ask her to come home? I need to talk to her."

"I don't owe you anything. Eat shit, asshole."

She hangs up on me without another word.

That went well.

Just as I decide that I'll give it another hour before packing up, raindrops start to fall. I take a deep breath, willing the tight feeling in my chest to subside. I close my eyes, letting the rain pour over me. I don't know how long passes, but when I open my eyes, Whitney is standing in front of me, her wet hair matted against her head.

I blink, sure that I must be imagining her, but then her expression seems to shift as she glances away from me. Her arms are crossed, and her shoulders are hiked up to her ears.

"What do you want?" she asks, her voice hard and cold. The sound of it is all wrong.

"Whit," I manage, my voice a rasp. Pushing myself off the ground, I stumble towards her, but she steps back, keeping distance between us. I swallow, trying to find my footing. "I got your message," I announce like an idiot.

She says nothing.

"Are you... can we go inside?" I ask, gesturing to the apartment. "You're getting soaked."

"No," she says, refusing to meet my gaze.

I shake my head. "I fucked up. Caroline told me that divorce is what you wanted, and—"

"She *what?*"

I draw my head back. Guilt swarms through me again, not only because I believed Caroline, but because Whitney still doesn't realize the extent of her mother's interference. I wish I didn't have to be the one to tell her, but we need to clear up this miscommunication. "What did Caroline say to you?" I ask her.

She shifts her weight and crosses her arms. "She gave me the papers that you'd signed and told me that you thought a clean break was easiest. That it was... better this way." Her voice cracks on the last word, and my heart drops to my stomach at the sound.

I shake my head. "I didn't say that. I'd never say that."

"It had your signature—"

"Caroline had your ring, and you promised me you'd never take it off. She knew I'd told you I loved you and that you hadn't said it back. I thought... I'm sorry. I shouldn't have believed her. I know that."

She shakes her head, disbelief coloring her features. "Wow. I can't believe she... " She turns away from me, wiping at her eyes, and I take a step towards her, wanting nothing more than to take her in my arms and comfort her. "She gets the inheritance money if we get a divorce."

Of course she had some ulterior motive. It's all starting to make sense now.

I run my hand through my hair in frustration, tugging at the strands. "Okay," I exhale. "We'll figure this out, baby."

Her gaze snaps to mine, anger still clouding her features. "You signed those papers, Liam. You can't just take that back."

"You are my *wife*—"

"Not anymore," she cuts me off, her chest rising and falling with angry breaths. My stomach bottoms out at her suggestion, a rush of panic hitting me.

"You signed them?" I ask, praying she hasn't. Something flickers in her eyes as she glances away from me. Clinging onto that hesitation, I take another half-step towards her. "Please say you haven't. Please say it's not too late. Let me fix this."

"How long did it take you to completely cut me out of your life? To throw away everything we had? Thirty minutes? Ten? Five? It was so easy for you to believe my mom—"

"*Nothing* about that was easy. I thought—"

She throws her hands in the air. "You thought wrong! You don't trust me. Maybe you never have. That's what this is about."

I'm losing my grip on this conversation. I don't know what I can say to get her to forgive me. Guilt and dread fog my mind, making it impossible to think.

"You know how I feel about my mom. You believe her over everything we had together? You trusted her word enough to just toss me aside?"

"You believed her, too. You thought the same as me—"

"Because you *signed* them, Liam."

"I'm sorry." I take a step towards her and lift my hand to her chin, tilting her eyes to meet mine. "I should have trusted you. I let my insecurities and fears control my actions, and when I was hurting, I protected myself the best way I knew how. It was selfish and stupid, and I regret it more than anything. Running from what scares me is all I know how to do, but I don't want to run from you, Whitney. You're my home."

She shakes her head and pushes my hand away. I'm completely helpless as I watch her eyes well with tears.

"You should go," she chokes out.

"I love you," I whisper, my voice raw. "You are the most important thing in my life. Please tell me what to do. I'll do anything."

My hand trembles with the need to reach out and touch her, to wipe away her tears and wrap her in my arms and tell her that everything is going to be okay, but I feel like I'm on the edge of a cliff, about to free-fall. Nowhere to land. No safety net.

"It's too late," she says eventually, her voice shaky.

An image of her standing barefoot in the kitchen flashes through my mind. The early morning light bathing her in a golden glow, my oversized t-shirt hanging off her thin frame. An ordinary moment made special simply by her being a part of it.

I shake my head, refusing to recognize what she's saying. Because it can't be too late. It can't be.

"No," I argue, my voice trembling.

"Please go," she whispers. "Please."

Something about the raw desperation in her plea sends a jolt through me, my spine straightening. I refuse to accept that we are over, but I have to respect her request and try again another time. Maybe once she's slept on it, she'll feel differently.

Swallowing my protests, I take a deep breath. "Okay," I say reluctantly. "I'll go, but this conversation isn't over. We can't just let her get away with this, Whitney."

Her eyes flare with anger, and I can't tell if it's for me or Caroline. "You made sure it was over the second you signed those papers."

There's nothing I can say. I feel like I'm grasping at straws trying to describe my rash decision, how the sickening pain of what I perceived as a rejection overruled any sense of logic and security. How the minute I saw her ring it felt like the world collapsed beneath me, and now I'm terrified I'll never find my way to solid ground. Not without her. Not without my anchor.

"I love you," I repeat, because there's nothing else I can say. "I don't want a divorce. I want to be with you, and I should have never given up on that. If you give me another chance, I will spend every day for the rest of my life proving to you how much I love you. I promise you that, Whitney."

She doesn't respond, and I can't tell whether my words have landed at all.

"I'll go now." I wrap my arm around her shoulder, pressing a quick kiss to her forehead. I'm surprised she lets me, and just the brief feeling of her in my arms seems to settle me. Hanging my head, I grab my bags and ramble down the sidewalk, walking away from the woman I love.

45

WHITNEY

Is this what dying feels like?

There's a hole in my heart the size of Everest. I can't keep a meal down, and no matter how much I sleep, tiredness seems to overwhelm me. Everywhere I look, the world seems dimmer somehow.

Gray.

Cold.

Empty.

I can't even take solace in my apartment because everything reminds me of Liam. He's woven into every part of that place, the memory of him following me around like a ghost. Even curled up in my own bed, I was assaulted with the memory of him pressed against my back, the two of us tangled up in my sheets. If I close my eyes and focus hard enough, I can almost smell him — that sultry blend of mint and clean linen.

So, here I am at a nearby coffee shop, trying desperately to forget the dead expression in Liam's eyes when I told him to leave and the reluctant acceptance of his goodbye. He said he wouldn't stop trying, but that was six days ago, and I haven't heard from him once. I don't even know where he's been staying.

I shouldn't care — I tell myself I don't — but the ache in my chest tells a different story.

I've ignored three texts from my mother. Every time I look at them, I'm hit with a wave of overwhelming sadness. I know I'll have to confront her at some point, but I don't know what to say to her. How can I ever forgive this? My own mother tried to sabotage my relationship. It's hard to believe she'd go that far just for money, and it makes me even more worried about what the hell is going on with her.

The only option for surviving right now is preservation mode: work, eat, sleep, repeat. I haven't been doing much of the sleeping or eating part, even though I've tried; I've managed to force down some white rice and miso soup, but the knots in my stomach seem to have moved in for good.

Tears, always fresh at the ready these days, prick at the corner of my eyes as I open my laptop. I force my eyes to focus on the website design in front of me and not on the memory of Liam's pleading *I love you*. Who knew that the three words I'd been desperate to hear for the past few months would hurt so much when they finally came? Maybe if I loved him less, I'd be able to stick to my conviction that things are done between us, but we've spent only a week apart and I feel like my chest has been hollowed out with a shovel. Regardless, as much as I want him to wrap me in his arms and hold me against his chest, I don't know how I can ever trust him again. I don't know how to forgive him.

All Rhodes is set to open in less than two weeks, and I'm working on getting our social following up leading up to the grand opening. We're teaming up with a nearby coffee and wine bar for the launch and offering free consultations for the first week. We already have appointments rolling in, mostly from Shatar's former clientele.

I've spent the past three days doing my best to avoid

anything even resembling an emotion, but despite my best attempts, my tears come anyway. I don't know if it's pride and happiness at seeing *All Rhodes* come to fruition, or my heartbreak over Liam, or both, but I can't seem to stop crying. Luckily, nobody in the coffee shop even glances in my direction. They have enough decency to let me sob over my latte in silence.

After my sobs subside, I head back home. It's not like I can avoid the place forever. I have to go to bed at some point, and once I do, it's another sleepless or nightmare-filled night in store for me. Last night, I finally managed a few hours when I suddenly awoke, covered in sweat, images of Liam's black-inked signature flashing through my mind.

When I get to my apartment, I find a bundle of tulips with an envelope attached to it. Furrowing my brow, I open it to find a letter that stops me in my tracks.

Dear Whitney,

It was my mother's idea to write to you. She told me that when she first met Simon, the two of them would write letters to each other anytime they would argue. Usually, she'd get out all her frustrations onto the page and then throw the letter away. When I asked Simon about this, he said that while mum was busy writing about what a fool he was, he would use it as an opportunity to remind himself of all the things he loved about her. I liked that idea more.

I love how passionate you are. Seeing your devotion to your dreams inspires me so much. It makes me want to be a better man.

I love how bad at karaoke you are. Like, truly awful. I've never been a fan of country music, but your rendi-

tion of *Before He Cheats* by Carrie Underwood has become my favorite song in the world. It makes me slightly terrified for what you have in store for me, and thankful that I don't have a car.

I love that you call me on my shit. You challenge me. Arguing with you is more fun than getting along with anyone in the world.

I love your smile. It deserves a fucking star classification it's so bright. I'm 99% sure your smile could power a small rat city. (Should we discuss this idea?)

I love your sense of humor. You make me laugh until my stomach hurts. You're the funniest person in the world.

I love your mind. The way you think about things, the way you solve problems and imagine things that I could never even dream of is so beautiful.

I love your eyes. When I look into them, I feel like I'm looking into my future. So deep and trusting and filled with warmth. Now, every time I picture those beautiful brown orbs, I'm reminded of the painful tears that filled them the last time I saw you, and it feels like a punch to the gut.

I love you so much. I know I don't deserve your forgiveness, but I wish you would give it to me anyway. I hope you will.

Yours forever,

Liam

My heart swells with an unexpected warmth. Gripping the letter in my hands, I try and fail to conjure up the anger and frustration of the past few weeks. Instead, all I can find is a sinking feeling of longing, deep in my bones.

I miss him so much.

How is it possible to be this angry at him and miss him this much at the same time? I try to imagine the two of us as we once were — dancing playfully in the kitchen, sleeping in too late, curled together in my bed — but I can't seem to hold onto it.

What the hell do I do with this? Not just with the letter itself, but with the gaping hole in my heart left in its wake. Part of me is aching to call him, just to hear his voice for a moment, but the other part, the part left bruised by his betrayal swims to the surface.

When I get up to the apartment, I stuff the letter into a box in the very back of my closet. Squeezing my eyes shut, I try my best to erase it from my memory completely.

THE NEXT DAY, I get home from a meeting with Sharon to find another bundle of flowers and a letter. The rational side of me knows that I should just stuff it in the back of my closet with the other one and forget about it entirely, but I can't stop my fingers from wrestling the envelope open and slipping the letter out.

> Dear Whitney,
> The florist was out of tulips, so I hope peonies are okay.
> Have you ever been to the Cloisters? I went yesterday, and it was beautiful. I tried to clear my head, but all I could think about was how much you would love it there. The blooming gardens, the architecture, the artwork. I've been staying with Darius and Jackson,

and Jackson had a school field trip, so I tagged along with him on the subway ride uptown. Maybe one day we could go back there together, if you ever wanted to.

I think it's easier, not being able to see you. I can imagine you reading my words and your face lighting up, the way it does whenever you see something beautiful. You see the beauty in everything. It's another thing I love about you — the way you see the world with such optimism and hope. You could even see something in me, and I never understood what that was. Why someone as amazing as you would ever give a guy like me the time of day.

I wish I could explain it to you, but it's difficult. Seeing those papers was like a confirmation of every awful thing I've ever thought about myself. It was almost like I'd been waiting for it to happen. Like I knew, deep down, that you wouldn't want me around for the long haul. That I'd let you down, just like I've let down everyone in my life.

I never told you this, because it's something I have a lot of shame about, but Luke called me that night. I ignored it. I was at a party, and I saw the incoming call, but someone was yelling something about shots, so I rejected the call. Later on, the phone records showed that I was the last number he dialed. I was the one who should have been there.

I'm losing the point. I don't want this to be my pity party. The point is... I'm terrified of letting the people I love down. When I saw that note, I figured I'd already messed up somehow. That maybe you knew the same thing I did. That I'd fuck it up.

The worst part is that I did. I took something beautiful and pure and perfect and destroyed it.

When I saw that voicemail from you, I can't describe how scared I was. It was just like that night with Luke, except so much worse. Because somehow, I survived his loss. I managed to get out of bed, feed myself, and keep going. But I know that if I ever lost you, I'd be destroyed. I can't lose you, Whitney.

I meant what I said before: I'm done running. Finding you was like coming home, and I never, ever want to leave. All I really want to say is that I love you and I miss you and I don't even know if you're reading these letters but if you are, thank you. Thank you for believing in me when I couldn't believe in myself. For loving me even when I can't love myself.

I was scared to tell you how I felt. I was scared I would lose you if you knew the depth of my feelings. Us starting out the way we did... it was like constantly walking a tightrope between real and fake. Never knowing how much you'd let me have. Never being sure if you were feeling what I was feeling. Settling for any tiny piece when I wanted everything.

I want everything with you, baby.

I miss you.

Yours forever,

Liam

Tears are streaming down my face in earnest. I try to catch

my breath, gasping for air, but the tears just come harder and harder.

God, I miss him so much.

Squeezing my eyes closed, I take a deep breath, imagining that Liam were standing here in front of me. Imagining him wrapping me in his arms and holding me against his broad, warm chest. His hands rubbing soft, soothing circles on my back.

How am I supposed to do this without him?

My phone buzzes in my back pocket and I wipe at my face, sniffling. I slip my phone out of my pocket to see Trent calling.

"Hello?"

"Ms. Rhodes," he greets me. "How are you?"

"I'm okay, thank you," I reply, sounding very much *not* okay.

"I just wanted to check in regarding our last conversation about Agnes' will. Shall I move forward with the redistribution with the understanding that you no longer meet the conditions of the inheritance?"

I open my mouth to respond but stop myself when I glance back down at the letter in my hands. At the words shining up at me.

I want everything with you.

"Actually," I say, determination spiking in my chest. "Do you think you could help me with something?"

46

LIAM

"**M**an, you really are pathetic."

Darius is joking, but he's not wrong. This is my fifth letter I've written to Whitney with not a single response. I pacify myself by thinking that she hasn't read them. It hurts to think she'll never know the true depth of my feelings, but it's worse to imagine that she read all of my confessions and still wants nothing to do with me.

It's been almost two weeks since I saw my wife's face. Two weeks since she asked me to leave her alone. Two weeks of utter silence.

"It's not pathetic. It's romantic," I argue, shoving Darius's shoulder.

He shoves me back, laughing. "Nah, you're a total simp."

I roll my eyes and put my pen down, distracted by his ribbing. He's not exactly helping me get into the right mindset with his mocking tone. I've been struggling to keep up with the letters, starting to feel, as Darius quite eloquently puts it, pretty damn pathetic. I've never tried this hard with a woman in my entire life, but with Whitney, I'm willing to do whatever it takes to get her back.

"I don't care if I am a simp," I tell him. "I'm a man on a mission."

"I'm just fucking with you. I believe in you. You're probably the most determined person I've ever met."

"Seriously?"

He nods, his face serious. "Yeah. You totally weaseled your way into our lives."

I shove him again, chuckling. Jackson comes bounding into the room, his backpack hanging off his shoulder. He's finished almost all of his college applications, so now we're just waiting to hear back. Columbia is his first choice, and I'm hoping he ends up there, too. It would be great if I could return to grad school with him.

"Has she written you back yet? Or texted?" Jackson asks, glancing over my shoulder.

I shake my head. "Still nothing."

He clasps my shoulder and smiles. "She'll come around. I know she will."

His confidence in me feels like a salve on my wound, but I wish I could share in his assuredness. Jackson and Darius make coffee in the kitchen while I finish the last few sentences of my latest letter with a sigh. I fiddle with my phone, debating. Before I can back out, I dial Abbi's number again, tapping my foot in anticipation. She picks up on the third ring, her annoyance immediately clear.

"I gotta give you credit for persistence, but you do know I have a life, right?"

"Please don't hang up," I beg her. "I have a favor to ask."

"Another one? You're starting to get pathetic, Liam."

I smirk, rubbing the back of my neck. "So I've heard."

She sighs. "What do you want?"

"You're coming back to the city for Whitney's opening tomorrow night, right?"

"Of course. You think I'd miss my best friend's big night?" she snaps.

Jackson waves goodbye from the doorway, coffee in hand, and I wave back. I cross the room towards the hallway, hoping for a semblance of privacy.

"I wasn't insinuating that. I just—"

"Make your point, Liam. I already helped you out once by convincing Whitney to go home and talk to you. I'm not on your side, so stop trying to loop me into whatever grand gesture you have planned."

"We want the same thing, which is Whitney's happiness, right?"

She clicks her tongue. "Yes, I want my best friend to be happy, but I'm not convinced you're the one to help with that, to be honest."

Running my hand through my hair, I suppress a sigh. I should have known calling Abbi would leave me on the verge of a verbal castration.

"I love her. You know I do," I point out.

"Sometimes that isn't enough, Liam."

"I know. I know, but tomorrow night is my last chance to show her how much she means to me."

Abbi hums on the other line. "And why is that? Why is her big night your opportunity to make everything about you and your fuck-ups? God, you're such a guy."

I consider her words. "Do you have a better idea? A man can only bare his heart out so many times before he gives up. I don't know what else to do."

"Just be there," Abbi says, her tone softening. "Don't come with some romantic proclamation or symbol of your dying adoration. Just show up for her. Let her know that you're gonna keep showing up, no matter what happens. If two weeks of unrequited letter-writing is all it takes for you to give up on your marriage, you aren't the man I thought you were."

"That was almost a compliment," I point out.

"Don't push your luck."

I rub at my chest, trying to dull the ache there. "She told you about the letters?"

"Yes," she replies, giving nothing away.

"What did she say? Does she like them? Does she hate them? Should I stop?"

"Goodbye, Liam."

Abbi hangs up before I can ask any further questions. I shake my head, frustrated. Still, I ponder her suggestion and find myself reluctantly agreeing with her point. The letters were meant to be a gesture, a vulnerable showcase of the depth of my feelings. She knows how I feel, so I don't have to keep reminding her. Tomorrow isn't about us, it's about Whitney.

My girl needs me to show up?

I'll show up every single day.

I HAD no idea what to expect for a grand opening of a salon, but when I get to *All Rhodes*, the place is packed, people milling about with mimosas or sitting in salon chairs with hairdressers running their fingers through their hair.

It looks amazing. I knew that Whitney spent a long time working with the interior designer to make the place stand out, but I didn't expect it to look like this. The entrance is like a garden, filled with plants and bright light that give the place an airy, welcoming feel. Beyond that, the chairs and vanities are a sea-foam green, channeling a more classic 1950s look. It's a perfect blend of modern and vintage, and it feels so indescribably *Whitney*.

Glancing around the room, I pat at my thighs nervously. I don't see Whitney anywhere, but I find Abbi across the room. She meets my eyes with one eyebrow raised, a challenge in her gaze. I offer her a small wave, and she pats Shane's arm, gesturing towards me. They cross over to me, the air thick and awkward between us.

Shane breaks the silence with a small smile. "How are you?"

"I'm okay. Been better." I glance around, still searching for Whitney. "Where is she?" I ask, unable to hide the desperation in my voice.

Abbi sighs and glances around. "In the back."

I move immediately to head towards the back of the salon to find her, but Abbi stops me, laying a hand on my arm.

"Remember what I said," she says. "This day is about her."

With a sharp nod, I slip away and weave through the crowds of people, ignoring the smiles from a few familiar faces and going straight to the back of the room. Taking a deep breath, I push open the door.

Whitney is standing behind a desk, rifling through a stack of papers. She looks beautiful. She's wearing a soft pink blazer with matching pants, her hair slicked back in a tight bun at the base of her neck. I don't know if it's because I haven't seen her in two weeks, but I swear she's glowing. When she hears the door shut, she sighs, a heavy, frustrated sound.

"Sharon, where did you put the invoices for the—"

She inhales a sharp breath as she glances up, shock coloring her features as she realizes it's me standing in the doorway. I take a hesitant step towards her, taking her in.

"Hi," I whisper with a soft smile, my hand going automatically to the nape of my neck. I'm not sure if she's going to kick me out or start yelling at me, but she just eyes me warily for a long moment before speaking.

"Hi," she replies.

The sound of her voice fills me with warmth. I want to reach for her and wrap her in my arms, but instead I fiddle with the hair at the base of my neck, my fingers itching anxiously.

"You look beautiful," I tell her, my voice scratchy. I clear my throat, trying to find steadiness. "How are you feeling?"

She swallows, her throat bobbing as she glances away from me, breaking our eye contact. "Good. Overwhelmed, but good."

I nod, tapping my fingers against my thigh. "That's good."

For a moment, neither of us speak.

"Everything looks amazing. I can't believe... I mean, I can believe it. You did a fantastic job, Whitney. You should be so proud."

She pulls her shoulders back, straightening. I expect her to make some excuse or try to downplay what an achievement this place is, but she nods her head, agreeing. "I'm very happy with how everything turned out," she says, meeting my eyes with a soft smile.

I try to hide my flinch at the deeper meaning in her words, praying that she's talking about the salon and not us. She seems to see it anyway, her brow furrowing.

Swallowing the lump in my throat, I glance away from her. "Well," I manage. "I just wanted to tell you what a fantastic job you've done. Not that you need me to tell you that, but I'm really glad I could see it. I know how much it means to you, and it's really special, Whit."

"Thank you."

My heart thumps in my chest, the sound of it echoing in my ears. Is this it? It all ends here, in a half-empty office?

"I won't stay long," I force out. "I don't want to... yeah, take away from your big day or anything. I just wanted to say congratulations, so..."

I reach for the door handle, but the sound of Whitney's voice stops me as she moves around the desk, meeting me near the door.

"Wait," she says, urgency in her voice. "I thought... do you have something for me? Another letter, maybe?"

There's a little humor in her tone, and I can't help the fall of my shoulders. She's laughing at me. I thought my words would show her how much she means to me and everything that I've been struggling with, but she thinks I'm a joke. I can handle her anger, I can even handle her hating me, but I don't know if I can handle her laughing at me.

"Don't," I manage on a whisper, my voice shaking. "I know I fucked up, but please don't be unkind."

I reach for the handle again, but she stops me, laying her hand over mine. My whole body stiffens at the contact, the warmth of her hand on mine causing my legs to lock up, keeping me in place.

"What? Wait, no, what's wrong?" she asks.

I whirl on her, anger rising in my chest. "What's wrong? What's wrong? Those letters were..." I squeeze my eyes shut, trying to ward off the flurry of emotions whirling through me, pushing the anger down. "Forget it."

Before I can move past her, she reaches for my arms, holding me in place.

"Stop, stop. This is coming out wrong somehow," she says, her voice pleading. "I loved the letters. They were perfect."

I force my eyes open, turning to meet her gaze. Her brown eyes are staring up at me with a familiar warmth, an adoration in her expression that I swore I would never see again. The sight of it is like a lightning bolt to the chest, a surge of hope spreading through me.

"You liked them?" I whisper.

She nods, her eyes shining. "I love them, Liam."

I shake my head, not understanding. "But I thought..."

"I love you."

My whole body freezes. I blink down at her, sure I must have heard her wrong. Sure that I must be dreaming, that I must have fallen into a fantasy of mine, because there's no way I'm hearing those words from her lips after all this time. She must read something in my expression, because she lifts my hand and presses her lips to the center of my palm, leaving a soft kiss there.

"I love you," she repeats.

"Whitney," I exhale, my voice shaking. I stumble closer to her, leaning my forehead against hers in disbelief. "Please... I can't. If you aren't ready, if you can't forgive me—"

She shakes her head, reaching her palm up to caress the side of my face, her fingers resting along my jawline. I lean into her touch unconsciously, my eyes fluttering.

"I already forgave you," she whispers.

Moisture gathers on my lashes, and I blink furiously, studying her expression. "How?" I ask.

She smiles brightly, pressing closer to me. "Because I love you."

My eyes flicker back and forth between hers, searching. Unable to wait another moment, I lower my head and press my lips against hers, kissing her with fervor. She meets my lips with a wild abandon, gasping into my mouth, both of us clutching each other wildly. It's a kiss that feels like the first day of spring, like a sip of ice cold water in an endless desert, like everything I've ever needed.

It feels like home.

I pull back from her, staring at her beautiful face in disbelief. I can't help the laugh that bursts forth, a gleeful feeling spreading through me. "You love me?" I whisper.

"Always."

A tear escapes, strolling down my face. I go to wipe at it,

trying to hide the overwhelming emotion coming over me, but she stops me, pressing her lips softly against the wet trail.

"I missed you so much," I confess against her neck, tugging her as close to me as I can. "I'm so sorry, baby."

She shakes her head, pulling back to meet my gaze again. "No more apologies. No more tears."

"I promise," I start. "I promise I won't run away again. I trust you with everything—"

She silences me with a soft kiss, her hands caressing the side of my face. I can't help but sigh into her arms, exhaustion overwhelming me, the torment of the past two weeks finally releasing from my body.

"Not now," she whispers. "I want to show you something."

She steps out of my arms, and I immediately miss the warmth of her. She goes back behind the desk and pulls out a piece of paper, crossing back over to me and holding it out for me to look at. I hesitate, unsure, but she pushes it towards me with a smile.

I take the paper from her hands, reading through it. I'm only halfway through when my mouth falls open in disbelief.

"Whit," I choke out, the tears I just swallowed resurfacing. "Are you sure?"

She nods, that calm, confident smile still resting in her expression. "More sure than I've ever been of anything."

I glance down at the piece of paper, warmth filling my chest.
Whitney Clark.

She legally changed her name. She's officially Mrs. Clark. My wife.

My fucking *wife.*

I sweep her up in my arms, pressing kisses against her lips, her chin, her nose, everywhere I can touch.

"I want to marry you," I breathe against her neck.

She chuckles lightly, running her hands across the broad

expanse of my back as her lips brush against my ear. "Last I checked, we were married."

I pull back and meet her gaze. "I mean for real. I want my parents there. I want Darius and Jackson there. I want everyone to know that you're mine forever."

Her eyes widen, a smile spreading across her face. "Really?"

"Whitney Clark," I say, just because it feels so damn good on my lips. "Whitney Clark is my wife!" I shout the words, and she presses her hand against my lips, muffling the sound. "Say yes," I beg her, reaching my hand up to intertwine our fingers and press a kiss to the back of her hand.

"Yes, Liam Clark," she announces, her eyes locking onto mine, shining with love and hope and a million other beautiful emotions. "I will marry you. Again."

47

WHITNEY

Liam and I get married for the second time on a summer evening at the Cloisters, surrounded by all of our closest friends and family.

It's perfect.

I wasn't nervous at all during the ceremony. I thought I'd be anxious walking down the aisle, but I was filled with a sense of perfect calmness and peace. Seeing Liam waiting for me, the excitement and awe in his expression, the tears swimming in his eyes as he took me in, I knew that I was exactly where I was supposed to be. That as long as I had him by my side, I could face anything.

Now, everyone is getting down on the dance floor while Liam and I hide in the corner like two horny teenagers.

"I thought you threw this party to show me off," I tease against his lips as he slides his hand down the line of my spine, the open back of my dress leaving it entirely bare.

He hums against me with a smile. "I changed my mind. I'm feeling selfish. I want you all to myself."

I chuckle, pressing a palm against his chest. "We're being terrible hosts."

"I don't care," he mumbles as his eyes darken, sparkling with desire. "How fast do you think you can get out of that dress?"

I can't help but smile at his petulant tone. Ignoring my rush of excitement at his words, I nudge his shoulder. "Be patient. You'll get your honeymoon soon enough."

He groans, then holds his hand out towards me. "M'lady, may I have this dance?"

I smile and place my hand in his. He guides me to the dance floor, gathering me in his arms and twirling me like a princess. I sway in his arms, somehow feeling even more in love with him than I did yesterday and the day before that. He whispers in my ear as we cross the floor, telling me all the things he's going to do to me later, his voice teasing and sultry.

We finish the dance, and Liam gets pulled away by Tim and some of his academia friends. Liam's starting back at Columbia in the fall, and since he's going to load up on coursework, it will only take him three semesters to finish. He just finished his summer internship working at a science journal focused on mental health and neuroscience.

Glancing at my phone, I see a text from my mom. Ultimately, I decided not to invite Caroline. My mother and I have a long road ahead of us, but with Liam's help, I've started to accept the reality of who she is and learned how to draw boundaries in my life without feeling guilty. Though I knew it might hurt her to miss her only daughter's wedding, this day was about me and Liam, and I didn't want her to ruin it. I didn't want her here, and that's okay.

After she realized that Liam and I were staying together and she wasn't going to get a cent of her mother's money, she called me nonstop. She left me a bunch of messages saying how sorry she was and how much she missed me, but I ignored all of them. Later,

I found out that the reason she needed the money was to pay her latest boyfriend's bail money. He ended up getting the charges against him dropped, so, eventually, she stopped badgering me.

Liam's arms wrap around my waist, his body hugging me from behind, his scent and warmth infiltrating my senses.

"You want to call her?" he murmurs against my hair.

I shake my head and turn to face him, wrapping my arms around his neck. "Not tonight," I murmur, pressing my lips against him.

"You two are relentless," Abbi interrupts from next to us, Shane at her side.

I roll my eyes. "You guys are worse than we are. Especially now that you're a trio," I argue. Abbi found out a few weeks after the *All Rhodes* opening that she was pregnant. Shane has been so excited to be a father, and even more so when he discovered that they were having a boy, filling their spare bedroom with basketball toys.

"Fair enough." She rubs her belly with a soft smile. "We're off. Too old for this shit."

I give her my best pouting expression. "Already?"

"Girl, you haven't realized because you two have been connected at the lips all night, but it's almost midnight."

Glancing at the clock with a guilty smile, I realize she's right. Liam just shrugs, pulling me tighter in his arms.

"Your dad is literally asleep, Liam," Shane says, laughing behind his hand as all of us glance at one of the tables in the back to see Andy leaning back in his chair, snoring. His wife, Stacy, realizes we've caught him and elbows him in the stomach, sending him straight up.

We all laugh, and I wrap Abbi in a tight hug. "Love you."

"Love you, too. Congratulations."

She hugs Liam and says something in his ear that makes him

look at her with confusion. She replies, her voice low, and pats his shoulder. He smiles widely at whatever she told him, then clasps Shane in a bro-hug, the two of them thumping each other's backs.

As they walk away, I turn to Liam. "What did Abbi say to you?"

He smirks, pressing a thumb softly against my lips. "Wouldn't you like to know."

I open my mouth slightly, teasing his thumb. "Don't worry. I can think of a few ways to get it out of you."

His eyes darken, and he chuckles. "Ah, classic torture techniques." He pulls his hand away before the two of us start down a path that is not at all appropriate for a room filled with most of our friends and family.

"She said 'you've convinced me'."

I furrow my brow. "What does that mean?"

"I didn't know either, but she reminded me. When we broke up, Abbi said she wasn't convinced I was the man who could make you happy. I guess I finally convinced her," he replies cheekily.

Stepping closer to him, I run my hands along the front of his suit, admiring the way it fits against his chest snugly.

"Have I convinced you, too? Are you happy?" he asks, staring into my eyes with a beautiful intensity.

I smile, reaching up to caress his cheek. "The happiest."

He kisses me again. "Come on. Let's dance until we can't feel our feet."

So we do. For the next hour, we dance until the garden is almost empty and the DJ comes on the mic to ask us if he can go home. Tomorrow evening, we'll depart for our ten-day honeymoon to Greece. Liam finished his internship a few days ago, and I'm leaving *All Rhodes* in the perfectly manicured hands of

Shatar. Spending ten days in paradise with the love of my life is the perfect way to end the summer.

Finally, Liam and I call a car to go home, and when we arrive, we stumble up the stairs, clinging to each other like life boats. I'm tugging at his tie when we get to the door and he searches for his keys.

"Slow down," he breathes. "I'm taking my time tonight."

He opens the door and lifts me in his arms, picking me up. I gasp, wrapping my arms around his neck.

"What are you doing?"

"Carrying you over the threshold, obviously." He grins, pressing a kiss to my neck. "I know you like your superstitions. Something old, something new."

"You were my something borrowed, remember?"

He carries me to the bedroom and sets me down in front of the mirror, his large form looming behind me.

"I'm your something forever," he murmurs, meeting my eyes in the mirror.

"Something forever," I repeat, my heart swelling with the love I have for this wonderful man in front of me. "I like that."

"I love you, Mrs. Clark," he says.

"I love you, too," I reply. "Mr. Clark."

And when he kisses me again, he feels like my something forever.

ACKNOWLEDGMENTS

Writing this book was truly a journey, and I couldn't have done any of it without my amazing community of supportive friends and family. I'd like to thank my incredibly patient and supportive editors Emma and Amy (@amyedits), my cover designer Sam (@inkandlaurel) for bringing my characters to life with such a beautiful cover, and my friend Sarah Kasha for proofreading. A huge thank you to my beta readers: Grace Downham and Hali Muhammad, my talented peers in craft, Meg Jones and Alexis Noel. To my cadre (you know who you are): you guys are my rocks and my constant reminder that my voice matters. A special thanks to my ARC reader team, and as always, to my friends and my family for their unwavering support. I could not have finished this book without any of you. Lastly, I would like to thank *you*, my reader, for trusting me and supporting my writing.

ABOUT THE AUTHOR

Rachael Harriet is an independent author and coffee lover with an addiction to grumpy love interests, enemies to lovers, and all things Romancelandia. She is a Wellesley college graduate and has been writing for over two decades (if you count her third grade diary). In her free time, Rachael is a member of an all women's improv group, a film enthusiast, and a voracious reader. She currently resides in Brooklyn, New York. Her debut novel *Love Marks* is available in paperback, e-book, and on Kindle Unlimited. *Something Forever* is her second novel.

9 798990 705708